T.A. TIERI

UNEVEN

It may seem "normal" to you, but it's an "ASD miracle" to Bradley...

First published by Tiwa Adetoye 2022

Copyright © 2022 by T.A. Tieri

This novel is entirely a work of fiction. The names, characters and incidents portrayed in it are the work of the author's imagination. Any resemblance to actual persons, living or dead, events or localities is entirely coincidental.

T.A. Tieri asserts the moral right to be identified as the author of this work.

Unless otherwise indicated, scripture quotations are taken from the The New King James Version. Copyright © 1982 by Thomas Nelson, Inc. All rights reserved.

Scripture quotations marked MSG are taken from the The Message: The Bible in Contemporary Language, by Peterson, Eugene H. NavPress, 2002. All rights reserved.

Tieri, T.A.

UNEVEN: a novel/fiction

First Editions—eBook & Paperback, published July 2022

Edited by Alison Imbriaco

Cover Design by Liam Relph

Author's Photo by Kelly Wilkinson

Visit website at www.tiwaadetoye.com

First edition

ISBN: 9798811791750

This book was professionally typeset on Reedsy.
Find out more at reedsy.com

Dedication
To David, in blessed memory, and Benjamin. I love you.

"Come to me, all you who are weary and burdened, and I will give you rest. Take my yoke upon you and learn from me, for I am gentle and humble in heart, and you will find rest for your souls. For my yoke is easy and my burden is light."

MATTHEW 11:28-30 (NKJV)

Contents

Praises for UNEVEN

A beautiful story about daring to believe in your dreams and the unlimited blessings God has for us regardless of what you've been through. A must read!

— **Marshawn Evans Daniels,** The Godfidence® Coach, Best-Selling Author, *believe BIGGER*

Uneven, an intriguing story of an autistic young man navigating the world of love, independence, loss, and hope. This book shows us that the same God over all, is rich to all that trust Him and depend on Him.

You can't help but love Bradley. You feel his struggle, cry along in his pain, and rejoice in the hope that it will turn out right at the end. It's obvious this is not the end of the story as T.A. Tieri leaves you yearning for more. *Uneven* is definitely a story everyone should read.

— **Abimbola Davids,** Co-Pastor, *Global Impact Church,* Nigeria, Speaker, Author and President & founder of *The women of worth foundation.*

T.A. Tieri's *Uneven* reminds us that even when we don't look and talk the same, the deepest emotions still tie us together. It presents a nuanced and layered lead character whose neurodiversity is just one part of his identity and not the entirety of his life. We very rarely get to see the fullness of characters beyond a diagnosis and this book will surely change the way you connect with people moving forward.

This is a wonderful story from a first-time author and definitely one

I'd recommend for your reading list.
— **Afua Osei,** Speaker and Entrepreneur, *Forbes 20 youngest power women in Africa,* 2014

Uneven tells the story of all of us. Navigating this world the way we know how, with our skills or lack of, hoping it turns out well by the grace of God. If I didn't know, I would think it was a Karen Kingsbury novel.
— **Adun, M.D**, advance copy reader, Canada

T.A. Tieri's *Uneven* is anything but—this novel is an elegant meditation on asymmetry in our relationships with others, ourselves, and our world. Her compassion for her characters and curiosity about the obstacles they face shines through every page. Tieri's vision cuts through challenging topics like gems until they catch an unexpected light.
— **Molly McGinnis,** featured writer in the *Grace and Gravity* literary series

I did not know much about ASD, or its effects on a person, but experiencing it through the eyes of Bradley has helped me put it to a different perspective. This book kept me engaged throughout the entire story, and I could not stop rooting for the characters.
— **Andrew Kim,** advance copy reader, USA

Wonderful story! I was so engaged with *Uneven* that it was hard to stop reading. It will open your eyes to the challenges that autism brings, but also warm your heart to know that the love of others, along with other factors, can help conquer them and promote a successful life.
— **Christy Young,** Home school Mom, and yelp elite, USA

Uneven is a riveting story that teaches the values of trust, faith, and perseverance. A perfect companion on that long flight, your leisure time or at home.

— **Omolara Cole,** Fashion Business Entrepreneur, Nigeria

The experience of reading *Uneven* was inspiring. I found it reassuring and enlightening, as it highlights some of the complexities of living with a neurodevelopmental disorder, dealing with grief, friendship, and above all, faith, hope and love.

— **Benedicta Dzandu,** Ghanaian book reviewer

Prologue

"Just great!" he muttered, his fist clenched. Like he needed a reason to spend more time at the Denver International Airport. The voice on the intercom had just announced a two-hour delay of his connecting flight from California to North Carolina. The weather report had indicated inclement weather in North Carolina, and the airline wanted to wait it out, or approach with caution. The months of December and January were usually the worst times to travel when so many people, including him, felt a need to be with family for the holidays. He didn't even have anyone to share his frustration since his best friend of almost twenty years had been unable to join him on the trip this year because of the workload from school. Being a second-year student at the community college at age twenty-seven, in addition to having a full-time job, wasn't child's play.

He was headed to the guest lounge when he saw a petite black woman with golden-brown skin, struggling to pull her oversize luggage across a floor break. His instinct was to go help her, but it seemed his legs wouldn't move until he had rehearsed his lines in his head.

"Hi, there. May I give you a hand with that?" He stepped beside her and inclined his head as he offered gently.

"Oh, yes, please. Thank you," she responded, panting slightly. Others had carried on as if she were invisible, even the airport staff members. Oh well, no one owed her anything, so all was well with the world. Once he had her luggage on even ground, he stretched out his hand for a handshake.

"Hi, again." he said with a smile.

"Hi...um, hello." She shook his hand. His palm was soft and warm.

"Thank you, again. I was hurrying to catch my connecting flight, but it seems I've missed it anyway. I did not anticipate a tedious luggage-check process, and the next available flight is not for another four hours." Her words tumbled out as she struggled to catch her breath.

He studied her tired face. Even though some of her now-loose hair had fallen across her face, he could see her eyes and thought she looked like she was about to tear up.

"My flight was delayed by about two hours. Care to join me at the VIP lounge? I hear the throw pillows are soft and the drinks taste better." He pressed his lips together and raised his brows invitingly, while he prayed silently that she would accept his invitation.

She couldn't trust her voice to not convey her queasiness, so she simply nodded. He smiled at her and led the way, wheeling her luggage for her. His suitcase was significantly smaller than hers, and he had his laptop bag hung on the handle.

A gorgeous gentleman with kind eyes and soft palms; that's rare! she thought. Clearly he made an effort to be neat, from his shiny black hair to his manicured fingernails and clean-shaven chiseled jawline. His checked blue-and-white shirt and dark blue jeans seemed to have been made just for him.

"Two guest cards, please." He handed over his credit card from his wallet to pay because he was not a member and was careful to make sure his driver's license was not visible to her. But two hours was definitely too long for him to sit uncomfortably.

She was suddenly conscious of herself and quickly undid her bun and ran her fingers through her long and wavy hair, not minding that some strands on her face still refused to fall in place. She hurriedly reapplied her now-dry light-pink lipstick and attempted to straighten the knee-length dress—red with black medium-sized polka dots—underneath her long black jacket. Thankfully the lower half of her dress was ruched to the left with frills at the ends so it could have been smooth or wrinkled.

He was right. The throw pillows were soft against her back on the lounge sofa. She had never been in the VIP lounge of an airport before. Both of the times she flew first class with her former boss, they had been running late and had boarded immediately.

A waiter brought them their orders—a vodka cocktail with an olive for her and a glass of fresh apple juice and a bottle of water for him. A few minutes later, accompanying finger food arrived.

"Feeling better yet?" he asked after they had both taken sips of their drinks.

"Yes, thank you. Flight schedules fluctuate a lot during these periods. But I am surprised going out of town could still be heavily booked in January. Are you from around here?"

"I stay in North Carolina. I went to California for the holidays."

"Really? Although I am flying in from Toronto—I attended a friend's wedding, I moved to Chapel Hill in North Carolina about the middle of last year with my mom and her new husband. I love the weather thus far and the community and work opportunities available. I currently work in an art gallery as an executive, so I get to meet new faces every now and then." She stopped suddenly when she realized she had rambled on, and he had barely said anything other than nod and listen intently. She usually wasn't that open with strangers, but he felt so warm and inviting. She sipped her drink and decided there was probably no harm, since they were most likely not going to see each other again. And stalkers or killers were probably not nice enough to help women in distress with their luggage at an airport and pay for their use of the VIP lounge. His strides had been calm and purposeful, nothing to set off her danger alarm. To top it all, he had two dimples when he smiled. One black man, two dimples! Just her luck.

He was intrigued by her free spirit. Her eyes were interesting to look into, and even though he'd been taught staring was rude, he found himself unable to tear his gaze from them. As he helped her out of her long jacket before they sat, he'd been sharply aware that she was the most perfectly shaped woman he had ever met. She had let down her thick dark-brown hair, and though it fell around her shoulders, he noticed her long neck. She wore simple silver teardrop earrings and no necklace, so naturally, he also noticed the low-cut neckline of her dress. It draped a little loosely on her frame, held by the thin straps on her slender shoulders.

Red was definitely her color. Or one of her colors. Her waist was small, but her hips were full and curvy, with the frills on her dress drawing attention to them even more, and the jacket had done a great job hiding her pear-shaped self. He concluded she probably wasn't big on accessories as the only other jewelry she had on was her silver wristwatch. Her black open-toe heels added a few inches to her petite height, but he still towered over her.

I have to say something smart now. He thought he should leave out the fact that he also lived in Chapel Hill, just in case she thought he was trying to impress her. Okay, he would like to impress her, actually, but not at the risk of her flying off in fear.

"Interesting. Well, I'm supposed to be a civil engineer, but I mostly play the piano for leisure, analyze data, or work with software. Of my past experiences, the structural engineering role has been my best times," he managed to say with a smile.

She laughed. "Supposed to be a civil engineer? I see. Well, I don't know who or what I'm supposed to be. Still figuring it out. I have modeled for a few fashion lines, but when some requests got too uncomfortable for me, my agent fired me. Shortly after, my mom and her husband and my step-brother moved, and I decided to start out afresh with them."

"Ouch. Sorry."

"It's fine. That has not been the worst really. I did get a personal assistant job with a CEO of a pharmaceutical at Clegg, about fourteen miles out from Chapel Hill. Barely three months of settling into my role, and he thought it all right to touch me inappropriately. The pig!"

She was still pissed about the incident and was glad she had been bold enough that day to slap his hand off. She had heard stories about him but was certain she could be different since she did not flirt at her workplace or behave unprofessionally. She had packed her bag that afternoon and had never gone back.

"Oh my. So much for a fresh start," he empathized, as he stretched his long legs in front of him.

"Mm-hmm," she muttered as she drained her glass and placed it on the table between them.

"But hey, it's okay, you know. The gallery doesn't pay as much now, but the few months I've been there have been wonderful. I've learned a lot about paintings, artists, and art supplies, and I enjoy chatting with the prospects and clients. While the actual sales are not my core responsibility, I'm always thrilled when I do make a sale, however infrequent that is," she shared excitedly.

"That's awesome. I love art, too, and actually paint a little myself. But just for leisure. Nothing consistent."

"No way. That's amazing! Who is your favorite artist?"

"Uh,"—he paused, considering—"right now, maybe Jadé Fadojutimi. She's not as popular as, say, Jackson Pollock, but I generally like abstracts with lines and color plays that have some illusion of a form. Makes any sense to you?" He massaged his forehead and chuckled.

"I'm more into music now, anyway. And sometimes good movies," he added.

"Mm-hmm." She managed to get out in a nod. She had been mesmerized by the fact that they shared an interest in art. And hearing him speak that long was like listening to music really. His voice was fluid. She took a deep breath. *I really have to get it together.*

"Hey, want to take a walk? My legs need to move," he asked after a few minutes.

"Yes, please," she replied eagerly.

He helped her up, and they strolled around the lounge. He admired the grace with which she swung her hips and walked easily with her six-inch heels. She was definitely super comfortable with heels. She was on his left side, so he had his hand in his back pocket as they walked, and he leaned in a bit to hear her, though she gestured an awful lot.

They shared their taste in music, and he obviously had more interest and knowledge than she did. The conversation went on to books and novels, then movies and actors, and by this time they were seated at the bar. She laughed freely and almost forgot her worries of having missed her flight.

So had he. It was refreshing to have a conversation caution and judgment free. But then his alarm went off. They could not believe they had been talking for almost two hours, but he had a flight to catch and could not afford to miss it. They hurried back to their table for his suitcase.

"I had you registered for a longer stay, so fresh snacks and drinks should be brought to you soon, I believe. It was a real pleasure spending the time with you. Enjoy the throw pillows," he said with a wink, then he leaned in to give her a quick hug and hurried out as he turned off his beeping alarm for the second time.

I

A DAY AT A TIME.

Chapter 1

B radley was stretched out on the long sofa for a second session, listening to the low classical instrumental playing in his therapist's office. He had a hooded sweat jacket on and a crew-neck teal T-shirt underneath, with knee-length black shorts, a pair of black calf-length socks, and white slides. Both hands were in the pockets of the hoodie. It had been eight years since he'd been in a room like this. He had thought he was done, but alas, here he was again because "it" had come and stolen his reason the last nine years had been almost perfect. One of the few reasons his twenty-eight years of living had a direction. He wasn't in denial, but it still didn't make any damn sense.

* * *

They had been on the tour bus for almost two hours, and he needed a break from his screen. He looked out the window and saw that they were on a long meandering road by a cliff. Definitely they would not be stopping soon. He was four years old at the time and had about three hundred phrases going for him. He screamed out in frustration and threw his headphones at his mom, who was seated next to him.

"Shh. Sorry, love. We will get off soon for some stretches, okay?"

His mom had tried to comfort him, but that was not helping this time. She had said that thirty minutes ago too. He increased his fits and fought to get out of his chair. One of the tourists, who had been asleep on the long chair at the back of the bus, woke up upset and yelled at him.

"Who the hell is that? I should give him a knock on the head!"

"Yes, by all means come over and see what happens, you idiot," Mom had retorted, immediately facing the woman with anger in her eyes.

The whole bus had gone quiet.

* * *

Bradley chuckled at the memory. His mom was crazy like that. She was strict, disciplined, and friendly at the same time and could pull out the guns in a flash if you messed with any of her family. The woman later apologized when they had a stop, but for the rest of their trip in the African country they had visited then, no one bothered his parents when he threw a tantrum.

Once his mom had wanted to take a picture with him on the personal watercraft. The beach attendant had explained that children were not allowed on the Jet Skis, but his mom had explained at length how they had traveled so far and stated that there was no way her son would not be allowed a ride and also not be allowed to take few pictures. She never had a problem creating a scene to get what she wanted if she had to.

His dad had long ago given up trying to talk her out of this behavior. He just stood with his hands in his pockets, waiting to be told when he could lift Bradley onto the watercraft for the picture. In the end, other families with children were able to take pictures, too, because he and his family had.

Bradley smiled as tears rolled down from the corners of his eyes, and he didn't bother to wipe them.

"So, did you meet anyone new today at the basketball court?" Dr. Heather interrupted his thoughts.

He shook his head. "No. I shot some hoops and left to jog as people arrived," he added.

"All right. Have you written the letter yet?"

The Letter. He couldn't. Writing it was confirming "it." He had started to type again the night before, but only one word was added. Now he had three in total. *"Dear Mom, I..."*

He clenched his fists inside his pockets and got up to walk toward the sandbox on the open bookshelf across the room. He raked it neatly and then formed a pattern. He did this for a few minutes and finally answered.

"Not yet."

He rubbed the back of his neck and then moved it sideways to give it a stretch. He had been struggling to sleep through the night, as well, and he was grateful for the quiet in Dr. Danielle's office. She was a very patient person, too, on the job or off.

A picture of two empty wooden chairs facing each other hung on the wall behind her desk. Next to it was a framed picture with three thick different-colored wavy lines and the message "Healing is not linear" in black along the top mustard-yellow wavy line. On her desk, a tray held a blue bird suspended on a silver pendulum at one end and a bowl of water at the other end. The bird swung left then right, dipping its beak into the water as if to drink but then swinging right back. The insatiability of the bird used to annoy him, but now he found it interesting because somehow it reminded him humans were mostly like that.

Danielle Heather, PhD, was Bradley's therapist during his time in college. When he turned eighteen, his parents thought a more young-adult-experienced therapist was best for him. He had missed Mr. Carly, his occupational therapist for five years, and initially struggled to have

5

a connection with Danielle. But with time, he realized the challenges he faced in college were different from those of his middle and high school years, and he was grateful the change had happened. Back then, kids initially teased him before they became his friends or left him alone. His best friend of almost twenty years was usually there to quickly talk down any bully who tried to mess with him. She reminded him so much of his mom.

Bradley smiled again at the memories.

* * *

When he was in kindergarten, a parent had walked up to his mom to express her concerns about her daughter always talking about her friend, Bradley, at home. But when she greeted him, like she would greet any of her daughter's friends, he had not responded. She thought to encourage his mom to visit specialists and pray more and maybe take him to a more appropriate environment with his peers. His mom had said nothing until the woman was done speaking, then responded, smiling, "I'm happy your daughter has a friend in my son. He is sweet and friendly to most people, really. Have a good one."

With that, they left for the parking lot, and after she buckled Bradley safely in the back seat, they drove off. He must have been five years old at the time, but he remembered his mom had wiped her eyes as they turned into the main street. They, however, still had their little moments on the drive home. She started a song, and he completed some lines. Then she leaned back, stretching her arm a little to tickle his feet at the end of each song.

By college, however, people treated him differently, special even, once they found out, and he did not always appreciate the excessive preferential treatment. He had accepted the fact that there were things others could do and he could not, not in the usual way anyway. But there were also things he caught on with easily that others struggled with. The problem was he communicated very little, so he didn't have many friends who took the time to get to know him. Especially since his best friend had not gone to college with him. She had decided to work, instead, to save and planned to study later.

He was fine with having basic conversations with people, but not everyone was patient enough to get past "basic." In addition, his interests appeared to be boring to college kids at the time. He seemed to operate at a level higher than most, except socially.

He had liked to go on his morning runs before most people got up and often ended at the basketball court. He would make a few hoops from several distances away by himself, but once others came around, he left. Three times, another basketball lover—Malik O'Neill, had met him on the court as he was leaving, but the third time, Malik persuaded him to stay. He eventually agreed to, but he did not join the game. He sat by himself and watched with keen interest. A few more games after that day, Malik challenged him to a one-on-one, which he ended up enjoying. Malik introduced him to a few other guys, and before long, he joined them in a few games.

When Bradley did not show up for basketball, Malik had checked on him. He really was determined to be his friend. On one occasion, Malik had helped him out when he noticed he was struggling with a girl who wouldn't stop bugging him. Malik had even tried helping him socially but was very understanding when Bradley needed his space, and eventually he gave up trying to change him and just enjoyed his company when he could. It was particularly helpful to Bradley to have a dedicated male friend he could speak with about challenges outside schoolwork. Well, another African-American male other than his dad. And thankfully, they took a few courses together too.

He had selected courses that coincided with his strength. Numbers jumped at him easily, and he understood how to work gadgets once he created a system around them. He had also discovered he was a creative, so he had chosen mostly engineering courses that focused on data analysis, computer software, and woodwork. Music and art he took on as minors. Though his certificate read "Bachelor of Science in Civil Engineering," he was just grateful to have stuck with college—the extended school years, the therapy sessions, and all—to graduation and to have made his parents proud. He had also connected with a professional pianist to perfect his playing and reading of musical notes during the summers. Now he had a grand piano in his living room, and he played really well.

* * *

"...Brad?"

He came to himself and tried to process what he thought Dr. Heather was saying. He picked up the lemon-shaped stress ball to squeeze, let down his hood, and walked over to sit on the wooden armed chair opposite her.

"Pending when your letter is ready, I need you to start a 'Gratitude' jar. Every other hour from when you get home till our next session, write on a small piece of paper something you are grateful for and toss it in the jar. It's okay to be grateful for the same thing more than once. If the jar fills up before our next session, you may stop." She paused for him to process what she'd said and for any questions.

"Jar. Gratitude. Every other hour. Got it," he confirmed.

"All right then. See you in ten days." She stood up and dropped her notes on the table, preparing to read up on her next client.

"By the way, how's the 'getting to know you' phase coming along?" She smiled at him.

"Good. Swell, actually. And before you ask, no, I haven't, but I bet she has a clue."

"Mm-hmm?" Dr. Heather lowered her face to look at him through the top of her glasses.

Bradley gave her a half grin.

"She's…she doesn't treat me differently, and I don't want to lose that, you know…" he answered her.

"I believe a month is long enough to tell if she will walk, but that's okay. As long as she allows you to be you and not someone else."

Bradley smiled wryly as he got to his feet and confirmed his uber ride on his phone.

"I am me with her, Dr. Heather. Always."

"Okay, then."

"Bye, Doc." He nodded curtly and left.

Bradley rode home in the back seat with his seat belt safely buckled, and his earbuds playing "Voice of Truth" by Casting Crowns. He rested his head and shut his eyes, recalling the events that had led him here.

Chapter 2

Bradley sat patiently in a booth at The Griddle diner, sipping his lemonade and waiting for his best friend of almost twenty years, Melanie Reed.

Melanie was his brilliant, carefree, five-foot-four, goal-getting, miss-independent friend, who currently worked as a supervisor at the diner to save up for her own business someday and to pay her way through community college. She'd never known her mom, who had left her and her dad when she was about eleven months old and had never come back—at least, so her dad had told her. Unfortunately, her dad fell terribly ill and eventually passed on when she was about five years old, and she had been put in a foster home in Nevada County, California.

Every day she'd longed to be adopted by a loving family, but by the age of eleven, she had given up on that dream and decided to make her life story better somehow. That began her journey to self-reliance and not expecting anything from people because, in the end, her hopes were always dashed. She had met Bradley when he joined her third-grade class and had since been his friend. Because she was used to fending for herself, she was happy to do the same for Bradley, and they were soon popularly referred to as "Super-boy and Ultra-girl."

Most kids did not have the patience to make sense of what Bradley tried to communicate, so he often retreated into himself. But not Melanie. She would force him out to the playground and take her time watching his gestures until she understood what he was trying to say. Sometimes he had words to express himself; other times he didn't. Thankfully their school was diverse, so their difference in color, race, or culture was nothing new.

* * *

One school day, Melanie was arriving as Bradley's dad dropped him off, and she called out to him.

"Hey, Brad." She waved at him with a smile and came over.

Bradley just stared at her and did not respond. She shook his hand and gave him a warm hug.

"How are you, buddy?" she asked him. Then she had turned to greet his dad, who was watching from the car.

"Hello, Brad's dad. I'm Mel, Brad's friend." She waved, smiling at him.

"Hello, Mel. Have a great day at school, okay," his dad had replied warmly.

Then his parents had gotten permission to have Melanie over for lunch during the weekend. They were excited to know Bradley apparently had a genuine friend. They took turns playing games on his tablet, she had even interacted easily with his twin sisters, who were five years younger, and she finally got to meet "Mr. T," his small brown teddy bear with a red bandanna around its neck, which had imaginary conversations with him and mom. It was one of the tools his mom had used to help him build his social skills and use his words and phrases in conversations. He had mentioned Mr. T a few times at school, and she had not understood him.

Bradley was good with numbers and science while Melanie was better with literacy and social studies. But unfortunately, he could not help her with the sums she struggled with—not because he did not want to, but because he did not know how to help her. Bradley had his own Individualized Educational Plan and received specialized instruction and related services different from what others had. By the end of high school, though, Bradley was better at having short conversations, even though he usually did not start one. He had a few other friends, but he and Melanie were definitely best of friends. The few times she had accompanied them to church, other than the fact that she wasn't black, most people assumed she was part of their extended family the way she blended in with them.

While he eventually continued to college, first at California, Melanie could not afford that and had started taking up a few jobs. She worked at a home decoration warehouse to start with, then a supermarket, a bakery, and finally a restaurant. Sometimes she worked a double shift. She was determined to move out of the foster home as soon as she could, and while by sixteen, she was legally allowed to, she still did not have enough saved up for rent, so she waited about two more years before moving out. However, she still planned to attend college, no matter how long it took, so when she got the opportunity to wait at a diner in Chapel Hill, North Carolina, and it included a better accommodation than the one she shared at the time, she jumped at the offer.

In the course of researching for a community college, even though she ended up not enrolling until another three years after her peers were done, Melanie had stumbled upon a school that was accommodating to someone like Bradley. Unlike the standard structured college he had started out with, this college would make it possible for him to take courses that focused on his strengths along with a few electives.

Bradley had been excited to be in close proximity with his best friend, who seemed to have changed in the two years since he had seen her and was fast becoming her own woman. His parents had also welcomed the change in environment for him and hoped it would help him develop his independence as a new adult too. They had made sure his apartment was fully stocked and would enable him to cope without their support. His mom had stayed a while until he found a housekeeper who could come by weekly to help with some chores, understand his routines, and provide support as he may have needed if Melanie was unavailable. Even though he did not intend to drive often, his dad had bought him an early Tesla model that came with advanced programming capable of providing autopilot features and full self-driving capabilities.

The transfer meant that he would lose a school year, but Bradley had never been one to be overly concerned about expected timelines anymore. He had missed a year switching in high school, as well, and he had long understood that he processed some things more slowly than most people, while other things came to him faster, and ultimately achieving his own goal was what mattered. His path was different. He did graduate from college after all, and he would always remember his mom's tears of joy and pride on his graduation day, reminding him he only needed to keep being a superior version of himself every day and never compare himself to anyone else.

* * *

Bradley was in the diner waiting for Melanie, who, encouraging as always, had promised to help him practice mock interviews and some case studies for the interview at an investment bank scheduled for the following day. She was studying business administration and was unfamiliar with some of the engineering terminologies. As a result, Melanie often had to google terminologies and do some research in preparation for their mock sessions. But the process had gotten easier with time. Bradley had done background research and learned about the bank. In this instance, he knew a few of the interviewing team members. This was not his first job interview, but he always liked to rehearse possible scenarios before any of his interviews, just so he was not taken by surprise. And while he had started out in his early twenties by seeing a career coach, he soon realized he preferred rehearsing with a less structured, and more familiar person.

It had been two months since his contract position at an engineering company ended, and he had been looking for something more stable. Melanie had been kind enough to have her boyfriend, Joshua Doyle, put in a word for him at his company, which was looking to fill a temporary role. Joshua was well respected, and Joshua's father was, in fact, influential in the financial industry, so Bradley had been granted the opportunity.

* * *

He remembered his younger days when he had sessions practicing his words with the use of flash cards and practicing his writing with his mom's hand guiding his. He had eventually learned to write on his own, but he usually wrote outside the line up until his last year in high school. There had been blending words and reading sessions with his mom, as well as many other lessons, from picking up his socks to throwing a ball, and many others when he was about six years old. He remembered the frustrations of painting outside the lines and mom still cheering him. He remembered their Mr. T moments.

As a child, he'd had so much energy it was necessary to go on walks or runs with his dad on the trails in their neighborhood, even on days he may have played hard at recess in school. On one occasion during a summer at their former house, he had clogged the toilet yet again with lots of paper towels for no apparent reason, and it overflowed his bathroom terribly. Unfortunately, no one knew until there was a leak several minutes later in the kitchen downstairs. His mom had run upstairs, and his dad had followed closely behind. They scooped the water as quickly as they could, but even the rug inside his room was already dripping. The vacuum was little help. His mom had been so mad at him, especially because it was not the first time he was being scolded for clogging the toilet. But this was huge, and it took weeks to repair the damage to the kitchen ceiling.

He remembered the many therapy sessions and daily prayers and confessions, all geared toward his ability to live a productive, satisfying life. "You are a child of great influence," "The peace of God is with you," "We wait on the Lord and our strength is renewed," "You are the salt of the earth,"—his parents repeated the promises from the Bible until the words were etched in his heart and he could absorb their truth. In addition, his mom had made sure he confessed the phrases, too, as early as when he turned five. He did not really start speaking coherent sentences till he was about four years old after his first year of speech therapy, but she believed "God answered Haggai's son's cries, not hers," so whether Bradley understood what he spoke or not, she made him say the words. Every day.

He knew at almost every point of his adult life that he was living the reality of seeds sown in the past, and he could not but wonder what the future had in store for him. He, however, was at peace each step of the way. There were too many contact points in his past for him to doubt the journey ahead was definitely not bleak.

* * *

Bradley was so deep in thought, sitting with a crooked smile across his worried face, it took Melanie a few seconds to get his attention.

"Knock, knock." Melanie snapped her fingers in front of him, and he came to.

"Sorry," he said with a genuine smile and set his lemonade down.

"Thanks for waiting patiently," she told him as she sank into the seat opposite him and fired up her laptop.

The diner was empty, apart from the few kitchen staff. Bradley usually hung out with her or their friends in the evenings anyway—if he had to. His natural preference was to order food to go or wait till the diner was virtually empty and sit in a quiet corner.

"What's the role again?"

"Statistical analyst. I'm part of the desktop-publishing crew. Again, not what I'm familiar with, but it's data so...," Bradley paused and then sighed. "And Mel, I really am grateful for the opportunity, but I can't help but wonder if I'll be successful at this."

* * *

When he had landed his first job at age twenty-two, he had ignored his parents' advice and taken on the associate consultant role without sharing his history with the talent acquisition team when he was interviewed. He was determined to blend in as much as he could, and fortunately for him, he had aced it and gotten hired.

Three weeks in, however, his supervisor began questioning his pace, as others who came at the same time as he did were catching on faster than he was. He was better at attaining his personal deliverables, but two out of the three projects he was involved in required a lot of teamwork. He barely contributed because, even when he knew what the end result would be, he was unable to explain his thought process to others as quickly as they wanted. He also always had an excuse to avoid hanging out with them, and eventually he was labeled as not being a team player.

But that had not discouraged Bradley. He was determined to prove he was as ready for the corporate world as his colleagues. He had been at the job six weeks before Human Resources called him in to discuss his discuss his reluctance to be a team player. They offered to have his department, and maybe his projects, changed, but he had refused because he knew that would mean explaining to his colleagues why he was being moved. However, about three months later, he observed a major inconsistency in data his team had worked on in the past, which would be referenced in the report they were developing. He flagged it to his team and manager, but they decided to "let sleeping dogs lie" and carried on with the client's project. He had not been able to handle the knowledge of the deception, and it ate at him. He had not backed off because he knew he'd been right. That was his first experience with politics at the workplace, and he knew it was only a matter of time before he made a slip. His inner turmoil affected his productivity, and the pressure kept building until he could not handle it anymore. The Human Resources person at the exit interview had pressed him for the genesis of his reason for his sudden resignation, and it eventually slipped out. He did not know what happened to his manager subsequently, but he did learn to play to his strengths rather than keep trying to be who he was not.

When it came to subsequent job offers and contracts, however, he accepted carefully and was as up-front as up-front could mean. Of course, that meant losing out on some opportunities he knew he could have excelled at, but he also trusted that as he progressed in his career, his success stories would eventually speak for him. And so far, they had. Not as much or as fast as he would have preferred, but he was grateful he was never at a standstill.

* * *

"You will, and it's temporary. We will still be on the lookout for what you want, and hopefully, it'll be a full-time offer. So man up, mister," Melanie said, drawing him back to their prep.

"Bully," he snorted.

"Tell me something new. A friend is coming over to my apartment for the night, though, so I can't be too long either."

"Fine by me. Thanks." Bradley sat up straight, ready for her questions.

"Here we go: Share with us a challenge you and your team encountered on a project and how it was resolved, if it was."

* * *

"Hi, Abi. Come on in. I arrived not too long ago. Just putting away groceries." Melanie chatted away as she opened the door for her friend and embraced her in a tight hug.

"Thank you. How have you been? Work, studies? It's been a while!" Abigail responded in one breath.

"I know, right! Stressful as usual, but good otherwise. Thanks. Help yourself to some plums and peaches in the refrigerator." Melanie pointed her toward the kitchen.

"Um, I think I'll have a shower first. It was busy today, and we had a lot of delivery logistics issues. Besides, I'm quite famished for actual food."

"Oh, that's okay, then. I did bring us packs from the diner."

Abigail made her way to her friend's room. It was a small but well-managed and neatly kept apartment with a large soft sofa in the living room, a television set no one ever watched, and an extremely organized kitchen and tiny pantry. Melanie even had a first aid-box. Her bedroom had the only bathroom of the apartment, so she rarely had guests over because that meant going into her bedroom to use the restroom. Melanie had mentioned to her that her brother-like best friend, her boyfriend, and Abigail were the only guests she'd had in over four years of living there. Although she seemed friendly enough to have acquaintances at school, work, and church, Melanie kept her life

18

as private as possible and safeguarded her privacy. "No expectations, no disappointments," she usually said.

Melanie had met Abigail at an interior showroom a few months ago when she was attempting to revamp her space. Abigail was, as usual, quick to warm up to her and helped choose her plants, ornaments, and even paintings. At the time, Abigail was working as personal assistant to a CEO and was picking up a few items for her boss's office. Melanie had been so grateful for her help that she had invited Abigail for supper at her diner the following evening. They hit it off easily and quickly became friends.

Melanie had also invited her to church a few times, but Abigail had yet to honor the invitation. Her weeks were so busy, weekends were when she rested and caught up on her social life. It wasn't as if Melanie was a regular attendee herself, especially because of her community college schedule, but she made an effort to make it at least once a month.

The smell of the pasta Melanie microwaved filled Abigail's nostrils, and she hurried out of the bathroom, changed into something more comfortable, and slipped back into the living room.

"Are you ready to eat now?"

"Yes, please," Abigail answered eagerly, rubbing her hands in anticipation as she salivated.

Melanie laughed at her dramatic friend. She added some sliced tomatoes and avocado next to their pastas and sprinkled some dried raisins on hers. Her phone beeped with a message from her boyfriend, Joshua. **Working late tonight. Call you tomorrow?**

Sure. She hit Send and set her phone down. It beeped again almost immediately.

I'm downstairs.

Melanie frowned curiously and then replied, **No you are not.** It took a few minutes for her screen to light up with a message again, and she half expected her bell to ring. But then she read his reply. **No, I'm not. I love you.**

She beamed. **Ditto.** She hit Send and finally sat down to eat, still smiling unconsciously.

"Aww. See, why can't I find that?" Abigail asked with a jealous smile on her face. She had watched the exchange and did not have to ask Melanie who it was before she knew why she had a smile plastered on her face. Melanie laughed with a forkful of food in her mouth.

"I'm serious! You seem to have it all together, Mel. I wish I was as put together as you. I just seem to throw myself at the wrong guys and end up with unfulfilling jobs despite my qualifications. And I have yet to muster the courage to move out from my stepdad's place—not that my mom is making moving out any easier, though," Abigail added.

"You are an intelligent and beautiful woman, Abi, with a sophistication any right-thinking man would want to show off. And I believe your job at the art gallery will pick up. You are very creative, you know?" Melanie encouraged.

"Yeah, I am actually enjoying this one. It seems promising," Abigail responded, her spirit feeling uplifted again.

"And speaking of men, while I'm not necessarily his fan, Malik seems genuinely interested in you, and I know deep down—like deep, deep down—he can be nice. But then again, who wouldn't be interested and nice to you, Abi? You were a model, for heaven's sake!" Melanie added with a wink. Abigail laughed.

Melanie had introduced her to Malik once when they met him at a club. He really was good looking with his well-built body, broad shoulders, and kissable lips, and he knew it. Most women flirted to get his attention, and who wouldn't? He was from a wealthy family and was doing well for himself, as well. They did have a good conversation and had exchanged contact information, but for reasons unknown to her, Abigail just wasn't interested in having a relationship with him.

Perhaps she wasn't sure she wouldn't be one of his conquests. Frankly, she could not handle any more of that. Her ex and her then best friend apparently were an item behind her back, and she had been stupidly blind to it. This was before she moved to Chapel Hill, and she didn't intend to be that naive lady anymore.

"I met someone about five weeks ago at the airport in Denver, on my way to Sacramento to visit my dad." Abigail started to share.

"Ah-h…do tell!" Melanie exclaimed excitedly.

Abigail chuckled, as she began to speak as if she were in a dream.

"He helped me with my luggage and then paid for my time to wait at the VIP lounge because I had missed my flight and the next one was not for another four hours. Anyway, he was sweet and respectful and good looking. No, scrap that. He was hot. Not all buffed up nor screaming-for-attention handsome like a knight in shiny armor, but he could have as well come with a warning label. And clearly, he picked out outfits that did justice to his body and perfect facial features," Abigail rushed out almost at once.

Melanie laughed till her side began to hurt, and she had to quickly calm herself.

"Oh my. I hope you got to breathe properly the whole time. What's his name? Why are you not dating yet? Or was he not into you?"

Even with her dark skin compared to Melanie, Abigail felt the heat on her cheeks. But she also laughed at the rush of questions.

"Um, I don't know if he was as into me as I was into him because if he was, he did a great job masking it. We just talked about work, art, and a few things here and there, you know, and he didn't, for once, make any rude passes or remarks. I do know he looked at me with such intensity, Mel, I felt tingles, butterflies, and goose bumps all at once."

Then she sighed.

"Unfortunately, like I said, his flight was about two hours earlier than mine, and he left in such a hurry, you would not have guessed we had spent about two hours together. We did not get to exchange names, let alone contact information."

"What? Oh wow. Sorry about that, Abi," Melanie added quietly. "But are you seriously holding out for him? I mean, you met at an airport. He could be anywhere in the world!"

"Yeah, I know... It's just...I keep hoping we will run into each other someday, somehow... He did mention he stayed in North Carolina too. I have replayed it in my head several times these last five weeks, wondering maybe if I had flirted with him a little, or added a little extra in my steps, things may have ended differently," Abigail responded with all seriousness.

Melanie chuckled. Abigail usually had guys flocking for her attention. This mystery guy had certainly gotten under her friend's skin for her to have the tables turned for a change.

"I wonder what his hair would feel like with my hands in it," Abigail blurted out in a whisper.

Melanie almost chocked on her drink laughing.

"Oh, dear heaven. Abi, you've got to get a grip. Even if you do meet again, and I'm almost convinced you may not, but if you do, and he's really as hot as you say, he may not even be available. And you would have wasted time daydreaming about a man who isn't or cannot be yours. You really don't want to do that to yourself."

"Oh well, till then a girl can dream, right? And girlfriend, you do not want the details of our imaginary kisses." With that Abigail finished her meal and stood to clean up.

Melanie chuckled and stared at her friend, as she was short of words.

"The movies make being in a secure and healthy relationship look easy. I hope you realize how enviable you and Josh are. Like he's super busy being an investment banker and all, and you are not exactly ever not busy yourself, but you are so good together. You make it work.

Why are the rest of us so unlucky?" Abigail continued as she made her way to the sofa.

"Thanks, I guess. But I did have my fair share of frogs, too, you know," Melanie said with a soft smile. Abigail laughed.

"Anyway, so what good movies are there? And you are joining me. No schoolwork tonight, please."

"Yes, ma'am." Melanie laughed as she cleared her plate.

"Which reminds me," Melanie said, "We are getting together tomorrow evening at the diner. Joshua helped Bradley get an interview spot at the bank. It's not set in stone, but chances are Malik won't be in town if or when he gets to begin the temporary job, so we decided to "celebrate in faith" tomorrow. Except Brad informs us otherwise. You want to come?"

"Mel, are you trying to set me up with Malik again?" Abigail asked suspiciously.

"I cross my heart! Not this time. Besides, you'll finally get to meet Bradley. Speaking of, please do not go all 'Abi, the irresistible model' on him."

"Hey, that's so not me."

Melanie gave her friend a lazy smile. "Right. But still, Brad is... He's super nice to everyone and innocently doesn't even notice when it's misinterpreted," she explained with an added seriousness in her tone.

"Uh-huh. Well, rest assured. I've got my mind set on my mystery man, so we're good, okay? I'll meet you there after work." Abigail winked with a smile. "Can we watch our movie now? I'm in the mood for a comedy."

Melanie laughed and grabbed her throw as she joined her friend on the sofa.

* * *

As soon as Bradley saw her step into the diner on 4th Street, their encounter at the airport VIP lounge came flooding back like it was yesterday, because he had replayed it several times in the past five weeks. And he was staring again, willing himself to wake up from what was looking like a dream, but she drew closer still. But then he realized he had to be awake because Melanie was suddenly next to him about to introduce her.

"Hey, Brad, meet my friend, Abigail Sogal." Melanie gave Abigail a hug and chatted on. "Abi, meet Brad. You know Malik and Josh." She concluded the introductions and made her way back to Joshua.

"Hi, Brad. Please call me Abi. Pleased to meet you." With an emphasis on meet, Abigail smiled and stretched out her hand for a handshake. She was sure that if she hadn't been dark skinned, she would have been red all over. She prayed he caught on with her charade and played along.

Bradley was confused. Did she really not remember him? Or had he made it all up in his mind?

"Hello, Abi. Bradley Madison. Same here." He shook her hand with a smile.

Abigail gave Malik a quick hug, and he flashed her a charming smile, clearly happy to see her. She waved at Joshua as she took her seat opposite Bradley but next to Malik.

Bradley barely spoke except when he was spoken to. He studied Abi. Abigail. He would never have guessed. He liked her name. And her smile. And her eyes. Her bishop-collar, sleeveless plain-white blouse with the big bow in front really brought out her eyes. She seemed lovelier today than he remembered. Perhaps because she did not seem under any stress. Her flared knee-length and high-waist skirt had abstract patterns of sea-green, light-brown, cream, and dark-gray, and it had swung nicely when she walked in on her heels. She had seen him staring at her once, but he held her gaze rather than look away

24

until she averted her eyes.

"So when are you looking to get a call back?" Joshua interrupted his thoughts.

"Well, they did not say exactly. Something vague about 'within a week or two' or so. But I'm optimistic," Bradley responded with smile and took a sip of his drink.

Abigail felt willing to give anything to get out of the diner. She had shared so much with Melanie there was no way her friend would believe her if she told her he was the same man she'd specifically warned her not to get involved with. Not like she would set out to hurt Bradley, but she could not risk losing her friendship with Melanie if it didn't work out. Even though it had been a different situation, her former best friend had hurt her, so she knew how that felt. Thankfully Bradley had caught on quickly and had not mentioned anything about their meeting before, either.

If only she was as drawn to Malik as she was to Bradley. She had unconsciously compared every other man she'd met subsequently to him, and none had matched. Perhaps because he was coming from the interview, they were supposedly celebrating in anticipation of him getting the job, he looked even hotter in the black suit and lavender shirt. His facial hair had grown out but was neatly cut to shape his jawline, and when he had stood up to greet her, she'd noticed how his clothes fit, all the way to his shoes. His pants sat nicely on him, and she could imagine his long legs stretched out underneath the table like they were at the airport.

Malik had tried to engage her in private conversations, but she felt Bradley's eyes on her the whole time. He did not say much except when he was asked, which seemed strange because she remembered him being free enough with her when they had just met. Maybe she made him as uncomfortable as he was making her at the moment. And it was totally her fault. She needed to find a way to apologize to him later and explain to Melanie. For now, she smiled along and counted the minutes as they went by, hoping they would go a little faster.

In the end, she called it a night and made up a story about an early delivery at the gallery the following day. Bradley asked for her complementary card since he was an art lover himself, which she happily shared. She hugged and waved everyone a goodnight, and Malik walked her to her car. She knew Bradley would have questions, so she dreaded his phone call. But till then, she had to figure out a way to tell Melanie or forget any possibility of her and Bradley happening.

* * *

Bradley was thankful he'd gotten her contact information this time. She had dominated his daydreams since they had met at the airport, and he'd had to keep believing he was going to run into her again. The only other explanation was she had been an angel sent to keep him company in the flesh that day. The only person he had mentioned their encounter to was his mom when she'd visited a few weeks after they met, simply because he still was not sure it had really happened and somehow he raced off without even getting her name.

He contemplated if the following day was too soon, but he had figured out where her art gallery was, and he decided to visit at noon.

"Hello, I'd like to see Abigail Sogal, please," he told the receptionist.

"Oh Abi. She'll be right out. Who may I say is here to see her?" The receptionist flirted, but Bradley didn't notice.

"Bradley Madison. Thank you," he added with a smile.

Abigail had seen him walk into the gallery in his navy chinos, brown long-sleeve top, and dark-gray hoodie, which he left unzipped. She had hoped he would call her to give her a chance to apologize and explain, but he'd decided to show up to make it more difficult for her. Oh well, she might as well get it over with.

"Hi, Brad. Nice of you to stop by." Abigail stretched out her hand with a professional smile.

"Hey. Glad to know I don't have to re-introduce myself today," Bradley replied with a smirk.

"Ouch. But I deserved that. It's about my lunch break now, so could we go someplace to grab a bite? There's an Italian place nearby."

"Sounds good."

"I'm sorry about yesterday," she whispered as soon as they were out the door.

Bradley walked quietly beside her with his hands in his pockets, hoping she would share more.

"You are not going to make this easy, are you," Abigail said with a sigh.

"No," he replied with a mischievous grin on his face.

"Fine. Here we are."

They placed their orders and sat at an outdoor table. The restaurant was on a busy street, and Abigail thought she could do with some noise around for a while before returning to the quiet gallery. Plus, it was a beautiful day, and the weather was nice.

"Why are you in a hood anyway? It's so nice and warm today," she asked.

Bradley shrugged. "An old habit, I suppose. You look really good," he added, staring intently at her.

"Oh, thanks." Abigail smiled and was suddenly very aware of herself. She had received compliments before, but when he said it, looking at her like that, she felt warmer on the inside. She had gone simple that day with a plain forest-green mono-sleeved puffy top, a white midi gypsy skirt, and her floral shoes. Her hair was pinned up nicely, and she'd let a few strands fall by her cheeks, which showed off her pearl studs. Perhaps if she had known he was stopping by, she might have put in a little more effort. But somehow, he seemed to believe she looked good. *"Really good,"* she mentally corrected. *Oh dear, this was not the plan.*

Their meals arrived: shrimp alfredo, calamari, spaghetti with homemade meat sauce and marinara, and lasagna. Abigail added a cocktail to her order, but Bradley had water.

"Mmm. I did not realize I was this hungry. Are you fine with your meal?" Abigail asked after a while.

"Yeah, it's good, thanks. Abi, why did I have to 'meet' you again yesterday?" he asked quietly.

Abigail set her cutlery down, wiped her mouth with her napkin, and took a sip of her drink.

"First, meeting you at the airport was"—she paused and cleared her throat—"was awesome. Great. Incredible. Magical, even. And even though I had hoped and wished every day since then that we would somehow meet again, I didn't think we would. Even more, that you'd turn out to be my good friend's best friend."

She paused and pressed her lips tightly to gather her thoughts. He just looked at her, listening.

"I had never met you before nor seen your picture...you know how serious Mel can be, right. But I knew she had a best friend she cared deeply about, and when she invited me to join you guys for the evening, she explicitly asked me not to flirt with you. Something about you being nice and innocent to everyone." She sighed deeply as she tucked her hair behind her ears.

"Brad, I shared a lot with Mel about my...our encounter at the airport. There was no way she would not have flipped if she found out the said person was you." She finally looked up and saw him smiling.

"You can be intimidating, you know?" she said in an accusing tone.

Bradley laughed quietly before settling to speak. "Meeting you was awesome for me, too. Great. Incredible. Magical even," he added with a grin and leaned forward.

Abigail blushed.

"You do understand, though, right? Why I…we…at least not for now, yeah?" she pressed on.

"Hmm. Is that what you want?" he asked.

She thought for a while with a frown on her face. If she was being honest with herself, she still wasn't sure what she wanted with him. She was trying her best not to end up with another jerk, but she found herself wanting more from this human she was meeting for only the third time. And for the life of her, she knew it had to be more than just physical. She just could not explain how. She was sure, though, that she did not want to hurt Melanie as a result, especially if her instincts about him turned out to be wrong again.

"I want not to have Mel disappointed. She is my friend, Brad," she answered slowly.

"Uh-huh." Bradley nodded and then gulped down some more water.

"So, how's work?" he asked warmly, changing the subject.

Abigail laughed, appreciating his attempt at lightening the mood.

"It's good. I'm now a senior executive, so I get to attend to a few more clients on my own now, voluntarily. I hope to be a manager someday. To have my own clientele to manage, but more importantly, to be an art curator. Beyond enlightening clients about paintings, organizing exhibitions, and making a few sales, I'm particularly interested in discovering new talents. There are some new artists with exquisite styles that big art galleries, like ours, are not giving the opportunity to be seen. In the end, we keep recycling the known and famous and lose out on the unexplored, and possibly highly as profitable, level of artistry. Oh well, I'm probably just…I don't know. I haven't even been bold enough to move out on my own, so there is no way I'm bringing that up," she explained, chuckling at herself.

"Most people try and then fail or succeed. I'm not saying I'll turn out to be who you have imagined. I could be better, or not, but I'd really like to be given my own opportunity. So, Abi, unless you are seeing someone or you really would just want us to be friends, I'm going to have to figure out a way to speak with Mel eventually." Bradley said after a while, his voice an octave lower than it had been as they were conversing. He sounded serious.

Abigail stared at him dumbfounded. Had he seriously just said that? She had thought he was simply listening to her talk about her work and possibly her dreams. Not to mention, he was giving her an out. He was going to speak with Melanie if he had to, just to be with her, even though they had been together for only a few hours. What if it did not work out and she hurt him and lost Melanie too? Or worse still, he decided she was not all that he expected, after all? She still didn't know the answers.

But she did know it was more than his looks that got her having butterflies when she was with him or away from him. Even when his dimples had haunted her for weeks. She also knew she did not have him figured out yet with his invisible wall she was sensing, but she was eager to find out. She had a comforting feeling that, despite his intensity, he wasn't going to hurt her intentionally.

Bradley decided to take her pause as consideration. It was her lunch break, and he was running out of time. His alarm would be going off soon, as well, and he really needed her to know that even though he would respect her decision, he really wanted more with her. For five weeks, he had struggled to find the right words, when or if he eventually met her again, and here she was, and he still did not have the words. She was passionate about her career and had dreams, and like him, she had fears too.

He did not know if she was going to be fine with him once she found out more about him, but till then, he was willing to risk it. She looked at him and spoke with him differently, not "special" like most people did once they found out, and he really treasured that. Aside from his immediate family and Melanie, she'd been the only woman who had got him conscious of his masculinity and certainly not in a family kind of way. It felt strange and really good at the same time.

"Abi?" He tried again.

"Um, no."

"No?" he asked with a worried expression, running his hands through his hair.

"Yes. No, I haven't seen anyone since we first met. Yes, I want more than just friends with you, Brad. And no, I'd rather be the one to tell Mel. Please."

He had studied her face while she spoke and seen the waves of emotions as she answered him. She was sincere about wanting more with him, and that gave him so much relief. He did not like the Melanie part, but if that's what it took, so be it—for now, he hoped.

"Bradley, I've been wrong before about...about this. So...one day at a time if that's okay." Abigail added with a little tremble in her voice. She did not want to get her hopes raised and dashed, so she thought it best to let him know she was not putting her guard down entirely for him just yet.

"One day at a time. Thank you." He breathed with a wide smile that popped his dimples.

Abigail laughed. He really could almost switch emotions like a weathervane.

"And," Bradley added, still smiling, "I know you'll make a great manager and an art curator when you muster up the boldness. As to moving out, just take it a step at a time. Get an agent, look at places. Maybe when you find the one you like, it'll make the moving fun rather than terrifying. That helped me when I had to move."

"Hmm. We'll see. Thanks. So, tell me something I don't know," she continued as the waiter brought the bill.

Bradley reached for it, but she snatched it up.

"Hey, this is my treat. My 'I'm sorry for the charade' treat," she explained.

"Oh, come on. Water under the bridge. But that's fine. My treat tomorrow?" he invited.

"Sure," she answered with a smile.

"But I have a busy day tomorrow with a couple of deliveries, so maybe evening? Except we do another—"

"Evening is perfect," Bradley cut in. "And I'll cook," he added with a wink.

"You cook? Real food not just toast or a sandwich?" she asked, eyes widened in surprise

"Yeah…well, enough to have not poisoned anyone thus far," he added with pride.

"Hmm. Well then, I'll look forward to it." She grinned.

"Do I pick you up from here, or…?"

"Oh no, just send me your address. I'll drive down. I really don't know yet how my day will end."

"Great. And I'm afraid of crickets."

"I'm sorry?"

"You asked to know something about me, yes? Crickets scare me. Among other things about life, but that comes to mind."

Abigail laughed hysterically till her eyes had tears in them.

"Please don't," Bradley said with a wry smile. "They are small but make loud noises and hop suddenly…argh," he continued with a frown.

She wiped the tears off her eyes and eventually sat still with a smile.

"I'm sorry," she apologized.

He waved it off as he reached into his pocket to shut off the alarm from his phone.

"Hey, I have to go now. But I hope you enjoyed having lunch with me as much as I did with you," Bradley said, his voice echoing his seriousness and sincerity.

His looks were warm this minute and intense the next. Not that either made the butterflies in her tummy flutter any less, but she really needed to get used to the switches.

"Yes, I did. Thank you very much. I also have to get back to work anyway." She tried to sound casual. It was too soon to be mushy, right? *One day at a time,* she reminded herself.

Bradley helped her up and gave her a hug. She smelled really good too. Or maybe all his senses had just decided everything about Abigail Sogal was good. Either way, it was fine with him. Even with her heels, he still towered above her like he had observed at the airport. He had to bend his head to give a light kiss on her cheek, then he released his hold on her.

"I'll hang out a while waiting for my ride. Have a great day," he told her as he put his hands into the pockets of his hoodie.

"Okay, then. See you tomorrow." She smiled up at him.

He watched her walk away, admiring how the gentle breeze made the skirt snug around her curves. She must have felt his eyes on her because she turned around to smile and wave at him as the breeze blew her hair on her face, as well. He waved back with a smile and finally pulled out his phone to order his ride when she disappeared around the bend. He sat down and plugged in his earbuds to listen to "Already Home" by A Great Big World while he waited.

* * *

"Hi, I'd like to order some flowers, please," Bradley spoke up when his call was answered. He had woken up with a smile, and he knew absolutely nothing could ruin his day. He decided to dial a local florist to order flowers for Abigail before he went for his morning run.

"Something beautiful," he continued.

"Very well, sir. We have prearranged bouquets, and you could also custom order your arrangements," the nice woman explained. "For example, we have roses, orchids, sunflowers, jasmine, tulips, lilies, and so on. We usually combine two or three complementary flowers or put a single type in a bunch."

"Oh. I think I prefer a single type as the bouquet, but none of the aforementioned does it for me. All nice, yes, but, if it's not too much to ask, something that says graceful, elegant, intriguing, sleek, sophisticated, and timeless all at the same time?"

The lady paused for a while, and Bradley was sure he had lost the connection.

"Hello?" He said into his mouthpiece.

"Yes, still here. I'm going through our collection," she responded.

Bradley chuckled. "I really am sorry for the bother."

"No, it's fine. What do you think of the calla lilies?"

"I can't remember what they look like at the moment. Please describe it while I google it as well."

"They are chic and modern, a single petal per stem that wraps itself to create a beautiful statement. The simplicity of the bloom lends itself to a soft yet unique appearance," she shared excitedly.

Bradley saw the pictures and loved them.

"Perfect. I see they come in various colors too. I like the pink ones if you have those. They seem to have a little white mixed here and there."

"Fantastic. Yes, we do have them in blush pink. How many would you want?"

"Uh, what number is not overwhelming but does not under deliver either?" he asked as he looked up at his clock.

He could hear the smile in her voice when she responded.

"I believe seven sounds perfect. We usually add a few lush greens to single-flower type bouquets, so they'll be sure to be rich. Also, would you want them wrapped in brown paper and a bow around it or delivered in a clear glass French vase?"

"A clear glass vase, please."

"Great. And the message for the accompanying card?"

"Hi, Abi. You look good. Brad."

"All right then. I'll need your card details and the delivery contact and address."

Bradley finished up with the florist and felt happy with his choice. He, however, had overshot his allocated time, so he decided to exercise indoors instead, since he had to do a few things before he got their dinner started. His workout room had a power tower dip station and pull-up bar strength trainer that had a red and black dumbbell bench attached, a smart black treadmill that could incline and decline, and a floor-to-ceiling mirror that covered the whole area of the small wall. The opposite section had black interlocking foam tiles, and arranged on a small movable stand were his adjustable dumbbells, each of which could be adjusted between five and forty-five pounds, a jump rope, and a twenty-five-pound soft kettlebell with a handle for swings and goblet squats.

He inserted his *Rush of Fools* 2007 album and started his workout on the treadmill. Then he worked his way to the dumbbells. And a little more than seventy-five minutes later, as the album ended, he decided he was done for the day.

Abigail had considered going back home again to change before heading out to Bradley's but decided against it. Consequently, she had taken an unusual amount of time in the morning deciding on her outfit for the day, knowing she would still be wearing it that evening. Even though it seemed and felt right this time, she really did not want to jump into the deep end with him too fast, like she had done in the past. She had asked that they take it slow, so she had to conform herself. In the end, she had settled for a V-neck black-and-white checked dress that ended with four corners that cascaded down just below her knees. It was a somewhat free dress that had a large silver safety-pin brooch at the V-plunge. The long sleeves were also loose but had buttoned cuffs, and she had added a solid black mini wrap to accentuate her waist and hips.

However, two hours after she arrived at work, she received the most beautiful blush-pink calla lilies bouquet with a note from him saying she looked good—without having seen her. She had been the envy of the gallery the whole day. She did not have an office to herself, so everyone who passed by her workstation gave her a wink, a questioning smile, or an outright grin. She had planned to use the flowers as an excuse to get home first but decided at the last minute to leave them at work. She did not need her mom asking questions either.

Thankfully, she had packed her red wedge sandals in case she could not make it back home to change. She sprayed her perfume, changed her lipstick to wine as well, and touched up her face. With one final look in her rearview mirror, she smiled at herself and headed out.

"Hi." Bradley smiled brightly as he opened his door for her.

"Hey, you." She smiled and he gave her a hug.

"Mmm, nice fragrance, too." he noted against her ear.

Abigail chuckled. "Too?"

"You look good. And smell nice, too." he said, looking into her eyes.

"*Oh dear*, she thought and swallowed.

"Thanks for the flowers. They were absolutely lovely. I loved them. So did every other lady at the gallery, but mostly me." She laughed.

Bradley laughed too. "I'm glad. You're welcome."

He ushered her in and handed her a glass of fresh orange juice.

"I'm just about making our crème broulee. Dinner should be ready in less than thirty minutes."

"Okay."

Abigail got busy with taking in his apartment. His living room was an open space that connected the kitchen to where should have been a dining area but instead there was a black grand piano and bench. As she entered, she had noticed a room to her left that she assumed was his home office because she had seen what looked like a work desk through the open door. Two flights of stairs meant his bedroom was probably upstairs, so the two closed doors opposite each other before the office had to be restrooms or something else.

Abigail wondered why a single man needed so much space. Perhaps he wasn't as innocent as she thought.

The colors he'd chosen were very subtle and toned down too. Shades of gray and one white wall. The wall of the staircase, though, was navy blue next to the white wall, which made a really nice contrast. Everywhere was beautifully lit, and his sofa had a similar chrome color. His kitchen was beautiful and neatly arranged; she wondered if his ex had that fixed for him. She was surprised at her jealousy but quickly moved on. Underscoring what he had told her about his love for art, Bradley had about four abstract paintings all around, one in the living room, one by the kitchen, and one behind his piano. The fourth painting was minimal, with words in a white rectangle in the middle. She moved closer and read, "Bradley, my grace is enough; it's all you need. My strength comes into its own in your weakness. Love, God" (2 Corinthians 12:9, MSG).

Abigail read it several times and wondered why she was seeing the verse in that version for the first time in a new light. *Perhaps because he personalized it? And why is this scripture personal to him?* she wondered. The only other picture was a large black-and-white picture of him when he was probably about three years old. He wasn't smiling or frowning, but he looked right into the lens of the camera with his head tilted a bit like he was studying the photographer. He still gave her that piercing look sometimes. She was drawn to the picture for reasons she did not know, wondering what must have been going on in his mind as a child and why that was the only picture of him or his family on display.

"Brad, are you an only child?" she asked.

"Nope. Got two younger identical twin sisters. Well, they used to be, not so much now. Emma is married to Ian, and they are expecting their first child. They live in California but not Nevada County. Emily is halfway through her residency as a medical doctor in another state."

Interesting, she thought. She moved on to a shelf that had about five rows of his music collection and two layers dedicated to his Sony PlayStation VR headsets with motion controllers, camera, the original box, and about ten different app cartridges and game CDs. He had an eighty-five-inch LCD television, which made some sense on seeing the PlayStation, but he also had a CD player. She had not seen that in years, but neither had she seen someone with so many CDs given the age and times. And some of his selections were not familiar. He had some mixes he must have compiled himself, but most were albums of various artists including Cory Asbury, Ed Sheeran, Owl City, The Fray, Rush of Fools, Michael Bublé, Kutless, Jeremy Camp, Casting Crowns, Hillsong, Joshua Radin, Phil Wickham, Parachute, Michael W. Smith, and Jonathan Traylor. The list went on for about two more rows. Some artists had three or five different albums next to each other, but other than that, Abigail did not notice any particular order to the arrangements.

After surveying the many CDs, Abigail turned to Bradley and asked, "First, you do have a smart television set, right? With this badass home theater. And I glimpsed an Echo Dot on your work desk, as well. So why do you have a CD player?"

"Because I have CDs," he answered with a smirk. He could guess what was coming next.

"Let me rephrase—why do you *still* have so many CDs?"

Bradley laughed.

"They are originals. I collected most of them growing up and have not been able to part with them. I don't buy as much anymore, anyway, and they have all been backed up, but putting them on still feels different from what we have now."

"I see. I recognized Michael Bublé, at least. And maybe two others. So what's your favorite collection?"

"Uh, that's a tough one. But as of today, Rush of Fools and Owl City."

"Rush of Fools?" she asked in confusion as she made her way to sit with him at the kitchen area.

Bradley chuckled.

"Before you get all judgmental, I read their band name was inspired by First Corinthians 1, I think 26 to 31 or so. How God chose the foolish things of the world to put to shame those who consider themselves mighty so everything and everyone can glory in God alone. Something like that. And being a living testimony that I am, I resonate with that."

Abigail listened with rapt attention, wondering why he would have taken the time to find out to start with. Or had he known she would ask?

"And what album are we listening to now?" she continued after a few sips of her juice.

"*Is There Anybody Out There* album by A Great Big World." He smiled as he hummed along.

"Are you sure this is not part of your favorites? You've sung along with almost every track."

"Nah. I like two—no, three—okay, four tracks the most." He laughed at himself.

"Yeah, right," she retorted sarcastically.

His kitchen was neat, and each time he added a seasoning, he but it back in place on the seasoning rack, with the label facing the front. He measured everything he cut or poured with precision, and he stretched the wooden spoon toward her for a taste of the soup.

For dessert, he was making them crème brûlée. He had his eggs yolks and egg whites already separated in small glass bowls next to measuring cups and spoons for the milk, flour, butter, and all. After he had combined all the ingredients, he filled the four white ceramic bowls with the batter, and there was no extra left.

Interesting, Abigail thought. He let it bake for about eight minutes while he dished up their food, and then he brought the bowls out to finish up the top crust with his torch. He could almost pass for a professional chef as he added three blueberries and figs on top of each cup. Watching him was already filling for her. Though her stomach thought otherwise.

Suddenly Bradley's phone rang, startling him, and he dropped the pan of the custard he was holding, which splashed on his T-shirt and shorts. Some also smeared his work top and socks, but he picked up his phone anyway.

"Hey man, you home?"

Bradley had answered without checking who the caller was, but he recognized his friend's voice.

"Hi, Malik. Yeah, I am. Why?" he asked.

"My date canceled. Wanted to come over for a game," Malik explained.

"Oh, I'm hanging out with Abi, so this may not be the best time. Tomorrow?"

"Abi? Mel's friend Abigail?" Malik asked again.

Oh crap! Bradley realized his error.

Abigail's face was horrified, and her hands went over her mouth and nose as her eyes shut tightly.

"Yes, that Abi. Malik, this has to stay between us for now, though. Please." Bradley tried to rectify the situation.

"That's fine. I was just surprised."

"Not Josh, not Mel. I can trust you with this, right?" He pressed again, especially because Abigail still looked worried.

"You have my word, Brad. Later then."

"Thanks. Bye."

Bradley dropped his phone carefully and stared at her, willing her to look at him.

"I'm so sorry," he said softly when she finally did.

"It's fine."

"He gave me his word, though," he tried again.

Abigail chuckled.

"It's fine, Brad. I need you to feed me now, please." She smiled.

She knew, however, that her clock had started ticking. She had to talk to Melanie soon.

Bradley led her to his balcony where he had two sets of tables and chairs but had laid out one for them. The dishes and cutlery were neatly set, and she was tempted to ask if he had a caterer come over just for this. He poured her a glass of wine and served her Swiss rolls. He placed the roasted chicken on the table with their bowls of potato soup and plates of steamed basmati rice sprinkled with parsley. Because he occupied the penthouse of the high-rise apartment building, he had quite a view from his balcony.

"Dig in," he announced with a smile.

Abigail was awed and sat down to start with the appetizer.

"I need to quickly clean the spill in the kitchen before it dries up and change my shirt, as well, so I'll join you soon. But please, by all means, do carry on." He dropped a kiss on her cheek and disappeared, but not before changing the album in the player to Michael Bublé, for her listening pleasure.

"You must spend a lot on your wardrobe and laundry. You do smell fresh and nice, though," she said with a smile when he reappeared about ten minutes later in faded blue jeans and a white and wine raglan long-sleeve T-shirt that sat snugly on him, showing off his abs.

He smiled but did not comment.

Abigail reminded herself for the umpteenth time that she needed to stop staring at him so she could enjoy the actual food he had worked hard preparing for them.

"You have a very lovely place. Hope your bills are not killing?" She tried to sound casual and to distract herself, although she really had been wondering.

"Not so much. I did not need to move here till about four years ago. The piano had been a gift from my parents and my flat screen from my sisters. My smaller TV set moved to my bedroom, and my old digital keyboard I donated to my church, though I intend to get another when I get a bigger place. I have saved over the years though, so spaces like my home office happened over time. So did my workout room."

"You have a gym in here?" she asked, really surprised.

"Um, not quite a gym. Just two major equipment pieces and a few smaller ones. I usually run in the nearby park or around the block, and I play basketball a few times with the guys."

"It's just so much space for…well, only you."

He laughed at her expression.

"The guys come over to play games, as well, or just hang out," he explained.

"Still. But that's fine." She gave up and continued eating her food.

He chuckled.

"Everything tasted delicious. I must confess, I think you are a better cook than I am," Abigail added, then wiped her mouth to take some water.

"Hmm, thank you?" He raised his brow with a questioning smile.

"I am serious, Brad."

He stretched his legs and took some water.

"I know. Thank you." He smiled as he wiped his mouth.

He was looking at her intently again. The sun had set, and it was a little chilly, but his gaze made her all warm and fuzzy inside. Then he spoke and brought her wandering mind back.

"Would you want to experience a virtual reality game?" he asked softly.

"Yes, please," she answered excitedly.

Bradley was not sure why he had asked, but he felt compelled to share his world with her. Well, almost all, for now. And he was trying hard not to be the jerk he'd heard some guys could be on first or second dates, but he had been staring at her full and inviting lips for so long, he had to come up with something. Although technically this was their fourth meeting, it was only the second date, as it were. But how was he to know she would be excited about his virtual reality game? Abigail Sogal was definitely a piece of work.

They cleared the table and went back into his living room for him to make the connections.

"So it's pretty easy," Bradley explained as he helped her get the headset on and wrapped her hands around the console as he handed it to her. Then he put on his own headset and grabbed the control console.

"I'll just pick out a basic arcade game for us where we are a team and shoot down the bad guys, all right? Call out or spell out your character name, then choose an avatar."

"All right. So far so good." Abigail was grinning as she did this. She had also taken off her shoes to get more comfortable. It felt strange not looking at a screen but rather into the simulated-eyes-monitor thing and feeling alive at the same time.

"By the way, there is a camera recording when we start, so you can watch your movements after the game if you want. It's usually interesting seeing yourself move your arms and body in thin air."

"Oh! I'm definitely up for that." She giggled along with him.

"Okay then, so I'm ready when you are. Are you in yet? You should see some sand dunes and big rocks and drones flying about."

"Yes, I am. They all seem so big and high up, though."

43

"Strange. I can't see you either. I'm the purple dude with the mohawk haircut. Do you mind doing something with your hands or so?"

Abigail pressed a button on her console and jumped. Bradley jumped backward in fright and fell on his sofa, as he yanked off his headset. His console fell to the floor, and his hands came to his chest and eyes as he tried to steady his breathing. Abigail removed her headset and was laughing aloud till her eyes had tears in them. She placed her console down carefully and sat on the sofa next to him, still laughing till her sides hurt and she had to hold on with her hands. She had selected a rather large dark-brown cricket as her avatar, and the jump and sound had both surprised and freaked him out. She had meant to just tease him, but his reaction was more than she had expected.

"Abi...?" he finally managed to say, but she was still laughing and didn't hear him. He liked her laugh. Probably loved it. And he wished he could be a part of it, but he just couldn't right then.

Abigail felt his lips on hers, and her laugh faded slowly into him. She opened her eyes slowly to look at him, and then he raised his head a few inches from hers. He had moved in front of her and was on his right knee, with his hands at each side of her on the sofa.

"I do love your laugh, but please don't...don't do that again," Bradley whispered in all seriousness as he stared intently at her.

"Okay. I'm sorry," she responded, slightly out of breath.

Then he bent his head forward and kissed her again, this time with his hand in her hair. She wasn't sure what to do with her hands, but one found its way up and rested gently on his jawline. His facial hair felt nice against her palm. And just as suddenly as he'd started, he moved away and sat back down next to her. Abigail licked her lips and willed her body not to show the shudders going through her.

What just happened? she thought. She had not meant to give him a panic attack, but then, *Who ever had a panic attack from a virtual cricket jump?* She had imagined their first kiss many times before they met again at the diner. In her imagination, there had been sparks and drum roll moments that would lead up to it. The kiss in her head had been great. Longer and great. This, however, was nothing like she had imagined. She had not seen it coming nor envisioned that she would be feeling apologetic, but it was definitely better than great. It was near perfect. Unfortunately, it was shorter than she would have wanted, but he tasted and smelled so good she was surprised she found her voice to respond. Worse still, the seriousness in his voice did a little more than he probably intended. It was a good thing he stopped when he did, because she clearly could have scared him off with her naturally bold instincts. This was "new Abi." She could not afford to be too forward or get tangled too soon again.

She straightened her dress and arranged herself on the sofa as she faced him. He was looking fine again, and he offered to play the game again—right this time—but she declined.

"Maybe some other time. It is getting late, and I have some emails to send out before tomorrow, so I should get going," she said with a smile.

Bradley smiled back but with a questioning look. He stood up to get her wedge sandals and sat across from her, watching as she slipped them on. She grabbed her purse, ready to leave, so he stood to walk her out but stopped in front of her.

"We are good, yes?" He took her free hand in his and lifted her chin to look at him with the other.

"Yes, we are. I had a great time, Brad." She smiled up at him.

He studied her face for a few seconds before responding. "Okay, then. Me too." He smiled back and hugged her tightly. He had been worried that perhaps he had been a jerk after all. He was grateful he had been able to get his panic attack under control before she asked questions he was not ready to answer. He walked her to her car and gave her a light kiss on the cheek before he waved her off.

* * *

Bradley exited the elevator to wait in the lobby while he ordered his ride. He had just signed the contract offer and completed the onboarding documentations, after waiting nine days, hoping that the call would come soon. Everything was going according to plan, and he could not be happier.

The premises were big and looked so quiet from the outside, one could never guess so much activity went on in the different companies that occupied various floors. The few people he had come across had been welcoming. A stranger would have thought he was already a part of the team, rather than a new one coming on board as contract staff. His own department and open floor plan had a lot of buzz going on, though. Names and numbers were shouted from across the floor, screens were everywhere, and everyone walked around staring into a document or device. He was concerned that may get to him initially, but he felt up to the challenge and believed he would overcome the uneasiness after a few days.

He had held off telling his parents and siblings, just so they would not be as anxious as he was. He had also wanted him and Abigail to be on the same page before he told his mom he did meet her again. So as soon as he left the HR office, he had placed a call to his mom to share the good news, but it went to her voice mail. He had also tried his dad and got the same thing. *Perhaps they are at a weekday function*, he thought. He had asked after Joshua and been told he was out of the office all day, so he proceeded to order his ride, intending to call Melanie and then Abigail on his way home. He was in the middle of the process when he looked up and saw Melanie's car through the glass door. She was parked outside the front of the building, and Joshua was walking speedily toward her. She seemed to be in deep distress. He stood up to join them, but then his phone rang. His dad was calling back.

"Hello, Dad."

"Hi, Son, have you seen Melanie?" His dad spoke so faintly, Bradley almost did not hear him, despite the earbud firmly stuck in his ear.

"Uh, I'm walking toward her now. Why?" he answered with a frown.

"Oh, I thought that was why you called."

"No. What's going on, Dad?" Bradley's heart was beating fast. He did not know what it was, but he sensed it was heavy. He was closer to Melanie now, and he saw she was crying and shaking so badly that Joshua was practically all that was keeping her from falling. They saw him, and she tried to wipe her face as she started to move towards the building to meet him.

"They lost her, son," his dad said after a few seconds.

Bradley stopped in his tracks and narrowed his eyes. He tried to catch his breath and adjusted his earbuds to be sure he heard his dad well.

"Who lost who?" he managed to ask through his clenched jaw and worried brows. Melanie and Joshua had gotten to him, and she was saying things he could not make out. He felt like his skies were darkening as he dreaded what his dad was about to say.

"Mom."

Time stood still, and all Bradley could hear was his own heartbeat slowing down.

Chapter 3

"I can't believe you're here!" Bradley hugged his mom tightly with a broad smile and helped with her bigger suitcase as they made their way out of the Raleigh-Durham International Airport.

"Well, I am." She gave him a kiss on the cheek and wheeled her carry-on.

"And don't get me wrong—I am happy to have you here, mom, but how and why did dad ever allow you leave?" Bradley asked as soon as he had buckled his seat belt in the back seat of their uber.

"Argh! First, I talk my way out of the house, and now I have to convince you to have me here with you?" His mom rolled her eyes at him.

He laughed.

"Of course not, Mom, and you know it. I left home barely a month ago. Imagine my surprise when you call to say you were arriving today to spend some days with me," he explained, not that he thought she did not get that, but he was used to explaining just what he meant, and this time was no different. He nudged her gently with his elbow when she still refused to give him her attention. Then she finally looked his way.

"If you must know, I'm on a holiday. I enjoyed having you all around for Christmas, but you know how tiring hosting can be. So, I decided I'll start out with you, then fly to Emily, and lastly visit Emma and Ian," his mom told him with a smile.

"And dad?" he asked quizzically.

"He chose not to come along unless we chose a later date, but I really wanted to do this now, so here I am." She ended with a shrug and turned toward the window of the car on her side to soak in the city as they made their way down the streets.

"Okay. That's fine, Mom." He smiled.

His mom had visited several times, but each time she looked around, expecting something new to catch her interest. And because she was meticulous and observant, she easily spotted the new eateries or renovations or new buildings or parks. Bradley was convinced he got his childlike mind from his mother.

"Would you want to stop by at Mel's?" he asked after a while.

"I definitely will see her, but maybe not now. Plus I have some items that need refrigerating immediately." She added the last bit in a whisper and with a straight face.

"You have what?" Bradley asked surprised. "Mom, you traveled over two thousand miles with cooked meals for me?"

"Don't act so surprised! This won't be my first time," she responded defensively.

"I was what, eighteen? Nineteen? And I remember we agreed that was going to be the last time. I have a home, I cook, and I have a housekeeper," he said laughing. There was no way he could be upset with his mom. The woman just did what she decided was best, no matter the circumstance, and they all knew even when she disobeyed, as it were, it was out of love.

Bradley's mom decided to go jogging with him the following morning, so he took a shorter route and went more slowly than he usually did. They ended up at the park near his apartment, and they decided it was a good day for some outdoor time. He ordered a beef po'boy and iced tea while his mom had a club sandwich and a bottle of water. They headed back to the park, sipping on their drinks while they looked for a spot. For a weekday, quite a number of people were already out with their toddlers, either in strollers or just taking walks. Some were gathered at other tables having a bite, as well, as they hung out. Most were casually dressed, but a few looked dressed for the office.

"How about here?" Bradley asked as they drew close to a bench and table that were well shaded by giant trees.

"Perfect," his mom agreed, and they placed their meals on the table.

Bradley took his seat opposite his mom, then lifted his legs one after the other to take off his running shoes and socks. He always loved the feel of the earth or grass under his feet and between his toes. His mom smiled and did same.

Bradley laughed. "You really don't have to, Mom."

"I know. But I ended up enjoying it myself back then. What's one more day?" she said with a wink. Bradley chuckled. When he was growing up, his mom or dad had usually joined him in taking off their footwear when they went to a park, just so he would not feel weird or different. Naturally, as he grew older, he had overcome feeling odd with some things that he felt good about, but he could not stop loving nature.

"This looks good," his mom said as they unwrapped their sandwiches.

They took a few bites and savored the taste. The wind blew gently as the sun warmed the day.

"So, how are you? Really? What's new? Or old?" she asked after swallowing her third bite. Bradley shrugged and took some of his iced tea as he swallowed a large bite of his sandwich.

"Not much really. Still applying here and there, hopeful something will come up soon."

"And it will. I'm actually concerned Emily may be too busy to hang out much with me like you are, but that's fine. I'm happy to be with her any way I can be this time," she added.

Bradley stared at his mom. Something told him her trip was not ordinary, but he let it be. She was here, and she was always welcome.

"Are you still on the medications?" he asked quietly.

"Yes, I am. But I'm fine, son. Not to worry." She smiled and gave his hand a squeeze.

"Okay then. That's good." He told her with a small smile lurking at the corners of his mouth. He had not totally agreed, but he was not about to make her feel worried that he was worried about her.

"I met someone," Bradley started after a few minutes of silence as they enjoyed their food.

"Uh-huh." She grinned and widened her eyes in anticipation of him sharing more, which made him laugh.

"It's not like that, mom. Well, I don't know yet. We met last month at the airport when my flight was delayed. She was stressed out, and I helped. But then I invited her to wait out our delayed flights with me at the lounge." He stopped for his mom's reaction, but she just stared at him, smiling.

He chuckled. "You've got to say something. I know you want to."

Mrs. Madison was overwhelmed already, irrespective of how the story ended. Her son who did not like being touched growing up was now a huger and voluntarily trying to have a romantic relationship without external influence. She was forever thankful for their journey because it had taught her tolerance and love and a different way of seeing things.

The hardest parts had been the fights for services, the fights for people who mattered to understand who he was and what he needed, the fights for knowledge, and the many quiet fights within herself, mostly on her knees, wondering if they had left no stone unturned. Even when she was tired and stretched thin—not like she knew where the strength came from in the first place—she always believed God was up to something good. All the time.

They had dealt not with tattoos or alcohol or his keeping the wrong company but rather with his communication, his independence, his social etiquette. They had encouraged him to learn to be employable by joining a vocational support group. And all the while, they chose to ignore the snide comments, the unending unsolicited advice from people, the pitying looks despite the supposed awareness in the twenty-first century. She had trusted her gut and heart even against the doctors' advice, knowing when to give him his space, especially when he was a teenager and then as a young adult, choosing to allow him to make his own mistakes and learn from them.

She was so grateful for the bond they had. That they all had with him. If there was ever anything they made sure he knew, it was that he was loved. They all loved him, and she was happy he knew that because he showed and expressed his love for his family too.

"Nope. Do go on," she simply replied with a smile.

"Uh! Well, we had a great conversation. She spoke so intelligently, and we had some common interests in music and art. Well, I was more into music and she into art. She worked in an art gallery, she said. Anyway time went by faster than we knew, and I rushed off to catch my flight without realizing we had not exchanged names," he concluded with chuckle, imagining how lame he sounded to his mom. He had decided during his flight that he wasn't going to tell anyone that story—unless by some divine order, he ran into her again. There was no point making himself a discussion topic to be laughed at. Although he hoped with all his heart that he would run into her again. But he had been compelled to share it with his mom. Probably because she was there in person with him. They had spoken over the phone a few times since he got back, and he had not felt a need to share.

"She was pretty, wasn't she?" his mom asked, still smiling broadly.

Bradley laughed.

"That's your takeaway from this?" he asked after a few seconds.

"You conversed for almost two hours without asking for her name!" She shook her head at him and finished her sandwich.

"I know. I know." he muttered as shook his head at himself and covered his face with his hands.

"But yes, she was very beautiful. And I'm not proud to say this, but I did stare at her. A lot." He added and averted his eyes, knowing his mom would convey unspoken words with just a look. He finished his iced tea instead and waved at a woman who pushed a stroller nearby. He and his mom knew the dance, and she laughed at him.

"I hope your paths cross again, and even if they don't, I'm proud of the man you are. Any lady will be blessed to be with you," she told him with a warm smile.

"Thanks, mom."

His phone beeped with a message from Melanie.

"Mel says would you prefer to come by her diner, or may she drop by the house after her work hours?"

"Let's go to her diner. It's been a while," his mom confirmed as she put her running shoes back on. Bradley replied to Melanie's message, and they head back to his apartment.

"And please, not a word about what I told you to anyone, especially not Emily or Emma. My ears will be full," he pleaded as they strolled off. His mom laughed, but nodded in agreement and gestured a "zipped and locked" sign across her lips. He chuckled and leaned in to give her a kiss on the cheek.

* * *

It was dark, and the rain kept pouring down. Bradley was sinking in what seemed like a pool, but he stretched out his hands to fight the waves. *Why won't she save me?* He could hear her calling out for him to not give up. Would it not have been easier to pull him out? The waves crashed even harder, and he sank deeper. Her voice grew fainter, and he knew he was deeper than ever. He needed to swim, as he could not hold his breath much longer. He was running out of time and options. He could either open his mouth and call for help, at the risk of the water filling his lungs, or fight with the little strength he had left before giving up.

Bradley sat up on his bed with a spring, sweating profusely, even though the rain poured hard outside. It had been a dream. He tossed his drenched short-sleeve pajama top into the laundry bag and went downstairs for some tap water. His digital wall clock read 2:27 a.m. His bed would need to be aired, so there was no point going back in there. He could sleep on his couch or his guest room, but he headed for his study instead. Even though the rest of his house was different shades of gray, his study and bedroom had at least one white wall each.

"Alexa, shuffle songs by Owl City," he called to the Echo Dot on his white desk. Bradley reflected on his last conversations with his mom. He should have insisted she stay longer than four days. *How was I to know that was the last time I was going to be with her?* She had been full of life as always. Except it was two months later, and he'd been made to perform some rites at her funeral. He felt so lost. He chose to believe it was a bad dream he was going to wake up from, and he had left the family house the very next day. He was still angry. He also had questions. Questions he was not sure anyone could answer for him, so he kept them to himself. Even though it was a Saturday, he fired up his Mac desktop to do some work. He seemed to be losing his edge these days, and as much as his manager was accommodating, he really did not like to be the reason for errors. Hopefully he would eventually be tired enough to fall into a dreamless sleep, he thought. He rubbed the back of his neck and stretched. He picked up the little photo frame on his desk, and he felt a half smile curl on his lips. It was a picture of him and his identical twin sisters at ages ten and five. They were struggling with him for his PS5 console, even though they clearly could not play his video games. Their mom had taken the picture for one of the many scrapbooks she put together.

A sixteen-by-twenty-inch framed picture of him and his parents at the airport hung on the light gray wall opposite him. He had a similar size photo in his bedroom with Second Timothy 1:7: *"For God has not given us a spirit of fear, but of power and of love and of a sound mind"*.

His parents had spent about a week with him that year, and he was dropping them off at the airport when his mom insisted on the picture to tease his sisters. It was unplanned, taken with his phone, and their smiles were genuine. She had unexpectedly pulled his head down to give him a kiss on his cheek so the "ladies" could know that no matter how tall he got, she was still his mom. Bradley chuckled at the memory. Next to that was a smaller framed watercolor of a fern leaf that Melanie had brought him from her weekend away with Joshua. He placed the picture of his sisters back carefully and connected his external keyboard as he sang along with his Echo Dot.

* * *

"Hi." Bradley opened his door and hugged Abigail tightly, giving her a kiss on the cheek as he helped her in.

"You look good," he added with a smile.

"Hey, love. Thanks. Sorry to barge in on you. I'm picking up artwork nearby to be ready for Monday and thought to stop by since I'm running early," Abigail explained again.

"It's fine really. I am expecting Mel later, so I was surprised when your call came in. Hey, I was about to play a cover of "Gone, Gone, Gone", one of my favorites by Phillip Phillips, so perfect timing."

She grabbed one of his high chairs and sat across from him by the end of his black grand piano, crossed her legs, and leaned on the piano.

He sat on the front half of the cushioned bench, with his back straight, and started with a few keys, alternating the black ones and white ones with his left hand before the right one joined in, and then he started to sing. She had thought it was just his piano arrangement he wanted to share, and it turned out she did not know the song, but he was doing a great job so far. She had to listen attentively, too, to catch the lyrics as he started out by looking at her as he sang, which was, as usual, super intense and distracting. Eventually he had shut his eyes and still played on. And now he had a frown across his face.

The fluid movements of his fingers on the keys grabbed her attention, and she made her way to sit next to him on the bench. He seemed to have taken complex instrumentations and boiled them down to a simple yet effective series of piano chords. He must have included bits of his own in some verses and interludes, too, but above all, his voice was smooth and intense. He shut his eyes for most of the parts he sang, and because she wasn't familiar with the song, she didn't know if the song was dedicated to her or his mom. Or both. The lyrics sounded like he was communicating things he struggled to say in regular sentences. Some parts of the song were upbeat and fast, others had a slower tempo, and he knew how to accentuate the lyrics. As he wound down, he played slower and opened his eyes to look at her as he sang.

Then he took her right hand and placed his over hers to strike the last few keys, still singing.

At this point, Abigail decided, *It has to be about his mom, except I'm not giving him enough reasons to...or is he wondering if I'm going to leave him? Why would he think that? But again, he seemed to always need me to not forget—*

Bradley interrupted her thoughts by lifting her hand to his lips for a soft kiss against her knuckles. He smiled at her.

"That was so beautiful," she whispered.

56

Placing her hand on his cheek, she made him look at her and asked softly, "Bradley, are you okay?"

"No." He winced and shook his head.

"No. But I will be. I have to be." He sighed and tried to smile at her.

Her heart ached to see him in pain, and she wished she had the right words to soothe him. She reached up and kissed him softly at first, unsure if that was the right thing at the moment. She really just wanted him to know she was there for him, but his hand went around her waist to pull her closer, and he kissed her back. Not softly like she had done. His kiss was hungry and needy, and he cradled her head gently as he slid her in front of him onto his lap. She had to tuck a knee underneath her other dangling limb, and even though he had moved back a notch to accommodate her, she felt the hard piano pressed against her back.

Her hands had been around his neck and head, but his tongue was demanding. His hot kisses moved to the column of her throat, along the pulse point, and then he was at her collarbone. She reflexively held on to the piano and struck some keys in the process. She felt him smile against her, but he was not slowing down. As much as she was enjoying their passionate moment and was wondering why she was considering what she was about to do, she knew she had to think straight for both of them. He was hurting and vulnerable at the time, and there was no telling if they would regret what may or may not happen.

"Bradley," Abigail managed to breathe out, even though her eyes were still shut.

"Mmm..."

"Bradley, Mel will be over soon," she tried again, opening her eyes this time. He slowed his trail of kisses and finally came to a stop as he kept his face buried in her neck and tried to catch his breath. His hands were still around her and hers around him. He looked up and tried to straighten her tank top and arrange her blown-out hair with his fingers.

"I'm sorry" he started slowly.

"I'm not," she cut in with a smile. She lifted her hand to his face, her thumb moving over his brow, down to his jawline, to where his dimple would be if he was smiling, and then across his lips. And he let her do this with his gaze locked on hers the whole time.

"I just don't want us to regret anything later. You know, with you hurting now and all," she continued and pulled his black hood over his head playfully, to ease the pressure that was fast building again. He smiled and gave her hug.

"I love you, Abi. Don't forget, okay?" he whispered into her hair.

"Okay. I should get going though. Anytime now—" Abigail continued, but they were interrupted by his buzzer. He went to the intercom to buzz Melanie up, while Abigail tried to get her hormones under control, in preparation for Melanie meeting her there. She still had not found the right time to have the talk with her friend, and she hated hiding out as much as Bradley hated not telling Melanie. And worse still, Malik knew. He had promised Bradley not to say anything, but she wouldn't put it past him to slip up, and that would be worse than her speaking to Melanie first.

"Hello, Mel." Bradley smiled warmly as he opened the door.

"Hey, buddy, you good?" Melanie gave him a peck on the cheek as they hugged.

"Oh, hi, Abi. Came to extend your condolences too?" she greeted in surprise.

Abigail hugged her tightly with a smile.

"Hi, Mel, you could say that. But I'm on my way out anyway to pick up a replacement artwork for a client. This was a pit stop."

Bradley excused himself to pour Melanie a drink in the kitchen. He did not want to get involved in case Melanie pressed her, but thankfully, she did not.

"Oh, right. Well done, and thanks a lot for checking in on him. Very thoughtful, really," Melanie added as she made her way to get the glass Bradley had poured for her.

"Well, you guys have fun." Abigail headed for the door.

"Hey, Mel, I'll be right back. I need to walk Abi to her car."

"Yeah, sure, I'm good. Bye, Abi."

They waved at each other.

The elevator ride to the parking lot was a quiet one. Bradley stood at the opposite end with his hands in his pockets, except when he had to press a button, and seemed deep in thought. Abigail wasn't sure if he was upset about earlier or at her delay in talking to Melanie about them or if he was just grieving again. But his posture made her feel he was distancing himself from her somehow, and it did not sit well with her. They got off the elevator and made their way to her sky-blue Hyundai accent. She had her back-up work shoes in the back and a work binder on the passenger seat near her mint gums by the gearshift, but otherwise, her car interior was neat.

She opened the door, tossed her small purse to the back seat, and turned around to give Bradley a hug. But he kissed her. Slowly and intentionally. This time he was gentle, and his hold at her waist was firm but not too tight. It communicated what she would have preferred he said. Nonetheless, she was relieved to know he wasn't shutting her out.

"Thank you," she whispered against his lips with a smile.

"Thanks for stopping by. Really." He held on to her.

"You're welcome. Bye, love."

Bradley watched her get into her car and stayed till she drove off.

* * *

Bradley took to the long couch again at Dr. Heather's office. The length seemed to work for his legs. She had called to mention she had an urgent stop at her daughter's school and could reschedule, but he'd opted to wait. Her receptionist had chosen to play Enya that day.

"Hi, Brad. I'm sorry to have kept you waiting," Dr. Heather greeted as she walked in fifteen minutes later.

Bradley opened his eyes and smiled at her.

"Hope your daughter is fine. Catherine, right?"

"Yes, and she is now, thank you," she said, appreciating his concern. She fished out her notepad and took her seat, ready for their session.

"I had a dream yesterday. I remember a similar incident did happen, only it was not raining that day. In my dream, it was pouring, and I had gone outside the house by myself. I must have been about five or six years old or so. It was at night, and our neighbor had seen me and raised an alarm as she dashed out. My dad ran out, too, and thanked her. I do not remember her face now, but she was not Mrs. Johnson, and he hurried back inside with me. Mom was holding out a big towel to wrap me with. Dad had been very angry and scolded me as that had not been my first attempt to go outside by myself. Mom wrapped me and was muttering things I later understood was 'speaking in tongues'. Then I woke up." Bradley shared.

"That's good. Having other characters involved and a connection from a past memory means you are accepting better," Dr. Heather noted as she jotted a few things.

"How was the gratitude jar exercise?" she continued.

"It went well, I suppose. I almost filled a two-quart jar." He sat up, smiling as he put one foot on the other knee.

"Awesome. Care to share some of what you wrote down?"

He thought through the times he actually wrote down, and most of it had memories attached to the gratitude.

He had been grateful for his childhood. The tears and the smiles and laughter.

For their family trips, which were usually stressful on his parents, but they still went on them for him and his sisters.

For Melanie.

For Malik.

For the high school and college days he had to form and defend his faith.

For his dad's leadership.

His dad's strength and resilience.

His sisters' love.

For his mom.

His mom's cooking.

Her constant outpouring of love.

Her patience.

He was grateful for the times he was rushed into the ER because he had swallowed a coin or crayons, and it had not done him harm.

He was grateful for the favor he'd enjoyed from people.

For good health.

For his ability to cook well.

For joy in his heart that usually overflowed its banks.

For those who encouraged his parents.

For his therapy sessions since the age of two and a half.

He was grateful for his teachers.

For Mel and Josh.

For Ms. Lopez and others from back home.

He was grateful for understanding neighbors.

For the swimming lessons.

For the testimony of graduating high school.

For his college degree.

For his work projects.

He was grateful for his ability to have intelligent conversations on his own.

For understanding and wisdom.

He was grateful for his local church here and back home.

He was grateful for his journey. Not once had he felt alone, even during times he was frustrated.

He was grateful for support.

He was grateful for God's grace always sufficient in his weakness.

He was grateful for the times he wrote outside the lines, and when he wrote within the lines.

The times he colored outside the lines and when he drew and painted within the lines.

He was grateful for musical ears and the ability to play excellently. For his voice.

For the highs and lows. For those who were clearly orchestrated by God to help him or his parents along the way.

And last and certainly not least, he was grateful for Abigail. The timing of her arrival could not have been more perfect.

And he was indeed grateful for his dimples. Because Abi loved them.

Bradley knew he could tell his therapist what he'd written, or some of them, at least, but she probably wouldn't appreciate why he would have been extra grateful for what he had on his list, so he decided to keep them to himself. She had been patient not to interrupt his thoughts, and he still had to give her an answer.

"Maybe not today," he finally said.

She smiled briefly at him and added, "That's understandable. Feel free to discontinue, though. But if you ever feel the need to, leave the jar open for more."

He nodded in acknowledgment.

"Right. We have a short exercise today. Please join me at the round table," she invited as she headed over to take a seat herself.

Bradley walked over and saw a partly put together jigsaw puzzle on the teal-colored table. He wondered why he had not noticed it before. The eighteen-by-twelve-inch puzzle had over one hundred pieces, and the picture on the box was a landscape of white mountains on the left side, green trees on the right, and a still, clear, mirror-like blue river between them. He took his seat opposite his therapist and stared at the puzzle on the table.

The corner where the sky and the woods connected had been done, then there were spaces. But on the lower parts of the middle, some paths of the river had been done. The peaks of some mountains were also formed, and lastly the stumps of some trees. Clearly, whoever had put together the pieces did not follow any particular process or pattern. Whenever he and his dad put together his Legos or puzzles, they started with the instructions. Then they began at the corner closest to them and worked their way up. That way even if they did not finish, they could easily pick up where they left off. progress with the pages or process.

Bradley remembered one of his early sessions with Mr. Carly, who had started out as his second speech therapist. He was about seven at the time, and his parents wanted to increase his vocabulary. Mr. Carly was proud of his progress thus far and had commended his parents for their hands-on and modeling approach. But he also wanted to test Bradley's vision and cognitive skills. Bradley was familiar with the Picture Exchange Communication System (PECs), even though it had benefited him only a little. It had been one of the many approaches his parents had attempted earlier. Mr. Carly needed him to put together something that looked like Humpty Dumpty to him. It turned out it was Mr. Potato Head from *Toy Story*. He was given the PECs to choose which part of the face he wanted each time. He had never seen the completed object before, but he intuitively knew where things went—the arms, eyes, tongue, nose, and moustache. When the hat and legs kept falling out, he had dragged his mom's hands to help him. She had insisted he use his words if he wanted help, which he did, and then she had helped him.

The therapist was obviously impressed and revised his program for a higher deliverable than what he had planned. He also had Bradley and his mom read a picture storybook about different emotions, and Mr. Carly had marveled at how he attempted and successfully blended the new five or six letter words he came across and how he and his mom had played out the emotions of the characters. Needless to say, it had been a struggle to let go of the Mr. Potato Head when their test session was over, but that had birthed the beginning of a productive time in his journey.

"Brad, are you still with me?" Dr. Heather prompted.

"Yeah," he said as he looked up.

"I said I need you to complete the puzzle. Take as long as you need. You may even choose to finish next time," she explained again.

"Uh-huh. All right."

Bradley stared at the picture on the box for a while and shuffled through the loose pieces for the two corner pieces closest to him. Then he fished for the adjoining pieces to form a straight line to connect the two corners. He usually would have moved on to the next line either diagonally or horizontally, but he saw some pieces that seemed to belong around the far corner that had been put together. Unfortunately, he did not find a spot next to any of the existing ones, so he left it at a space he thought it should sit later.

"So, how are you and your friends? And Abigail?"

"Very well, thank you. We hang out a few times for virtual games, basketball, or just talk. When we are not all so busy, anyway, which is rarely. And Abi…" He smiled at the thought of her but did not say any more than that.

"That's great. And how is work going?"

Bradley was fixated on the puzzle now and had a frown on his face. He had not heard her last question. He broke up some of the already put-together parts of the farther corner, so he could have less floating pieces while he progressed with the ones he had started.

She observed him and noted his changes. About half an hour later, he had broken up about 90 percent of what had been done on the puzzle previously and also had the puzzle about half done, with three of the corners in place and no spaces nor floating pieces as he worked toward the last corner.

"Bradley, I know you probably want to finish it, but could we take a pause?" his therapist interrupted gently.

"Definitely." He stood up to stretch his legs and flex his neck, which was stiff from looking down the whole time. He also walked to her table for a bottle of water and sat on the chair next to it.

"Did you observe that most of the pieces that had already been put together, you took apart eventually to build up what you were working on?"

"Interesting," he commented after a few seconds.

"I know. You seem to have a methodology that works for you, and your instincts went with that irrespective of what was already seemingly being built. Do you see where I'm going with this yet?"

Bradley thought for a while. The pendulum bird dipping its beak in the water caught his attention.

"I'm sensing something about not being able to complete what may look already built but needs rebuilding? Maybe?" he asked after a while of ruminating on it.

"Right. And like you saw, it may take some time to even make sense of all your thoughts and dreams, but don't hold back because sometimes the only way to heal or build back is when we tear it apart first," she concluded, observing him take it all in.

Bradley looked at his Fossil wristwatch and knew his alarm would go off soon. He stretched out his legs and rested his head farther back on the chair.

"Work is more of a struggle these days, Dr. Heather. And I hate to be ungrateful to Josh."

"Bradley, the sooner you stop bottling up, the better for you. Clearly you are hiding behind your routines. Do you mind taking some time out?"

"I don't know. I'll think about it," he responded after a while and sat up.

"I do know I'm running out of time with Abigail, and it's scary. No matter what or how I do that now, I'm definitely coming off as deceptive." He sighed into his hands. Then his alarm went off.

"I won't worry about that too much now. If you do decide to take some time, let me know so we can reschedule. And Bradley, please write the letter."

He got up after a few minutes and slipped his hands in his pockets to feel for his car key fob.

"I'll be sure to. Thank you, Doc." He said with a smile and left the room.

Chapter 4

"Hey Brad, please could you pick me up instead? My car won't start." Melanie said, sounding frustrated.

Bradley chuckled and got up to grab his shirt.

"I'll be with you soon."

Great! she thought. Joshua was going to have a field day when he found out. He already believed "her girl" had done her time, but Melanie really loved her old-but-sure VW Golf car and was not willing to part with it just yet. She sighed and rolled up her window to go back inside the diner to wait.

"Hi, guys, thank you so much for coming." Abigail greeted Melanie and Bradley with warm hugs.

"Are you kidding? Would not have missed it for the world." Melanie smiled back

"Everything looks amazing. Well done to you and your team," Bradley added with a smile as well and slipped his hands into his pockets as they made their way into the gallery.

Abigail had been really occupied with the preparation for the exhibition all week, and they had not spent any alone time together except over the phone. She believed it was her chance to demonstrate she was ready to be an assistant manager, and she had gone all out to ensure the event ran smoothly and perfectly.

Bradley could not have been more proud. Even though he was not in the best mood to socialize, he had missed seeing her and being with her was going to be a great and a needed distraction from his heavy heart. It turned out, however, that Melanie also intended to go, and she had offered to give him a ride. Hanging out with Abigail around Melanie meant they had to be "just friends," but she was going to be working and attending to clients, so Melanie's presence was welcome company.

"Wow! Apparently, my being with you is no threat to them," Melanie scoffed, interrupting his thoughts.

"Excuse me?"

"Those ladies keep batting their lashes at you and laughing louder than they should, as if I am invisible. I really should set you up as soon as possible," Melanie muttered with a raised brow and took a sip of her drink.

"What now?" Brad laughed. "Thanks, but no thanks. I'm good, Mel," he quickly added, before she got any other ideas.

"I'm serious, Brad."

"Can we not do this here? Please," he scolded with a sigh. He might have been embarrassed with someone else, but he knew Melanie only meant well. Except, she did not know he really was good—with Abigail.

They walked around and stopped to admire a few paintings more closely. Bradley was more interested and fascinated in the strokes and finishes than Melanie was, as she was basically there to support her friend. If it was colorful and neat, it was good to her.

"Hope you guys are doing okay?" Abigail joined them again.

"Yes, thank you. I see you are really busy tonight, so just in case we don't get to see you before we have to leave, thanks for inviting us." Melanie gave her a hug

"More like thank you for honoring my invitation."

"Which one of these is your favorite?" Bradley asked, interrupting their girlfriend moment.

"Um, I doubt I have just one," she said after a few seconds of thinking.

Bradley stared at her, waiting patiently. He had wanted to hug her longer and tell her she looked stunning as always. He had caught glimpses of her as she answered questions and moved around attending to clients graciously in her heels and was tempted several times to go whisper something or anything to keep her smiling and going, but he had kept his hands in his pockets and willed his legs to walk around with Melanie, just so he did not embarrass either of them.

"Fine, since I absolutely have to choose one, that one," she finally said, pointing to a large sixty-three-by-thirty-seven-inch painting on a canvas. It was a gradation of colors from red to violet that blended into each other, all starting from the same point but flaring out and fading into light gray like a blazing fire. The strokes of the brushes were prominent, and thin black-and-white lines had been added, as if splashed across. The artist had also coated it with high-gloss varnish to prevent the color fading.

"Hmm. Interesting," Bradley said as he studied the vintage beauty. It was an original painting he had also admired earlier.

"Well, thanks again for stopping by. I have to hurry along now. Take care." Abigail gave him a hug and waved at Melanie as she disappeared back into the small crowd.

"Do you need me to drop you off at home?" Bradley offered Melanie when they were ready to leave.

"No, that's okay. I already ordered my ride. I'm spending the night at Josh's, so he'll also help me get a mechanic tomorrow. Thanks a lot, though."

"Awesome, then. Tell Josh hello from me." He hugged Melanie with a smile and then headed out.

* * *

"You bought the painting in my name?" Abigail asked in utmost surprise.

"Hello, love," Bradley answered softly with a smile. He loved when she was a bit feisty. Her voice had a fire in it.

Abigail laughed and took a deep breath.

"Hi. Why did you buy the painting in my name?" she tried again, a bit more calmly.

"You looked great today." He said as he stretched out on his sofa in his living room. He had been itching to tell her all evening but decided to wait till they spoke when she got home at night.

"Bradley Madison!"

He chuckled. He could picture her eyes. He found it strange that she was the one person whose impatience made him beam.

"I don't like spam or marketing emails, so I avoid dropping my details. And I did buy it for you, except it's in my house, so you can come over anytime to see it," he explained.

Abigail's bedroom was in one word—quirky. Even though the exterior of the house was brick, the inside was fully plastered, except the garage and storage area, but she had asked that the wall next to the door in her room be brick too. The adjoining wall was swathed in light-purple and her dark-brown headboard rested against that wall. Her quilt was pale-blue with a flowery designed at its base, and her worktable and chair were unfinished wood. She had placed them opposite the only window in the room for adequate lightening without blocking the ventilation. Her other books, however, had remained on the floor in neat piles since she moved in because she knew her time there was limited, but she had made the best of the space. She had a Bill Cosby–looking sweater her dad had given her in college hung behind her door, not because she wore it, but she had liked it then, and it reminded her of him despite his distance from them. Above her lamp and nightstand was a framed watercolor of a vibrant, shimmering hummingbird painted in motion as it approached loose, impressionistic pink flowers. A smaller pencil sketch was on the wall next to the light switch. Because she shared a bathroom with her step-brother, she had bought a full-length movable mirror for herself, which she placed next to the white standing wardrobe.

She lay on her pillow and stared at the small pencil sketch of a dress on a hanger. It was his gestures like these that got her speechless, and Bradley had a weird way of making her feel really special without even knowing he did.

"Do you want to see it?" Bradley continued when she did not speak for a minute.

"Yes, please," she managed to whisper as she propped her pillow to sit up.

He switched their call to FaceTime and moved to his piano area. He had hung it on the wall behind his piano and had moved the smaller painting that was there before to his workout room.

It was beautiful, and it stood out nicely in the room, with lighting over it too.

"Thank you, Brad. It's beautiful." She smiled at him.

"You're welcome. But if you do want it with you, you can take it anytime."

"Okay. I'll keep that in mind."

His alarm went off, and he proceeded to his kitchen to check on his macaroni and cheese.

"Did you have a good time yourself?" he asked as he set his phone down in its docket and moved around his kitchen to fix his dinner.

"I did. I am exhausted at the moment—both mentally and physically—but it was worth the time," she shared. He could hear the delight in her voice and saw the joy in her eyes as she recounted the challenges she had faced in the week and how that in turn had helped her and the other executives anticipate and plan for any other hurdle during the exhibition. The turnout had also been great, and the sales were more than anticipated too. Her boss had been really proud of them, and she was happy the exhibition was a success.

"Sorry. You know how I get to talking a lot when I'm excited," she apologized softly when she observed he had started eating and she had not taken a break in minutes.

Bradley chuckled.

"I'm always happy to hear your voice, Abi. You know that."

"Okay."

"Do I get to see you tomorrow?" he asked softly after a while.

"I'm not sure. I promised my step-brother we'd bake chocolate chip cookies for his bake sale. It's usually a half-day project, but chances are he'll also want me to go to his school with him in the evening for the event. And then on Sunday I'm celebrating with my colleagues with some Cosmo drinks, basically for the success of tonight's exhibition. I'm sorry," she added with a wobbly smile.

"You don't have to be sorry. It's fine. I just really miss you. Enjoy the bake sale, and have fun hanging out. You all deserve it," he told her with a lazy smile.

"I'll save you some cookies." She hoped that would cheer him a bit.

"I don't eat cookies."

"Cake? Pizza?"

"No. And only the crust."

"Has anyone ever mentioned you are weird?" she asked, amused

"A few times." He smiled and got up to put away his empty plates and clean up the kitchen.

"But my mom always made sure I knew I was different, so it was okay if I seemed weird to others," he continued with a straight face.

Abigail was quiet for a while and pondered the statement. *What does he mean by "different"?*

"She was a wise woman indeed," she finally said with a smile.

"Yeah. She also believed 'one doesn't go through a fire and not come out a fighter.' I really hope I do come out as one…" He covered his face with his hands and took a deep breath

"Brad, do you want to talk about it?" she asked softly after several minutes

"No." He shook his head. "No. Not tonight anyway," he added with a sigh, and then he smiled lazily at her.

"Okay."

"I'm yet to find any apartment I'm thrilled about." Abigail hoped the change in subject would lighten their mood again.

"Oh, but are you warming up better to the idea of moving out?"

"I am actually. Though my mom keeps reminding me of reasons why she would miss me around, but hey, a girl's gotta do what a girl's gotta do." She chuckled and Bradley laughed too.

"That's great," he told her. Abigail yawned and stretched out to lie back on her bed.

"I need to sleep now, Brad. It has been a long week."

"I see that." He smiled.

"Goodnight, love," she whispered with a smile.

She looked peaceful, and her face was radiant in the low light of her bedroom. He had seen her a few times before she applied her makeup or after she wiped it off, and each time he wondered why she even bothered. She was gorgeous either way. It was a good thing they were on the phone tonight and not together, as he really wanted to kiss her goodnight.

And because he was currently short of words, he waved at her with a smile after a few more minutes of staring at her sleepy face, then hung up.

* * *

Bradley's struggle in dealing with the loss of his mom, however, was telling on his productivity at work. Some tasks that had come easily now needed a lot more of his concentration, in spite of his anxiety medications. Joshua had spoken to him about requesting more time off, and while he was honestly considering it, he was concerned his idleness would only make him worse off. Melanie had taken a few days off herself after the funeral, and she came over as often as she could. Thankfully when she had met Abigail at his apartment once, she hadn't given it much thought, given the current circumstance. Bradley felt guilty each time he knew one more day had passed without his best friend knowing he was with Abigail.

His therapist, however, was more concerned about his declining interest in his responsibilities at work. The job was supposed to be temporary, anyway, until he found a job he actually wanted, but he thought he needed the work distraction now more than ever and had not put in much time searching for something else.

He had woken up feeling really low and had not bothered with his morning run or worked out. He showered with all four faucets and slipped on his shorts and a short-sleeve Henley.

He knew he could not go to church feeling the way he did, so he turned on his flat screen to play Psalms. The male voice-over of the audio Bible came with a piano playing lightly in the background, and he hoped that would lift his spirit. Other than their most recent trip to the art exhibition, He had not hung out Melanie in a while, and he knew she would be at school that day, so he sent her a text. **Hey, I'm going to be home all day today. Let me know if you get off early or if you can stop by. Thanks.**

He dragged himself to his pantry to decide his cereal for the day. He loved cereals and had quite a number to choose from.

He brought out his bowl and spoon and the milk, then heated some water and was searching through his measuring cups when his phone beeped. *Mel is probably responding to my message,* he thought, but it was a message from Abigail.

Up for some company?

He thought for a few seconds, wondering what she could mean, then he heard a knock.

"Abi? How are you here?" He greeted in surprise and gave her a hug. She grinned and leaned up to kiss him on the cheek.

"Hello, to you too. I thought to surprise you so slipped into the building with another occupant. Since you had not sent me a message about being off to church, I figured you were still home. I'm still hanging out with some colleagues in a few hours, though. How are you?"

"Oh. Thanks. This may just not be the best of times, but I'm good, I think."

"Uh, are you expecting company? Maybe I should leave."

"Please don't. I'm always happy to have you around, Abi," he said softly but made no attempt to move closer to her.

"O-kay." She was not sure why, but she was sensing some distancing again, so she headed for his sofa.

"My housekeeper should arrive soon, though, but she has a key so no issues," Bradley added and headed back into his kitchen.

"Would you want some cereal too?" he offered.

"Yeah, sure, thank you."

He had made a mess of his cabinet searching for a particular measuring cup, and he did not like it. He could easily have changed his mind about breakfast and placed an order, but he had offered Abigail cereal, so he had to make some, at least for her. He heated some milk and poured some into the bowl, added some water, a teaspoon of sugar, and then added the cereal. He stirred it, and it was watery. He emptied the bowl into the trash and made another, changing the order in which he added each item and tried reducing the volume of the milk and water. It turned out thick, and he could not stir it well. He emptied that bowl and took another bowl. He also grabbed another brand of loose cereal and tried again.

"Argh!" He slammed the third bowl in frustration into the trash, and opened the cabinet for another bowl with a force that made his elbow tip the milk cartoon over.

Abigail looked up from her phone and walked over to him.

"Hey, love, can I help?" she asked softly.

"No," he snapped.

"What happened?"

He ignored her and grabbed paper towels to clean up the milk on the kitchen floor. Abigail grabbed some more and joined him, but he got up almost immediately and backed away, his breathing becoming more rapid.

"Brad, can I just make us the cereal? You don't look too good." She stared at him with a worried frown.

"Abi, I know you can, but I need to, okay? So just...I'll fix it."

"Why?" she asked in confusion, feeling a little angry at his attitude.

There was a knock, and then Ms. Lopez let herself in. She was about to announce her arrival with morning pleasantries when she saw the mess in the kitchen and Abigail and Bradley looking like they were at a standoff.

"What happened?" she asked gently as she set her bag down and moved closer to them.

"I'm not sure... He spilled some milk, and it seems to be big deal that he makes the cereal himself," Abigail summarized in a rush with her hands in the air, still upset at him.

"Have you seen the light-blue measuring cup?" Bradley muttered without looking up at either of them.

"Oh my, I'm so sorry. It got broken in the dishwasher last week. I was going to replace it today when I went for the monthly supplies," the housekeeper explained.

"What? This is because of a flimsy measuring cup?" Abigail yelled at him in frustration. She could not believe her ears. She had tried the best she could to be there for him and to be understanding about his grief, but her patience was wearing thin.

"Miss, please, could you not raise your voice? He probably just needs some space or his anxiety medications. I think his therapist placed him on them again, if I remember well," Ms. Lopez said as gently as she could, then left them hurriedly for the living room. She put the television on mute and inserted one of his mixed CDs.

Abigail's head felt light, and she had to sit on a nearby kitchen stool as she tried to connect the dots. Could her hunches have been right? Anxiety medications? Again? Therapist? She had considered, but also dismissed, the possibilities of Bradley having general anxiety disorder, or OCD. She had also heard of adults with Asperger's syndrome, but she had not had the opportunity to interact with an adult with any of those disorders, especially not at the level she had with Bradley. He had some peculiar behaviors she had observed but nothing outrageous. For example, he always wore footwear, or at least his socks, around the house but sometimes walked barefoot on the grass when they spent time in a park nearby. But his ability to communicate and have friends made her conclude that maybe, just maybe, he had a hint of Asperger's. Again, she had excused a lot of other self-absorbed traits he showed because he was taking his loss really hard. But he surely did not have difficulty in showing his romantic side to her. And in all honestly, she was always more than happy with the undivided attention he gave her.

Bradley just stood there with his fists clenched, as if he was in trance, and had not said a word since Ms. Lopez arrived.

The music seemed to be working, though, because he finally moved and went to lie on his sofa without glancing her way or saying a word. The mix had started out with "Tell Your Heart to Beat Again" by Danny

Gokey and then "Breathe" by Jonny Diaz. He shut his eyes and turned his back to her.

Ms. Lopez went back to the kitchen to clean up, rearrange the cabinet, and begin her shopping list as she looked around.

Not wanting to disturb Bradley, Abigail moved closer to the other woman to whisper, "Please, is Brad ill? As I was not aware he was on any medications." She felt willing to risk sounding stupid.

"Oh, no, not ill, as it were. Just the autism spectrum disorder. I guess his mom passing made the anxiety waves come back." Ms. Lopez smiled kindly at her.

Abigail stared at his housekeeper as if she had spoken in a language other than English.

"Does Bradley Madison know he is autistic?" she choked out, just to confirm it was as real as it got.

"Of course! But believe me, this is not a common occurrence." Ms. Lopez seemed to read the fear and shock on Abigail's face and feel a need to reassure her all was well. Except it wasn't. Not in Abigail's world, anyway. She asked for a glass of water, drained the glass in seconds, and asked for another. Her eyes had gotten moist, and her head was swarming with questions.

What were his plans? Why had he kept lying to her? Or, okay, technically he had not lied. He had just kept her in the dark about it. So was it his intention to leave her deceived? For how long could he possibly have kept up the act? She should have trusted her guts. Except it would have been insensitive and maybe rude of her to have asked her grieving boyfriend, since he did not think it was important to reveal the information himself.

The tears dropped, and she quickly wiped them. She would have to deal with herself later.

"So, what could I do to help? Should he not have an EpiPen or something?" she asked after a few minutes of catching her breath.

"No, he doesn't have nor need one. Just give him some time alone for now." The housekeeper squeezed Abigail's hands with a smile and left to go about her tasks.

Abigail went back into the living room, sat on the couch that was farthest from him, and wrapped her hands around herself. She was confused, and he was shutting her out again.

She heard him singing along softly with the song that was playing, and she recognized it as "Till I See You" by Hillsong United.

As he sang to himself, his housekeeper moved about quietly and avoided the living room, while Abigail's head felt swamped with questions. Why had he never mentioned he had ASD? Or that he was currently seeing a therapist? Had he needed to take his anxiety medications the whole time they were together? How was she to deal with him? And with this knowledge? When he wasn't even giving her a chance to? His housekeeper had said to give him some time. She had sat and stared for about thirty-five minutes, and she was beginning to feel a little dizzy again.

When her colleagues buzzed her to confirm they were still on course, she realized she would need to cancel with them, as there was no way she could enjoy herself. No point bringing down their moods as well. But then again, the one person she really wanted to speak with about this was Melanie, but that could not happen, and she doubted being alone would do her any good at the moment. Maybe she would go be with her colleagues, after all, to stay distracted and keep her mind occupied until she was ready to deal with this. She was beginning to enjoy the songs, too, and Bradley had sung a few lines from "Walk by Faith," by Jeremy Camp, so she decided to try and reach out again.

"Brad, do you want me to leave?" she asked softly.

"No," he whispered.

"Okay. What can I do to help?"

He did not respond again. Abigail helped herself to another glass of water and walked around to stretch her legs.

"Could you please stop pacing?" Bradley asked so softly from the sofa, she almost missed it.

"Right. I can't... I can't do this. I don't know what to do or what not to do... And why did you decide to let your housekeeper do the honors of informing me? I'm leaving, Brad. Clearly you need space. Maybe me more than you at this point. I'll call or email you, perhaps," she told him in despair. She waited some seconds, hoping he would maybe stop her, but he did not move. She grabbed her purse and considered moving toward him for a peck or a pat or a hug or anything but decided against it at the last minute and left his apartment.

Later Bradley woke up with a start on his bed and could barely remember making it there. He was still wearing the same clothes, so he'd obviously been too tired to change the milk-stained T-shirt or shower. His Echo Dot was playing softly in the background. His clock read 4:06 p.m.

Abi! he thought, suddenly shocked and irritated. He shut his eyes tightly in remorse.

He remembered her saying something about giving each other some space...and she would call or email him, maybe?

He picked up his phone and was disappointed to see she had not left him either, so he sent her a message.

I'm sorry, Abi. Really. I woke up with a lot of pent-up emotions. I can't explain it, but I'm so sorry I hurt you. I will respect your request and hope you give me a call soon. Please.

Melanie had texted to say she was having extra tutoring sessions in preparation for tests coming up soon but she'd try to stop by later in the week.

He took a shower and felt better. His tummy rumbled, and he remembered he had not eaten all day. He went to his kitchen to find his bowl and cereal laid out in a tray. Ms. Lopez had also been kind enough to replace the broken measuring cup that afternoon. The new one was white, not blue, but all was well. He heated some milk and poured in three-quarters of a cup into his bowl, then half a cup of warm water. He added a teaspoon of sugar and lastly added five bars of his Weetabix cereal. He stirred gently with a spoon and had a taste. It was perfect. He turned on his television to catch some basketball highlights as he ate by his kitchen counter. He thought about his last session with Dr. Heather and decided she was right. He needed to go home. But first, he had to speak with his manager the following day and take his offer, if not more. He emptied his bowl, tidied up the kitchen, and went to his home office to book a flight to Nevada County on his desktop.

II

CHOICES. CHANCES. CHANGES.

Chapter 5

Not much had changed since Bradley had moved out. His old room still had the same wallpaper, and pieces of paper with bits written outside the lines were still stuck all around the corner wall of the room. His favorites to date were "God has good plans for me (Jer 29:11)," "I am fearfully and wonderfully made (Ps 139:14)," "The Lord your God says to you, Do not fear, I will help you (Isa 41:13)," "I am the vine, you are the branches (Jn 15:5)," "if anyone be in Christ, he is a new creature; the old is passed away; behold the new has come (2 Cor 5:17)," and the ones he also had on the wall in his house. His study corner still had his wooden table and white rotating chair. Along the other walls were his mini keyboard and seat, his whiteboard, and his bookshelf, which had loads of picture storybooks with activities, some scrapbooks, various flash cards, jigsaw puzzles of different sizes and pictures, and other sensory tools.

His custom "My First Calendar" magnetic calendar chart was set as Monday, January 4, the last time he was home for Christmas. He had not had the energy for anything when he'd come for his mom's funeral. He smiled, and took out the cards to place the correct date, season, and weather. Of course, he had outgrown it by second grade, when he had understood the concept, but he was attached to updating it first thing in the morning and had kept up with it and updated it whenever he was home. His sisters, too, had used it, mostly to annoy him because they never stuck them perfectly in the squares the way he liked, but they had also used it to learn. His parents did buy a calendar for them, but they always chose to meddle with his instead.

Some of his crafts and paintings were hung on the opposite wall in cardboard frames, along with some memorable pictures of him and his sisters and parents on different occasions. The picture of him at three years old was also displayed, but this one was the small-size, colored version. He had the enlarged one printed in black and white and framed for his penthouse. His room was smaller than his sisters' room, especially because, unlike him, they needed more space for friends, like Melanie, when they visited or had slumber nights. But even then, his sisters usually hung out in his room most days or disturbed him in the living room when he played his video games. His parents had insisted his video games were in the living room and not his bedroom to force him to keep interacting. His mom usually had exchange students over after he moved out to college and subsequently used their rooms to help new members in their local assembly who needed a few days to sort out their accommodation. Barely three months passed without a new name or face in the house when he called.

Bradley sank onto his old bed, stretched out, and pulled out his phone to place it carefully on his study table the way he usually did. There was no point switching it off Airplane mode too. He had given his two weeks' notice at work and called Melanie to leave her a voice mail of his whereabouts. He did not have to tell Abigail, since they were currently undefined and sort of awkward, but he did leave her a voice mail also. It had been four days, and she had not replied to his message nor called him.

She seemed to be more upset at the fact that he had not told her himself in the course of their over two months they had been seeing each other than the actual knowledge of him being autistic. He had apologized, but it seems it had been too overwhelming for her to take in, so he was going to give her space. In fairness to her, he also needed some space and time out, although definitely not from her. She just happened to have borne the heat of it all, and he really was sorry he had hurt her.

* * *

Today was going to be different. He felt it the moment he woke up from his dreamless night's sleep. He had been moping around for about three days, and his dad had given him his space, not saying much except when spoken to. He heard his dad a few times when he prayed, though, as his room was adjacent to the study.

He took a long hot shower, which felt really nice against his skin, changed into his gray joggers, white T-shirt, and a pair of black socks and headed out to look for his dad.

"Hello, Dad, what are we watching?" Bradley asked as he took a seat on the beanbag across from his father.

"The usual; football highlights," his dad responded with a light shrug, not taking his eyes off the screen. Bradley smiled. His dad usually avoided the live matches, just so he didn't feel under pressure—except when he had nothing else to do and his team was playing. But he never missed the highlights that followed.

Growing up, he had usually sat on his dad's lap or next to him, watching with interest, even though he had not understood the concept. But it was one of the many times he looked forward to sharing with him. That and their evening walks around the neighborhood. Sometimes during the day, when he was uneasy and cranky for reasons he did not know, his dad had taken him on strolls or even runs. Other times, his mom would use his sensory tools or sing his favorite songs and rhymes until he joined her. Melanie and his sisters usually just stayed away until he was okay to be approached again, and they would continue like it never happened.

Bradley made his way to the kitchen to grab a cold drink. The fridge was practically covered with pictures of them at different ages, some school projects, and postcards from some close relatives. There was a section that had some of their paintings from elementary or high school; he had drawn an angry banana and a smiling giraffe with a yellow helmet and square glasses. His sisters had drawn an oversize ladybug that did not have legs, a house with a smiley face, and a unicorn. He remembered he had added a robot on their unicorn just for laughs, which had not gone down well with the girls. Still, their mom had kept the drawings.

He sat on one of the high stools at the marble-top island and lowered his head into his hands.

"Son?" His dad had put the television on mute and walked up behind him to place a hand on his back

"I miss her, dad." Bradley answered without looking up.

"We all do. Terribly."

"And I'm not sure how to deal with it either. Time is supposed to ease the pain, right? Then why does it feel fresh with every passing day?" Bradley added.

"I know 'we walk by faith and not by sight' and all that," he continued. "I mean, we all sing it and love the way it sounds, too, but not until now have I found myself struggling to understand it. To understand what it really means now that 'the lights are out,' and I need something to hold on to. What's worse, I kept hearing whispers of how we can't question God at the funeral. Is that even fair? By the way, I'm sorry I left in a hurry the following day, Dad. I just couldn't deal with her absence just yet."

His dad sighed deeply.

"I still hurt too, Brad. So do your sisters and Mel and other family members and friends. Maybe we don't cry on the outside as much anymore, but no, it's not just time that does the healing. I am being intentional about it, and with the grace of God, the Holy Spirit helps, too, from the inside."

"Mmm." Bradley took a sip off his cold drink and listened.

"Two things that have helped me thus far: Your mom was sick for a very long time and held up as long as she could. I honestly believe this past year was an extra time the Lord gifted us. Her last week at the hospital was the worst for me. I wished I could take her place, as I hated watching her in pain and not being able to do anything about it. Worse still, she asked me not to tell any of you. She could not bear having you all putting your lives on hold to be with her. We believed she would get better and be out in no time, but the last day, I noticed she stopped praying for healing and sang mostly. She prayed for each of you and the grandchildren. She had many little fond memories that we laughed about, and I believed she had gotten rest from our healing prayers. I see now her 'rest' was different from what I had in mind."

His dad poured himself some cold fresh milk, took a few gulps, and sat back down next to Bradley.

"Secondly, and yes, this is the hard part, but I'm having to remind myself, faith is not just believing in God when things are going well, but also trusting God no matter how things are going. I doubt Joseph would have held on to his dreams if God had shown him the journey to getting there," he added with a smile.

"By the way, there is nothing wrong with asking God for clarity or understanding, as long as it's from a sincere heart and not in rebellion or mistrust. Or attacking the character of God because of a current situation. Even when it seems as if God isn't doing anything or has abandoned us, He is working behind the scenes. Remember, 'we know in parts, and prophesy in parts until that which is perfect is come.' I strongly believe your mom's passing is as a grain of wheat that falls into the ground to produce much grain. I don't know how, but that was the answer I got when I questioned God, as it were."

Bradley listened intently and did not even know when the tears he had held back for over six weeks rolled down his cheeks. His dad always knew what to say and when. He was not as hugging and physical as his mom, but their talks had always been full of wisdom and a balm indeed.

"So are we supposed to just 'move on' now?"

"Well, like every other thing in life, what you don't feed won't grow. So feed on the good times. Naturally something will trigger the pain again, but we'll keep praying for grace to heal and be comforted during those times. I'm convinced that, sooner than we know, her memory will bring only joy and smiles to us. Besides, now we have something to look forward to in the afterlife besides Jesus and the saints of heaven, right?" His dad smiled again and finished up his glass of milk.

"You may not remember the stares we got when you were younger, bud. The whispers, the unsolicited pity and overwhelming advice on what to do or what not to do. And you would think being in the Western world should have made it easier, with the awareness, but no. You even had questions of your own when you figured it all out. We had done everything right to the best of our ability. Thankfully your sisters proved that in later years, but we had to learn to wait. Wait on the Lord and hope, worshiping in faith. And not one, not one of those seconds, would we have traded for less time being your parents, Bradley. He will come through again for you. For us all. I love you, Son. You are one of our many testimonies. Don't ever forget that, okay?"

Bradley and his dad hugged for a few minutes, then his dad left the kitchen, leaving Bradley to ruminate on their conversation.

He listened to Psalm 121 with his earbuds, and it reminded him of the lyrics in Don Moen's song, "He Never Sleeps."

He eventually left the kitchen and decided to go for a walk. It was a fine weather for a stroll around the neighborhood after all.

* * *

"Hi, Bradley, good to have you around." Mrs. Johnson waved cheerfully from her front porch

"Hello, Mrs. Johnson. Good to see you too. How is Mr. Johnson?"

"He's fine. You look very well, son," she added with a smile

Bradley chuckled. He could trust their neighbor to always be a mom figure, no matter what or where.

"Thank you, ma'am."

"Headed somewhere?"

"Er, just a walk around. You know, the usual." He shrugged.

"All right then. Regards to your dad." She smiled warmly

"Will do. Have a good one." He waved with a smile and hurried along in case she decided to continue their conversation.

His neighborhood was very aesthetically pleasing, with low white fences that separated each person's front lawn. The outer structures of the houses looked similar, but some people had renovated and repainted theirs over the years. Very few still had the original brick exterior, but at every corner were trees, whose flowers blossomed beautifully in the spring. And in the winter, during the rare snowstorms, the white was as beautiful against the brown of the bare trees and the black lampposts.

His street was connected to another community that was a cul-de-sac, so they had some traffic go by their own drive. This encouraged people to get to know and be fine with each other, even with 77 percent of them being white, while the remaining 33 percent were African American, Asian, and Latino. The street began at a fairly busy minor road that connected two major streets, which encouraged businesses to spring up there. Bradley's neighbors had the luxury of a gym, a library, and various eateries within walking distance.

Bradley walked past a big supermarket that had been there for years.

UNEVEN

In the past, when the store was much smaller, he and his dad had sometimes shopped there if they needed only a few things. When his sisters were old enough to run errands, they had taken over the responsibility. Now the supermarket even had a pharmacy.

As he walked, Bradley saw shops he recognized and others that seemed new. Some of the old buildings had been renovated, so he could not tell if the shop was new or had been there before. He noticed one that stood out, with a sophisticated looking sign and glass wall, and was surprised to find out it was a salon. He was intrigued at the detail whoever owned the place had put into the sign. As he passed the building, the door opened, and a woman called his name.

"Brad? Bradley Madison?"

Bradley turned around and stared at the cute young woman behind a pair of nerd-but-fashionable pair of glasses. She looked like she was in her late twenties, and she definitely looked familiar. He just could not place how or where he had known her.

She smiled and moved closer, wiping her hands on her the apron at her waist. As she came close, she stretched out her hand to greet him.

"Hi."

"Elaine?" Bradley said, pulling the name from his memory.

She nodded excitedly.

He pulled her in for a hug and almost lifted her off the walkway. She had to stretch on her toes to match his height, so he released her to relieve the stress.

"Wow. So great to see you, El. You look amazing."

She laughed as she adjusted her glasses back on her nose.

"So do you, Brad. You've always looked good, so it goes without saying that you still do."

Bradley shrugged off her comment with a gentle smile.

Elaine had been his friend from his first elementary school before he had to leave at third grade for a school that could give him the support he needed. They had hung out a few times outside school but less often as they grew older. Eventually they saw each other only at church on Sundays. They had also attended different high schools, and then she had left town for college, coming home only during the Christmas holidays. Even though most people hoped they were going to be an item at the time, they kind of knew it wasn't going to happen after they shared a kiss one of those Christmas holidays and found it weird. They hadn't kept in touch since then.

"It's been what, ten years? I thought you left Nevada County for LA."

"I know, right? Yeah, I did. Moved back a few years ago to set up my salon. Got bored of life in the fast lane," she shared proudly.

"Wait, you own that place?" He pointed in surprise.

"Yeah. Do you have some time to come in?" she asked. "We have the male and female section kind of separated, and massage chairs to relax in while you wait."

"Sounds grand. And I can bet your services will be top-notch if your outdoor aesthetics are any indication. But maybe not today."

"Oh, all right then." She sounded disappointed.

"I'll be sure to stop by for a haircut before I leave though. I promise."

"Okay, then. We'll be looking forward to having you." She smiled up at him.

"Well, I have to go now. It was really nice seeing you, Bradley."

"Same here. Really proud of what you have going." He gave her a warm hug as he was about to take his leave.

"Thank you. My regards to everyone, if they still remember me." She smiled and waved at him.

Chapter 6

Abigail and Malik walked into The Griddle diner together, even though they had arrived separately that evening. They had bumped into each other in the parking lot, and Malik had reassured her she really did not have anything to worry about once she understood Bradley's moods, likes, and dislikes. He for example had met Bradley in college, and they had remained good friends because he related with him back then normally and respected his need for time alone when he needed it.

"So just give it some time, all right? You'll be fine," he had added with a smile.

Abigail smiled quizzically. "Thanks, Malik."

She wondered why she had never seen this sweet side of him before. Maybe, just maybe, she would have given him a chance with her.

"Did I miss something?" Melanie asked Abigail cautiously when she saw them being a little too friendly with each other.

"Am I that terrible a man you don't trust me to make an honest woman of Abi?" Malik responded with a hint of anger in his voice.

"Malik, your women give you high fives and send you a thank-you card for a great time. So no, I can't entrust my friend with you."

"Mel, no need to get worked up, hon. We are definitely not together. Just grabbing lunch, okay." Abigail quickly chimed in, not liking where the conversation seemed to be headed.

"And I wonder why that is. Ever wondered why 'your friend'—Malik added the air quotes sarcastically—is definitely not with me, Mel?"

"Malik, please stop," Abigail begged and stepped between them.

"What is he talking about, Abi?" Melanie looked between them in confusion.

"Well, she seems to have everyone judged and figured out but somehow missed her precious friend here and Brad have been hitting it for at least two months now." Malik announced with a malicious smile.

"I'm sorry?" Melanie was sure she had heard wrong and looked to Abigail, expecting her to cut in on his joke or whatever it was.

"And while we are at it, did you also know you were a bet I had with Josh, but clearly he won?" Malik added so softly, one would have thought he was having a business-related conversation.

Melanie went into a shock.

"Malik, you are way out of line, and Mel, I'm so, so sorry you had to find out this way. I promise you, I tried several times to tell you, and that's why I'm here. Brad and I were an item but not at the moment..." Abigail continued to explain, but Melanie had zoned out.

She left them for the staff lounge, where she sat down a while to catch her breath and hold in the tears that were gathered in her eyes. *Malik has to be kidding to get at me,* she thought. *But Abi has confirmed she is with Brad, so Malik has to be sure of all he said. Why did Bradley or Abigail not tell me? And more importantly, I was a freaking bet?* She brought out her cell phone to call Joshua. It rang unanswered. She thought to send him a message like she usually did, but she knew she would not function well the rest of the day until she was certain what Malik had said was a stupid joke or just a bad dream she was going to wake up from. So she kept calling until he answered.

The conversation was shorter than she anticipated, and it ended by him hanging up on her. She stared at her phone and finally let the tears fall. Her heart was beating so fast she could hear it. She remembered their first weekend out.

* * *

The week had taken a toll on Melanie, and she had her heart set on movie night with Joshua Doyle that Thursday night. Though she had Wednesdays and Sundays off for school—and occasionally on Saturdays if Elka asked her nicely, which she 101 percent of the time did—she seemed to have had backlogs of assignments in two of her four courses, which were due next weekend. She really hated last minute work and had decided her personal deadline was this Sunday. However, her boyfriend had been so busy these past weeks, the closest they had been physically was when he dropped by her diner for a quick bite the Saturday before. He'd had a meeting with a prospective equally busy client and that seemed to be the only available time he was able to schedule. They'd had to communicate via phone calls and messages. Some late nights she had fallen asleep while on the phone and woken up the following morning to a message from him—a weird emoji or smiley and **see you on the other side, babe.**

There was no way she was giving up her chance to see him tonight. She would have his undivided attention for about three hours as they watched a movie together. She had hoped to get off work early enough to have her hair and nails done to surprise Joshua. He always appreciated her efforts, no matter how little they seemed, because he knew she did not go huge often without a special reason. But she did every now and then for him.

However, that opportunity was gone now, and she was driving as fast as her old but sturdy 2002 silver Golf and the speed limit could permit. She wasn't always fancy, but she was a lady. She was going to have a shower and put on some makeup at the very least. Joshua was never late. If he had to be late for reasons beyond him, he always called at least an hour ahead. She'd had her phone charged and with her all day, so their date was on. He had said he would pick her at seven.

She made it home with minutes to spare. Her shower was hot and so refreshing, she was tempted to call Joshua and asked if they could stay in instead but changed her mind almost immediately. She had daydreamed about getting dressed up for him, so no point chickening out now. She applied her makeup—black smoky eyes and nude lipstick. It was just seeing a movie together, but the way Joshua's eyes swept up and down her length every time he saw her still gave her butterflies in her tummy.

"Make it worth his stare." She could hear Abigail's voice in her head and laughed as she made her way to her room and grabbed a plain rich-green dress she had tucked away at the end of her closet. That was the section for special-occasion outfits. It wasn't much, but each had a memory or was waiting to create one. She had bought the green dress as a gift to herself almost two years ago when she started at the community college on a part-time basis. She'd had dinner with Bradley and his mom who happened to be visiting at the time. They were technically the only family she knew and had now. It was a v-plunge midi dress with spaghetti straps and small buttons of the same fabric all the way down. Fitted at the upper body, it flared from just below the waistline to swish and swirl nicely when she walked. She wasn't big on fashion, but she knew what worked with her body shape without breaking her small bank. As much as she liked shoes, though, she had a lot of dreams and responsibilities to support, so stuck to the absolutely needed and turned away from what she just wanted. Tonight, like most times, she had the choice of black, nude, or gray heels. She settled for the black with the shimmery satin strap and black clutch purse. Her toenails were well manicured to the best of her ability although not polished tonight.

Melanie was in front of her mirror trying to decide whether to pin her hair up or let it down when the doorbell rang out. She looked up at her wall clock—6:55 p.m.

"Hi, stranger," she greeted him with her wide smile. Joshua always had a flower for her when they went on dates. Always. Sometimes he sent a bunch ahead, but most times he came with a stem. Tonight, he didn't have a flower in his hand. Instead, he held a paper shopping bag. *Strange. Maybe he has an errand to drop off on our way.*

His kiss brought her wandering thoughts back to him standing at her door. He continued the kiss as he entered her apartment and shut the door behind them. Her hands had found their way behind his head pulling him closer and removing his tie simultaneously, as he steadied them with his left arm around her waist and her back to a wall.

"Hey, babe. Thanks for the dress. These are for you," he said smiling down at her when they finally came up for air. Melanie looked at the bag and then at him and then at the bag, still shaken from the so-many-unspoken-words-kiss they had just shared. Her regular self really wanted to ask what occasion the big package was for, but the woman Joshua was fast making of her was curious as to see what was replacing her flower tonight.

"We really don't have time for the 'you don't have to spoil me' speech tonight, okay? Also, I'm still parched from how hot you look and need some water," Joshua said, answering her unspoken question. He led her to the sofa in her living area, dropped the bag, and got himself some water from the kitchen. After gulping down a glass, he turned away from the refrigerator to look toward her. He found her seated with her hands over her mouth as she stared at the box of shoes on her lap.

"Babe, is something wrong?"

"Josh, how did you...where did you...how...? I really can't accept these. Please don't make me."

"Hey, hey. Come on now, that'll be unfair." He put down the second glass of water he had poured and walked to her.

"Okay, I'm sorry I eavesdropped on your conversation with Elka about them. I did not mean to, honestly, but your eyes lit up while you described them. And as much as I knew you probably were going to save to get them—or not if you decided they were luxury to you—I really wanted to be a reason your eyes have a spark in them. Besides, you dressed up for me, and I do appreciate it. It's only fair you cut me this for being so busy these past two weeks." He paused, hoping he had made a winning case. She just stared at him. So he sat next to her and continued.

"Babe, do you mind putting them on? Or away? So we can catch our movie?"

Melanie's heart was racing. She could not believe he had gone and bought her a pair of shoes worth about a month and a half of her house rent. More importantly, he painstakingly found the time to google and find a store to deliver it by describing what he had merely overhead her whisper to Elka during her lunch break about three or four weeks ago at the diner. They were a pair of newly designed Sophia Webster butterfly six-inches heels. The lower foot and horizontal strap were mustard-yellow, and the back heels and butterfly wings were white outlined in black. The sole and thin ankle straps were black.

She had seen the ad on the screens in the metro on her way to work. Her car had refused to start that day, and she was running late. She had fallen in love with the pair instantly and was eager to share the news with anyone who would listen. She did not get the opportunity until lunch break with Elka. Joshua had sneaked in to surprise her, and he had beckoned to Elka to not mention his presence until a few seconds later when he tickled her. *Oh God.* She was going to cry. She wasn't even sure why, but she really wanted to. *Breathe. Breathe,* she told herself.

She had not yet put on her black heels and had opened the door to him barefoot, so she took the new sandals out the box and unbuckled them one after the other. She slipped them on, and they fit perfectly. Joshua helped her up and watched with a proud smile on his lips as she walked off to her room, hopefully to have a look at herself in the full-length mirror. He stood with both hands in the pockets of his suit pants, waiting for her verdict. She came out shortly cat-walking gracefully towards him with a smile on her face. Not as wide as the usual, but he took it all. Her eyes had a fire in them, and he was excited knowing he put that there.

Melanie stopped in front of him, placed one hand on his shoulder and the other softly on his cheek, and whispered, "Thank you, Josh." And before he could respond, she reached up and kissed him.

Joshua had not expected that. He always started their kisses. Always. His hands enclosed her waist, pulling her into him, forcing her hands to go behind his neck. She pulled his head down into her. He took the invitation and explored with his tongue. Her left hand moved and held on to his back for balance. His left hand remained on her waist while his right hand found its way to her head.

"Babe, we are running late if we are to make our movie."

"Mmmm... okay." Melanie moved her mouth to his neck, then down to his Adam's apple as she began working on undoing his shirt buttons.

Dang! Joshua thought. He was getting more than he bargained for. All good. Definitely all good. That night just happened to be their first time together, and he never liked to be caught unawares. He always showed up with his A-game.

Melanie's heart was racing again. *I'm really doing this, and I'm not scared.* She heard the voice in her head. Some of their past kisses had left her wanting more, but they had never gone past a few hickeys. And she definitely had never encouraged any more than that. She was surprised at herself and needed to constantly remind her hands and mouth to slow down. Problem was they suddenly seemed to have a mind of their own.

She unbuttoned his shirt, then took it off him and tossed it on the floor. When she moved her hands underneath his V-neck white T-shirt, she felt his skin against her palms. He led them to the kitchen top since it was closer than the sofa. He set her on it and bent on one knee to remove her heels. He was so gentle and precise, Melanie wasn't sure if they were that expensive or he was just that attentive. Somehow, she decided it must be the latter, especially when he kissed her toes after slipping each shoe off. He set them back gently in the shoe box on the sofa and went back to her. He kissed her slowly as he wrapped her legs around him. She pulled his head to her and slid the other hand inside his T-shirt. He deepened the kiss and slid his hands underneath her dress and up her thighs and her hips. She moaned and tightened her hold on him. While he wasn't certain, he could swear he heard her say something about trust.

He kissed her neck and trailed down her collarbone and cleavage. He started to unbutton her dress and stopped at the waist. He made a mental note to google and thank whoever invented front buttons, for it had revealed to him her black lace strapless bra. He swore at how so little of her almost made him go over.

"Joshua."

He looked up into her eyes. He definitely saw the desire that burned in them both, but something else he could not place at the moment.

"I trust you," Melanie continued.

She placed her right hand softly on his cheek like she had done earlier. He kissed her. And she held his head closely as if he might leave her. *I have to get us protection*, he thought. Joshua had been to Melanie's room very few times in their eight months of dating, for a quick trip or less, so he didn't know where such an item could be and was, once again, angry at his unpreparedness for the occasion. He hated to do this.

"Candytuft, do you have protection?"

"Uh, yeah. I think. My first-aid box. But I doubt my legs can hold me."

He chuckled into her hair.

"I'll be right back. I promise."

That's a first, he thought with disbelief. Most women had theirs in their bedroom dresser or purse or car, but not his little tornado. She had hers in a first-aid box. Seriously. That was to be discussed another day, not today. And definitely not now. He walked as fast as his tights could allow him to the kitchen cabinet that had the box, searching frantically. He found an unopened Durex box still sealed in its wrap. *Perhaps she restocks often,* he thought. He checked the expiration date and was pleased it had at least a year more to go.

For reasons he could not explain, Joshua wanted to make it to her bedroom. He lifted her off the counter top and headed for her bedroom while they kept kissing. With her hair in his face smelling so good from her shampoo, mixed with her perfume, he heard her soft cry, and it wasn't all pleasure.

He tried to raise his head, but she wouldn't let him see her. Had he hurt her?

"Mel?"

"Yeah?"

"Are you hurt?"

There was no answer. Crap! She had trusted him, and he had hurt her. How was he to know?

He had to fix this. He didn't know how yet, but hey, he advised people for a living. *Surely, I can figure this out,* Joshua thought. Her eyes were closed, and he saw a tear had slipped out. He kissed her neck and trailed downwards.

"Hey, Candytuft,...tell me...what you...want," he said between kisses. He nibbled on her lower lips, up her nose, her cheeks, her ears.

"I'm not sure."

"I totally love your dress, babe, but your body is blowing my brains out," he said, his voice husky as he undid the rest of her buttons and slid the dress from under her. She smiled up at him. Some confidence came with the compliment, and she reached to discard his T-shirt also.

"Josh…"

"I'm here, babe. All yours."

She was warm, and her embrace made him feel safe. At home. He didn't understand what happened to him at that moment, but he saw Melanie very differently for the first time.

She looked very vulnerable and more beautiful than he'd ever seen her. And she was all his. But how? How was she still a virgin? And in these times? She had an hourglass body shape. Her intellect was especially attractive to him, and her sense of humor was uncanny. Strong willed and fearless. Hardly took no for an answer and was too snarky for most people, but he was up to the challenge. She had trusted him with this. He had to make it right.

"Hi," he smiled several minutes later, lifting her chin up to look into her face. "How's my little tornado?"

"Never better," she smiled back. He kissed her lightly and laid her head back on his chest.

Melanie was still floating as she replayed the events of the night in her head. One minute she was getting ready for a movie, the next she was trying on shoes, and with a blink of an eye she was wrapped around his hips. She could not fathom how or where the boldness had come from. Joshua probably now thought little of her 'Miss-Independent' life, knowing she was a virgin until minutes ago. She thought she was mentally prepared for the physical hurt of it, but she'd had him all riled up; he'd assumed she was a pro. She should apologize to him for springing that on him. Now that the line was crossed, where did they go from here? She knew she did trust Joshua, but if having sex made him less interested in her, so be it. It was eight months well spent. Though she secretly hoped he didn't walk away.

"Babe, you need to soak in a warm bath and eat." Joshua's comment interrupted her thoughts.

"Oh."

He chuckled.

"You do need to heal. I'm so sorry I caused you pain. I'll make it right the best I can. I promise."

Melanie could not believe her ears. He apologized to her. She was convinced she was dreaming. Nevertheless, she sat up and looked into his eyes.

"Josh, I'm...I apologize for springing this on you. Believe me, I didn't plan this. I had missed you and was overwhelmed with work and school, your grand gesture with my new heels, and frankly, the topic just never came up till now. I know you would never force a woman to bed if she was not ready to anyway, not like any woman would hold out on you for so long...um, sorry. I'm getting off topic here. Basically, please don't feel obliged to make anything right. We are good. I am, anyway. Honestly."

"No." Joshua answered as soon as she was done speaking.

"No?"

"No, I'm not good with that. It was liberating for you to kiss me first—"

"Hey, I kiss you!" she interrupted.

"Not first, babe, and you know it. I kiss you and you kiss me back."

"Oh."

He smiled and kissed her. She kissed him back, and her hands were already behind his head drawing him closer.

"See, just like that. I kiss you and you kiss me back." He laughed.

She found a pillow to smack him with. "Cheat."

"Problem now is I can't guarantee it will start and end with a kiss Melanie Reed."

How am I supposed to respond to that? she thought.

"I'll have that bath now, thanks," she said and scooted away from him.

"Good call." He chuckled and walked to her living area to find his pants. He also picked up his briefs and shirt and tie. It wasn't too late to get to his house. He rarely slept in a bed other than his own, but he wanted to spend the night with her until he could figure out his next move. He had an early close-out meeting with his team and the prospect with a $64 million investment portfolio they had been following up with, so definitely he had to stop at home before heading out the following day. He went back to her bedroom and ran warm water for her bath, then added some bath salts. Candytufts included.

Melanie did not realize how weak she was till she tried to get up. She massaged her sore areas with olive oil and just enjoyed her body soaking in the salts.

Joshua had brought her a glass of juice, as well, for quick energy while he searched her small pantry and refrigerator for something to whip or heat up for them. He settled for toast, pork sausage, and scrambled eggs. He popped into the bedroom minutes later to check on her and was surprised to see her curled at a corner of the bed, asleep and hugging a pillow. He drew the comforter over her and went to fetch his laptop in his car.

After about thirty minutes of researching and a phone call to his colleague Jason, he was happy with his plan and decided to wake Melanie for their meal.

* * *

"So, what do you think, babe? Can you get this Saturday off work and

Sunday morning too?"

Melanie was seated next to him on her sofa in her shorts and T-shirt pajamas, her left leg tucked under her right thigh, and her right leg dangled over his left leg.

She had stopped chewing her food and stared at her man for what seemed like forever. First the expensive shoes, now a weekend getaway? She could not afford to get used to this kind of treatment, just in case he still walked away.

"Josh, isn't this too much? I promise you, I'm good, and I know how close you are to winning over this client. You say you're meeting tomorrow, but what if something comes up and he and/or his partners need to see you on Saturday?"

"I've rescheduled my other important meetings to tomorrow and Monday. Jason and Schmidt are all caught up with this and the other deals we're handling at the moment. We are a team, babe. No one person signs a corporate client as their personal investment banking consultant, you know. At the very worst, I'm a phone call away."

She really liked the idea of having Joshua all to herself for the weekend. She was scared it was still a dream and she would have to wake up pretty soon. Oh well, she might as well enjoy the dream to the fullest and face reality tomorrow.

"Okay, then. I'll speak with Elka tomorrow and inform Brad just so he knows I'm safe with you."

He smiled at her. "Thank you. I need you to finish your toast too."

"Should I expect Mr. Bossy all through the weekend or just tonight?"

He chuckled and moved her closer to take the fork of eggs he was about to feed her.

"Only when you starve my Candytuft. Those curves won't fill up themselves, will they?"

She frowned but did as she was told. She usually wasn't this mushy, and her recent reactions to him both annoyed and excited her.

"So, I could spend the night if you are fine with me here. And wake up very early to get showered and changed at home before I head out to the office. Or I could go home now. I'm totally up to it as well. It's just about 11:13 p.m., so I'll be home before midnight. But I should mention, I do want to spend the night with you. Again, only if you are okay with that—you know, first time and all. I promise I won't—"

Melanie kissed him midsentence. He had her when he said he wanted to spend the night with her in her tiny apartment. She had spent the night once at his, the night of his birthday. He had been really occupied the whole day and had done nothing special to celebrate his day, so she was determined to spend some time with him, no matter how late it got. But he had wanted her to spend the night. They ate, watched a movie, and talked till late, and when she started to nod off in his arms, he kissed her and left her in his bedroom, while he slept on the couch in his living room. He had converted the other bedroom—which should have been the guest room—to his home office. It was almost as if he did not want any guests.

Melanie knew Joshua Doyle was in every way a gentleman, but she had worried he might make a move she may or may not have been ready for that night. It turned out he had long decided he would wait until she was ready.

Several minutes later she was catching her breath. He on the other hand was breathing normally, staring intensely into her eyes, but some other member of his was clearly as affected. *This can't be good*, she thought. She had not meant for this to linger, but nothing about the night had gone like she'd anticipated. It had all been better. Every time he kissed her, the kiss seemed to trump the last one. His hands held her like she was the most fragile gem in the world, and he wasn't wasting any second not adoring it. She needed to cool it before she did or said something they were both sorry about later.

"I could get used to this...you kissing me first." He smiled. "It's consuming to finally know I'm not alone in this."

"Josh, I do want you to spend the night. Kissing you was me saying yes. But…"

"But?"

She bit her lower lip.

He groaned and moved his hand to her lips.

"I hope for my sanity, you do this only with me. spit out what's eating you. I am going home, all right? I just want to know what changed your mind."

"I do trust you. I just don't trust myself with you tonight. And last I checked, I don't have sixty-four million dollars, so I cannot be responsible for you being late or incoherent tomorrow," she explained.

He laughed out loud and threw his head back a little. Then he rubbed his forehead and brows with his free hand.

"Okay, love. I better head out now then. May I pick you up at six tomorrow?"

"I'll be ready." She got up to get his folded shirt and tie while he packed his laptop and then walked him to her door.

"I'll email you the brochure of the resort so you can see the activities and decide what to pack. Not that I'm promising anything, but I'm a gentleman. It's my duty to inform you."

Too late to back out now, she thought. He leaned in to give her a kiss on her cheek and whispered, "Get some sleep. I love you, Mel."

"Ditto."

Chapter 7

"Hey, you, how have you been?" she said cautiously when Bradley answered her call. Melanie had forgotten she had made plans to attend the Thanksgiving service with Bradley on Sunday. She knew Joshua had practically put a pause on his tight schedule to fit this in, and she had a deadline the following weekend. They would not be back until Sunday afternoon. She needed to cancel with Bradley or with Joshua. She already felt Joshua was doing so much for her, the least she could do was meet him halfway the best she could—not that it was ever an equal half and half anyway.

"I'm fine, thank you."

She could hear his smile in his response.

"Brad, Josh invited me for a weekend at a cabin & lodge in the Blue Ridge Mountains, and we won't be back till Sunday afternoon."

He did not respond, probably waiting for her to share more.

"I'm really sorry I can't make Sunday service with you," she added.

She had struggled to keep moving forward on the Christian path the Madisons had steered her to. Since she'd moved out to North Carolina, her job and school had been priorities. She had started attending church again occasionally after Bradley joined her in North Carolina because he was determined that she should take her relationship with God seriously. Because of her orientation as a child and having to fend for herself so early in life, she barely believed in miracles, let alone in an invisible heavenly Father who truly loved her with all her imperfections. Among those on earth, the Madisons were the closest she could associate with love. As far as she was concerned, every human was naturally selfish, and she'd long decided she would not be taken advantage of.

"Oh," he finally answered.

She really hated the guilt she felt at that moment.

"Will you be okay?" she asked.

"Yes, sure. Have fun."

"Brad, I could cancel with Josh, you know. I do miss him and long to spend this weekend with him, but I also did commit to attend this Sunday with you before this came up…"

"Mel! I am rooting for you both. Josh is good people." He chuckled.

She smiled. He did understand. Even when it was inconvenient, they could count on each other.

"Thanks, Bradley. We will go together, though, when next my schoolwork permits. Till then, I'll just watch a replay online or something."

"Sure. Call me," he added.

That meant he would stay out of her hair till she was ready. He always respected her relationship with Joshua, and that warmed her heart.

"Okay," she responded.

Great. Now she could enjoy her weekend. Elka had been more than willing to not need her for the weekend. Joshua had emailed the brochure for the Homefront Cabins & Lodge in Banner Elk, which offered an appealing indoor swimming pool and scenic hiking trails. Nearby was a mountain resort for climbing, skiing, and cable rides, as well as Seven Devils, which offered a mountain zip line tour. Melanie had called Abigail to confirm that she could get off work early to go lingerie shopping with her. Abigail was more than happy to join her, but she had insisted that Melanie be waxed ahead of their shopping.

"The product is as important as the package," Abigail had shrieked into the phone when Melanie started to argue. Out of three of Melanie's preferred choices, Abigail allowed her just one because it was "Mel"—a plain M&S black satin midi-length gown with spaghetti straps and a tiny bow at the plunge of the V neckline. It fell nicely on her curves with no emphasis on her waist but flattered her hips, and the fall of the V revealed a little rise of her breasts. For her second choice, she let Abigail convince her to fall in love with a maroon Shein floral lace teddy bodysuit. Okay, she did look and feel very feminine in them. The thought of Joshua being gentle with the lace made her blush. It had decorative pearl buttons in front, so she made a mental note to let him know the teddy did not open that way. Abigail was wiping her eyes from tiny tears of joy. She was so excited to have been part of Melanie's mini transformation.

"Will you knock it off? It's just a weekend. He put in the effort, and I thought it would be nice to reward that." Melanie rolled her eyes at her friend for the umpteenth time.

While she did love the glow of her skin afterward, she was tired and grateful she had decided to have her hair straightened and her nails done before the spa visit. She hugged Abigail tightly, thanked her for her time, and drove home to get packing. Joshua would be on time. He had sent a message while she was at the salon: **Babe**, nothing about running late. He was thinking of her in his crazy day. She had responded with the smiling-poo emoji. She wore a smile the rest of her stay at the saloon, knowing she must have made him chuckle. She had every other item she would need in her wardrobe, or at least could convert to make a nice accessory. Joshua was sure to dress appropriately. If there was a tennis match, he wore shorts, tucked in with belt and his casual shoes with sunglasses. The weather would be cool in the high country and there was a chance of snow, so deciding the clothing to pack was pretty straightforward. The only addition to her pile was a low-rise multicolored retro ruffled swim skirt with matching underwire halter-neck bra top, and as always, a pair of jeans, party tops, and an extra camisole. For footwear, her newest addition went in the small suitcase first, then ski boots and snow boots.

Melanie was applying the final bits of her light makeup when her phone chimed. It was a message from Bradley. **Okay, not too much fun to where you think about eloping. Mr. T and I will hunt Josh down. But you do deserve the time out.** She laughed out loud. Bradley could be a bully when he chose to be. Oh well, it was comforting to know her bones would never be buried unquestioned on a deserted island.

Minutes later, Joshua showed up with a single jasmine flower for her. He stood with one hand in his front jeans pocket, and his dark-brown leather jacket was unzipped over his dark-green V-neck T-shirt. *He smells of his bamboo shampoo. He must have showered before heading out,* she thought.

"Hey, babe, this is for you. Ready?"

She smiled and nodded. He kissed her lightly on the lips and then bent to pick up her suitcase. Melanie found a cylindrical water jar for her flower, grabbed her coat, and headed out with him.

He had swapped his dark gray 2018 Jeep Grand Cherokee, for Jason's black BMW 2 Series convertible for the weekend. Melanie thought she was probably overthinking it, but he had not complimented her appearance, and the ride was starting out too quietly for her. Maybe work was stressful that day. It usually was, but he thrived on the hustle and bustle. Or maybe he had second thoughts and was not sure how to inform her.

"How was your meeting? Deal sealed yet?" She tried to sound casual, hoping to break the ice.

"We had a series of meetings actually. I had to move some forward, but that acquisition should be concluded tomorrow when the attorneys sign off. Thanks for asking." He shot a quick glance her way and winked with a smile.

Melanie tried again a few miles later after the only change was the radio she had turned on.

"What's the fun of being on an open road with a convertible if you can't feel the wind in your face?"

He chuckled. "In this cold? You really don't mind the wind blowing out your ends?"

So he did notice my hair at least, she thought, *but decided to say nothing. Well, I'm going to have fun no matter what. When he's done sitting on his high horse, he can come down and speak with me.*

"No, I don't. Please fold up the roof, if you don't mind yourself, thank you," she answered without looking his way.

She heard the top begin to fold up slowly, and in seconds the wind was all over her face. She didn't need to wind the windows down. It was cool and beautiful and had her hair across her face. She had to use her hands to brush it back. She screamed in excitement and waved at strangers speeding past them. Apparently, Joshua had slowed down a bit because of the rush. It was exhilarating indeed. Joshua's hair was shorter, but still the effect of the wind was obvious. He seemed to concentrate on the driving, so she didn't bother him.

About thirty minutes later as it got darker, she felt chilled and asked him to put the roof up again so they could turn on the heat, which he obliged.

"Feeling better yet?" Joshua asked her a few minutes later.

"Yes, thank you." She still rubbed her hands to generate more heat, though, and tried to rearrange her hair to look better.

The map showed they were still about two hours away from their destination, so she grabbed a book from her purse to pass the time, and she eventually nodded off into a restful sleep.

Joshua drove into the parking lot and turned off the ignition. He'd made it. The plan was to check into their cabin first, but he had done a pretty good job making it to the parking lot of their lodge. He unbuckled his belt and turned to get Melanie's as she stretched herself awake from her sleep.

"Hi," he breathed against her cheek.

He didn't wait for her response before he hungrily took her lips in his. One hand went in her tousled hair and the other around her waist and up her back, pulling her out of her seat and on him as much as the gearshift and hand-brake area could allow. Thankfully she had on skinny jeans underneath her coat that made maneuvering around them easier, and within seconds she was straddled across his thighs. Melanie pulled at his hair angrily. He had ignored her all through the trip, and she should be putting up a fight but did not have the energy. It was a good thing he'd gone home the night before. *Why is he slowing down again?* she thought.

"Of course, I noticed your hair," he whispered against her lips. "And your skinny jeans and manicured hands and feet"—he ran his right hand over her hand and brought it down from his neck to his chest—"And your tanned skin and your eyes and your lips." He kissed her hand and her neck and back to her lips.

"Help me make sense of you, Joshua Herberman Doyle," she whispered.

"I did not want to lose the essence of this weekend, Mel. You kissed me once last night, and we ended up in bed for the first time. Getting you here was a priority for me. I am, in fact, sorry I could not wait to check us into our room." His voice was hoarse as he looked deeply into her eyes.

"Josh, I won't—I can't have a good time if you'll be following strict plans like your work deals. We are here to be together, not for you to be my bodyguard while I explore. At any rate, Bradley has promised to hunt you down if anything goes wrong with me. So just in case that happens, enjoy the rest of your life to the fullest. With me, not for me," she added with a smile, leaning in to give him a kiss.

"Agreed?" she pressed again.

"Sixty-four percent agreed."

She laughed.

"I'll take it. Thank you." Then she kissed him.

* * *

"Welcome to Homefront Cabins & Lodge. Do you have a reservation?" The woman at the reception desk greeted pleasantly with a wide smile. *She sure knows how to earn herself a large tip,* Melanie thought with a grin.

"Yes. Joshua Doyle. Two nights." He handed her his credit card while the porter loaded their luggage on the cart.

"We have the Love and Faith cabins available. The Hope cabin is currently occupied. All three are the same size and offer equal amenities, but their views are different."

"The Love Cabin will do, irrespective of the view."

Melanie had thought she had heard the receptionist wrong, but Joshua had carried on as though he was already aware, so she filed her questions for later.

Melanie was in awe of the room and thought she could easily stay the whole weekend indoors. She took off her shoes, her coat, and kimono top with the belt but left her camisole and jeans on to explore. The woody smell of the cabin was welcoming, and the ceiling to floor sliding door led to a private porch that had an outdoor BBQ grill and a spectacular view of a waterfall cascading down a mountain. The bed was large enough for five of her to sleep in diagonally, and a huge gold-and-blue abstract painting of a mountain hung above the headboard. The bedside lamp had a white shade and gold-coated rod, and suspended over each side of the bed by black cables were lamps with gold dome-shaped shades. Other ceiling lights were built into the quadrangle design. A curved lounge chair was placed next to a glass table with a small artificial potted green plant. The TV was on the wall to the left of the bed, above a reading table and minibar. The closet was a walk-in. The lights came on once you stepped into the corner. *"Whoever needed such a huge space for a weekend? Oh well."* The bathroom was to the far right of the room, separated from the room by a clear glass wall. Whoever designed this room clearly did not expect the occupants to entertain guests.

"Babe, we have about forty-five minutes to freshen up and head out to the lodge for dinner."

"This place is amazing, Josh. I bet it all cost a lot too." She walked up to him and placed her hands on his chest. He must have tossed his coat and jacket at some point, as he had just his T-shirt and jeans on.

"Thank you. Not just for the expense, but for taking the time out and the grand gesture." She stretched and stood on her toes to kiss him.

"You're welcome." He smiled down at her without releasing her. "In the spirit of enjoying this together, I'm totally okay with staying indoors tonight if you'd rather not go."

"Are you kidding? I want to see the lodge, and I think I heard music. Nice try, Mister." She wriggled out of his hold and went to look for her suitcase.

* * *

They headed to the indoor lounge to grab a bite. A band was playing on the stage, and people were on the dance floor. A group Melanie thought must be tourists occupied a table and were playing a board game she wasn't familiar with, and they had attracted a few others. There seemed to be fun on every inch of the room.

Joshua held her by the waist and led her to the bar to get drinks and something to eat. The bar was known for its creative cocktails, and the old school vibe made every customer's experience enjoyable.

"We'll have two burgers, fried chicken, and the accompanying sides. For drinks, two glasses of the signature cocktail and some water. Thank you." Joshua handed back their menu after they had decided. Melanie was swaying to the music on her chair and looking around, mostly at the dance floor. Joshua chuckled.

"You can go nuts on the dance floor if you want. I'm happy to admire you from here. I'm starving and terrible at the dance thing."

"Huh?" She raised one brow, trying to decide if it was another of his tricks.

Joshua laughed and helped her up.

"Have fun. And fear not; I won't touch your food."

She smiled, gave him a tight hug, and skipped away to join the others dancing to a country song. A few other couples joined them, and for a moment she felt as though it was just her having a private dance.

Water had never tasted so good to Joshua. Melanie looked angelic swaying her arms, swinging her hips, and smiling dreamingly. She had taken off her light sweater before leaving his side, and her movements made her dress cling to her curves. He hoped he was the only man staring intently at her—otherwise he was going to break jaws that night. He appreciated the fact that she could be happy and fulfilled all by herself. She did not hover. The two times she had decided to surprise him at work for a change, she had called him first to verify if it was okay. He was too busy to hover around her anyway, so her yes was yes to him, and no meant no. No dramas. Okay, a little drama here and there but nothing he could not live with.

He was falling fast and hard in love with her. And he knew she probably loved him, too, but it would take a miracle for her to admit that to herself let alone to him. She was not selfish. Her early independence just got the better of her so that receiving anything or allowing anyone in was like a war. Even with something as little as gifts, Joshua had to fight tooth and nail before she allowed him some of his rights as her man. She did not see a need for a gift if it wasn't her birthday or if there was no achievement being celebrated. She had even refused him tipping her when they had been close enough to being an item. And when they had started dating, he had to pay for his meals without leaving her a tip, unless someone else attended to him. Joshua chuckled to himself. Those were her types of drama.

The music had changed to a slower pace, and couples found each other to slow dance. Joshua got up to join Melanie, just in case she wasn't ready to leave but also did not want to be left out. Even if another man had walked up to her, he was confident she would have refused.

"Hey, care to be embarrassed for a few minutes?" he said with a straight face when he got to her.

"With you, yes, please." She smiled and connected their bodies.

She wound her arms round him and rested her head on his chest, listening to his breathing in spite of the music and noise around them.

"Babe, our meals may be too cold to enjoy by now," Joshua noted a few minutes later.

Melanie opened her eyes to see some new faces had joined them on the dance floor.

"Right."

They didn't get back to their room until after one, happily exhausted. Joshua took a quick shower and turned on his laptop. He had some mails to respond to. Melanie took her time in the tub to allow the salts to work their magic on her skin. Abigail had sent her a message earlier when they had just checked in. **I hope for your sake you**

118

are too occupied to reply to this message. Melanie laughed at her enthusiasm. She had planned to surprise Joshua with the maroon lace bodysuit lingerie but changed her mind, thinking they were both tired after the long evening, not to mention the long drive. With the Jacuzzi though, it seemed there was some energy building.

Joshua was catching up on some mails so she could not really tell if he was still as tired or had transitioned into work mode. She decided to try. She got out of the bath and went to slip it on in the closet. The lodge had provided a white robe, which she put on over it, and then went to lie down under the duvet. That way if he was tired, they could both just fall asleep without any pressure. She turned on the television but muted it so as not to disturb him. Nothing interested her, so she turned it off and watched him type away.

So many mails in a few hours. He had responded to the super urgent ones on his mobile earlier. As a project manager, he still worked as much as when he had started as an associate investment banker or when he was a senior analyst. He was working toward his dream of becoming a managing director of an investment bank, and Melanie could not be more proud of his drive.

She must have dozed because his weight on the mattress as he stretched out beside her woke her up. He had tried to place his arm behind her or around her, wanting to move her head to rest on his chest, when he caught sight of the lace fabric. They had turned out the lights except for a small one in the bathroom. Joshua pulled back and pushed the robe off her shoulder to see what she had on. He swallowed painfully.

"Babe?"

"Mmmm..." she mumbled as she stirred.

"Mel, can you be awake? I need to see you." His heart was beating fast, and he could feel his blood rush to other specific parts of his body. He turned on a bedside lamp and helped her get out of the white robe. He sat at the edge of the bed in his cotton long-sleeve pajamas dumbfounded, while she stood between his legs. Melanie tried to rub the sleep from her eyes.

"I wanted to surprise you, but I guess I dozed off. Do you like it?" She smiled shyly at him.

* * *

Melanie opened her eyes slowly and replayed the events of the early hours in her head. She wasn't sure she'd heard any response to her question from Joshua, but oh, she had felt his answer. A lot. Everywhere. If what he did to her was his answer, then that was a definite yes. He had been so gentle. And as she had predicted, he had been disappointed to find out the buttons on her bodysuit were decorative, but he had managed to gently slide it off her anyway. A smile crept up her lips.

She wanted to look into his sleepy face but did not want to wake him. His head was on her chest, and picturing it brought tears to her eyes. They had been together for eight months, and she had tried several times to tell him but just couldn't find the words. Even when he said it to her.

"I love you, Joshua Doyle." She placed her hands on his head and fought to keep the sob from escaping.

She felt his grip around her tighten, but he didn't wake up.

"I love you," she said again, more to herself than to him. This time she smiled and drifted back into a deep sleep.

Several hours later, Joshua opened his eyes and tried to remember. Melanie had said she loved him. He was sure he had heard it. Twice. He didn't see himself as being Prince Charming at first sight, but he knew he was fantastic between the sheets. Satisfying his woman was one thing he carried out excellently, next to closing deals at work, but he had no doubt that was not why Melanie finally uttered the words he'd waited so long for her to admit to him—although he was sort of asleep, so technically, she'd admitted it out loud to herself. She was still asleep curled up beside him with her arms wrapped around a pillow. He smiled. He did not understand her obsession with pillows when she slept. He needed to get back on track.

He really was going to send Abigail a thank-you note. And to think he almost missed it because he was working.

He sighed deeply and rubbed his face with both hands. Thank heavens she really was understanding. He was brought up to be disciplined and taught to thrive on success only. No one remembers the runner up, his dad always said. His longest relationship had lasted barely three months because he was "too busy." His few close friends had not exactly approved of his ex anyway, but he had been so determined to make it work that he ignored any red flags. Eventually she had walked away on her own. He did not want to lose Melanie. He could not afford to. And even though his mom had been weighing on him since he turned thirty to introduce her to his woman, his desire for more with Melanie had nothing to do with that.

He grabbed his camo pajama bottoms and went to the bathroom to freshen up. They did not have to get out till later in the morning for the zip line and the other activities for the day, so he let her sleep in while he ordered their food.

Melanie opened her eyes to search for what smelled so delicious. Joshua had ordered them a feast in the small kitchen area, but he was on a phone call by the sink in the bathroom, and spoke softly, his free hand gesturing as he paced the floor. She was unsure if he had heard her earlier, but she was too chicken now and did not plan to bring it up unless he did. Even if he did, she wasn't as sure as before anymore. She concluded the events of the weekend were overwhelming her, and her hormones were taking over her thinking faculty. She decided she needed some space away from Joshua for a while. She slid off the bed as quietly as she could and headed for the closet. *A swim should do me some good,* she thought.

"Where are you going?" Joshua asked in surprise when she stepped back into their room with her coat and a mini sling bag dangling from her hand.

"Hey, you, good morning." Melanie walked toward Joshua and gave him a quick kiss. "I didn't mean to disturb you. I need to go for a swim in the indoor pool," she added.

"I'm not using the bathroom now. You can take all the time you want in the Jacuzzi."

She laughed. "It is not Olympic size, I know, but it's still a swimming pool, not a tub. Not the same, Josh."

"But I had plans for us to have breakfast together. By the time you return, we'll practically be headed out again. Although we'll have a car to ourselves, the group leaves for the Hawksnest Zipline in an hour, and I'd prefer we moved together." He protested with a frown.

"Thanks, but you'll barely notice I'm gone before I return. I promise."

"I can turn off my phone, Mel." He tried again, unsure why she suddenly needed to swim, especially since she had not mentioned it before.

"Certainly not! It's just not advisable to swim right after a full meal."

Joshua studied her for a few seconds and then decided to let it be.

"Fine. This was supposed to be our private breakfast, so you owe me for blowing me off."

"I'm not blowing you off, Josh. I'll eat my share when I return."

"It's not the same, babe."

"How can I make it up to you?" she asked with a tease in her voice after a few seconds of silence and drew closer to him.

"Will you have dinner with me tonight? Just us. That means skipping the chocolate and wine tasting event the lodge has planned for its guests tonight," Joshua said, looking down at her face, his arms around her.

Melanie frowned, surprised. "Is that all? Sure. Dinner sounds great."

"I already got you a dress and was cooking up a reason to give it to you. So for skipping breakfast with me, you will accept it without questions or arguments. You don't have to wear it tonight, though, if you already have something. Also, I ordered you a dozen purple orchids."

"Thank you," she responded softly with a smile.

Joshua's phone beeped. He looked at the screen and apologized to Melanie, saying he had to take the work call. She nodded and waved him off, thankful for the distraction as she slipped out the door.

* * *

Melanie had not been on a zip line before and was looking forward to experiencing the views of the mountain from a high and exhilarating level. As they drew near the mountain, they could hear music, and she was glad she had decided to come after all. They joined the first group in getting their safety gadgets in readiness for the zip line ride, and Melanie almost changed her mind about going on the zip line, but Joshua requested their harnesses be attached together so they could ride together.

"It's tempting to keep your eyes shut throughout but trust me, after the initial rush, you want to take in the view." Joshua spoke softly into her ears.

Melanie giggled. "Easy for you to say. But I'll take your word for it and try my best to keep my eyes open."

The guide checked that their helmets were buckled safely; he also checked their lanyards, carabiners, and their pulleys.

They started off slowly, and Melanie squeezed down tightly on Joshua's hand around her as they picked up speed. But in a few seconds of them soaring over the mountain landscape, she was experiencing the surreal and natural beauty of the snow-covered Blue Ridge mountains. Melanie as grateful she had summoned the courage to open her eyes because the scenery was absolutely breath-taking. She felt like a bird in flight and was surprised when they came to the end of the one-thousand-foot line. Joshua encouraged her to have a second ride by herself, but not sure she could survive it knowing he wasn't right there with her, she declined.

They spent the later part of the afternoon at Sugar Mountain Resort skiing, and Melanie was great at it. She particularly enjoyed watching Joshua try but fail to keep up with her. Sometimes he fell, and other times he made her trip along with him.

On leaving the resort, their dedicated driver took a longer route to allow them to see some more of the town. Melanie's eyes were glued to the window, taking in all the town had to offer—which was mostly other climbing mountains, or lodges that had existed for decades, but she asked a few questions when the driver shared some historical stories about such notable places. Joshua sat quietly beside her, mostly on his phone, but he drew her into his arms a few times to drop a kiss on her hair or her cheek when she pointed out something fascinating to her. Melanie took a lot of pictures of the places, and then stopped by a local store with unique items. She got Abigail and Elka handmade bracelets, a framed "shades of green" watercolor painting of a fern plant for Bradley, and a dyed multicolored neck scarf for herself.

Melanie thought they were going to the café at the lodge or a nearby restaurant, but when they got to their cabin, she discovered that a table for two had been set up in their large living room, and a second table had covered dishes of food. A low fire burned in the fireplace, and the sound of soft music drifted from a cordless speaker. She wondered if Joshua had this planned all along or if he arranged it after last night, which meant all this was because he had heard her say she loved him.

Whichever, he sure knew how to pay her back, because otherwise, they might have been in an argument by now. Luckily Joshua had gone to shower immediately when they arrived so that she could have the bathroom to herself later. She then noticed the medium-size ivory paper bag on the mahogany table. "For my little tornado" was written on the small card. Her dress.

Melanie sighed. She might as well wear it tonight. Knowing Joshua, he probably had a tux planned. No point showing up underdressed and ruining his efforts. When she stepped out of the bathroom, Joshua was still not back from the errand he had said he had to run. She packed and pinned her hair so that it fell nicely in front of her left shoulder. She applied her makeup and added a little extra glitter to her eyes to complement her dress. It was a slightly stretchy but straight and short shimmery-black long-sleeve evening dress with a boat neck in front and a cowl low back that stopped just below the small of her back. Even with the straight cut, it fell nicely on her curves without effort. This was the perfect time to wear her new Sophia Webster six-inch butterfly heels. Boy, was she glad Abigail made her wax this one time. Her legs were inviting even to her. She wore silver rectangle earrings and was about to wear her black-leather strap wristwatch when Joshua came into the room.

"I was about to send out the search party after you," she teased as she turned around to see him.

He was in a white shirt tucked into black pants that she suspected were from a tux. He had no tie on, and though he left the top button of his shirt undone, his shoes could not have been any more formal.

"Yeah? You're going to have to re-apply your lipstick, though."

"Oh." She stood up with the intention of checking the mirror, but he got to her in time to plant a heavy kiss on her. She seemed to match his height better with her heels and wound her arms around his neck and shoulder. His hand was warm against the small of her back as he pulled her closer still.

"Sorry. These are for you." He smiled and gave her a black circular box that had on its side "The Million Roses" printed in gold. She opened the lid slowly and saw the beautifully tucked in purple roses, each wanting to be picked. They smelled heavenly. She had promised herself she wasn't going to cry tonight, but he was making it hard not to.

"I was expecting orchids."

"I'm glad I could still surprise you."

"Thank you," she said smiling at him.

"You're welcome. Let's feed those curves."

For starters, there were bread rolls and garden salad with cucumbers, cherry tomatoes, carrots, and other garden vegetables, served with red wine vinaigrette. They also had spiced red snapper filet with grilled pineapple and mango salsa. For the main dishes they had the penne pasta puttanesca with plum tomatoes, capers, garlic, roasted red peppers, and olives in a rich, burgundy-based tomato sauce.

They had chatted lightly about her school and her dream of owning a diner or restaurant, starting with saving to be part owner of Elka's family diner. He had shared more about his childhood, the business-like relationship he had with his dad, and the more warm and friendly one with his mom. Each of his parents was now remarried, but they had a respectful and cordial relationship with each other.

After the meal they had some wine and danced to Ed Sheeran. Actually, she danced a little while he sat at the edge of their table and watched her or twirled her around.

She started to bite her lower lip, and he pulled her into him guiding her hands on his shoulders.

"Josh?" she started slowly.

"Babe."

"Did you do this because you heard me last night?" She looked into his eyes intently.

"Heard what?" he pushed with a straight face.

"Uh, what I said to you last night. Or the early hours of this morning."

"Hmm…What did you say?"

Melanie could hear her heart beating fast. She could not tell if he was kidding or not. She could dismiss it right now or admit it again. She hoped for her psychological and physical health that she wasn't trading with the devil. Bradley always said he prayed for her, right?

"That I love you." She swallowed and waited.

"Could you be audible? I don't want to miss this, babe." He edged closer, looking serious still.

Okay. He's yanking my chains this time, Melanie thought with a smile.

"I said I love you, Joshua Doyle," she repeated.

"I love you too, Candytuft, but you already know that." he responded with a very wide smile, and then he kissed her.

"And yes, I did hear you in the course of the night too," he added with a chuckle. "But I like to hear you say it to me when I'm awake to kiss you."

"Come on…seriously!" She laughed and held him tightly.

Joshua was the happiest he could remember ever being. He cradled her head and held on to her just in case she thought to take it back. He knew it took her a lot to get here, and he prayed he did not mess this up.

"Mel, I can't promise it'll be all roses and candlelit dinners. But I will fight hard to keep earning your trust. And I promise to always handle you with care."

"That's all I'm asking." And then she finally allowed the tears to roll down.

* * *

Bradley got a call from Joshua that he needed to speak with him. He hoped all was well with Melanie. He answered the door and was relieved to see Joshua smile and stretch out his hand for a handshake.

"Hey, man, enjoyed your weekend?"

"I did. We both did. We both have school and office work piled up naturally, but I would not have had it any other way."

Bradley laughed. "Nice. I'm glad. How's Mel?"

"She's good. Dropped her off a few minutes ago and headed here."

Joshua took his seat on one of the couches, while Bradley walked behind him and took the opposite three-seat sofa.

"Um, Mel told me she loves me." Joshua leaned forward with his elbows on his knees and paused for a bit.

"Ah. Finally," Bradley answered, smiling but with a raised brow, wondering what the issue was. Perhaps he had missed something.

"Yeah? I knew she did and hoped she allowed herself to see it too. It's just she finally says it, and it's surreal. In a good way anyway," Joshua rambled on, running his hands through his hair.

Although he had not understood why at the time, he had later realized Melanie freaked out the morning after, using her desire to swim to put some distance between them. She had reconsidered her decision to trust him with her heart, and at that moment he knew he would do everything in his capacity to make sure she never regretted choosing him.

Bradley was surprised at how it was affecting the usually calm and collected Joshua. He grinned and got up to pour them both drinks. A shot of bourbon for Joshua, but he had sparkling grape juice.

"Josh, Mel telling you she loves you means you have done right by her, and she does love you. She's the most uptight and difficult to woo human I know. Believe me, I've seen guys try." He laughed and handed Joshua his glass as he sat down.

"I'm going to ask her to marry me, Brad." Joshua finished without taking his drink.

There was silence.

"When?"

"I don't know yet. Maybe in a few months? Or a year? I haven't thought that far. I just know she's home for me, and for as long as she will let me, I intend to be the same for her. God help me."

Bradley took a deep breath and finally leaned forward to shake his hand.

"Congratulations, man. You have my blessing." He smiled at Joshua and raised his glass to him.

"Thank you." Joshua released his held breath in relief and finally drained his drink.

Bradley did admire Joshua and could not see a better fit for his childhood friend. He was particularly honored that Joshua deemed it fit to tell him first, and for that, his respect for the man just doubled. Most guys might have felt threatened by his relationship with Melanie, but not Joshua. He knew his place and trusted it to hold.

"Hey, got time for a quick bite?" Bradley offered.

"Oh no, thanks. Jason and I have an informal meeting with a client tonight. I need to get up to speed with his intel among other things," he explained as he got up to take his leave.

"All right, then. Have a good one."

* * *

"Hey, Abi," Melanie answered her beeping phone.

Abigail squealed into the phone, which made Melanie move the phone away from her ears in shock, trying to make sense of what her friend was saying.

"Abi, please calm down. I can't understand you." She tried again, smiling at the excitement in her friend's voice.

"Tell me everything."

"My weekend? I'm not one to kiss and tell, but it went well, thank you," Melanie told her, grinning.

"Just 'well'? Then why do I have a thank-you card and a small box of chocolates from a Mr. Joshua Doyle delivered to my gallery on a Monday morning?"

"What? Josh did that?" Melanie asked in surprise, as her face turned red.

"Yeah…" Abigail laughed joyfully.

"Sorry."

"Why? I'm not complaining. Happy to have been of help." She grinned.

"I got you a little something myself. See you later? Customers are waiting." Melanie moved on eagerly.

"Yeah, sure. Thank you."

"Bye."

"Bye, Mel."

* * *

It had indeed been the perfect weekend etched into Melanie's heart forever. They had been together for over a year now, so it just did not add up. *Why does it hurt so much that he didn't give me a direct and reassuring response but instead just hung up? Maybe it was true? Maybe it had started out as bet, and he'd had a change of heart? Or the bet included making her fall in love with him and walking away in the end?* She did not need him to be perfect, but this was not handling her with care. Melanie was breathing heavily into a paper bag to calm herself, but it did not seem to work. She decided she needed to get out of there.

Chapter 8

Joshua was beginning to lose his mind. He hated not having his mood controlled, and not getting a hold of Melanie was setting him on edge. Her call had come in at a bad time. The due-diligence team had overlooked some red flags, and a $17.3 million deal was almost slipping through their fingers. The team was brainstorming how to salvage the situation without placing blames, and they were in the heat of things. He was one of the responsible project managers, so technically, his ass was on the line. Melanie usually sent him a message if he didn't pick up her call, but she had kept calling so he excused himself and rushed out in a panic to speak with her. He had expected there was an emergency and was shocked to hear her ask if being with her had been a bet with Malik.

"What?"

"Was I a bet you won?" she repeated.

"Babe, I can't do this right now."

"It's a simple yes or no, Joshua Doyle. Was I bet you made with Malik?"

"I can't believe you'd even ask me that! Seriously?"

"Well, I am," she choked through her tears.

"Mel, I really have to go," he'd responded angrily, and then he had hung up.

He had called her several times since he left the office and left about five voice mails asking her to get back to him. She was not at the diner nor her house, and it was not a school day. He had also tried Bradley but got his voice mail too. He wasn't the type to barge in on people, so he refrained from going to meet Abigail at her workplace. He had wanted to be good with Melanie first before facing Malik, but he needed to let off some steam, so he drove to Malik's place. He wanted to see him rather than talk over the phone, and he was glad to see his red 2012 Lamborghini Aventador parked in its spot. Malik called it "The chick magnet," and he was right. A good-looking, financially stable man in a good-looking financially stable ride always did the trick for him.

Joshua buzzed his apartment, but it went unanswered. Thinking Malik was probably at the gym or pool, he went around to the entrance and told the receptionist at the lobby that he was an expected guest of Malik's. Joshua found him getting out of the shared pool, about to grab a towel, and walked up to him as calmly as he could. He was brought up to not wear his emotions on his sleeves.

"Hey, man, I did not hear my—" Malik was cut off by a hard blow to his left jaw that sent him crashing back into the pool. He was sure he may have needed a stitch if the towel had not been over his head to cushion the punch a bit, but he definitely needed an Advil right away. Malik stepped out of the pool again carefully and sat by the pool chair rubbing his jaw. A few swimmers in the pool had stopped to watch what had transpired, looking alert in case there was a need to call an authority in the event a fight broke out.

"Are we good yet?" Malik finally spoke, his hand still on his jaw. He did not need to ask what it was about because he had it coming.

"You are going to find Mel, apologize for the story, which you and I know you spun ridiculously, and promise to stay the hell out of our business. You got that?" Joshua told him sternly without raising his voice. No need to draw any more attention than they already had. Malik looked up at his friend, still in shock at his reaction. He had never seen Joshua so angry. He had been mad at Melanie and spoken without thinking things through, but he was fast regretting his actions.

"Fine. I'm out of town for the next two or three days, though. Business," Malik replied flatly.

Joshua stared at him a few seconds, rubbed down his mouth with his hand, and walked off without another word to Malik. He did not have many people he called friends, and Malik was his friend. He could not cut him loose over this. Besides, he had met Melanie because Malik took him to her diner. He just needed him to know he had crossed a line he wasn't taking lightly, and he believed his message had been understood.

Joshua sat in his car for a few minutes to get his emotions under control. His suit had been splashed with water when Malik fell into the pool, so he removed his jacket and his tie and flung them in the back seat. His mind wandered back to the day more than a year ago when he went to the diner with Malik for a quick bite during work hours.

* * *

Joshua'd had a meeting in the area with a client and rather than go back to his office all the way in Raleigh, he called Malik to recommend a good place he could grab a bite in peace. He was in no mood for loud music or anything overly fancy. Malik had assured him her diner served the best ribs in the area, so he had agreed. Melanie's name tag had "supervisor" underneath her name, but she had brought them the menu. She wore a short-sleeve flared jeans dress that he suspected had buttons all the way down behind her apron, which was tied around her slim waist. She wasn't wearing any makeup other than lip gloss, and her hair was hidden underneath the disposable hair bonnet each of the diner staff wore.

"Welcome to The Griddle. I'm Melanie. I'll be back for your orders in a bit." Melanie had welcomed them with a smile.

"Are you on the menu?" Malik winked at her.

"As it says on the sign outside, we serve cooked plants and animals to humans and not the other way around, sir," she retorted and handed Joshua the menu.

"Thank you, Melanie." Joshua smiled at her as he took the menu.

"Malik, what the hell was that?" he shot at his friend after she left.

Malik laughed and waved it off.

"Mel is a friend. I just like to get under her skin."

"She seemed to have it out for you, as well. I think that's the first woman I ever met immune to your charm. I like her already," Joshua added with a smirk.

Malik laughed.

"Don't waste your time, man. I bet you she'll wear your chase out," he informed Joshua confidently.

Joshua scoffed at Malik. They both knew he was not one to indulge in anything he did not want to, solely out of pressure or a flimsy bet. But he did find Melanie intriguing. Besides, he thrived on overcoming challenges for a living. True to Malik's recommendation, Joshua had enjoyed his ribs and fries, but he also enjoyed watching Melanie go about her work. She welcomed customers politely, not overly friendly as to send a wrong message, and she handled any rude advances professionally. Even though she seemingly looked plain, he liked the fire in her eyes and caught the swing of the hips she tried to hide underneath the flared dress. He usually met his women at exotic places where he met his clients or VIP sections of clubs or casinos that other clients or Malik dragged him to and did not bother if he wasn't sure he had a shot. But Melanie definitely had him reconsidering his rules.

She greeted a tall and handsome black gentleman warmly with a kiss on the cheek, and Joshua could swear he felt a little jealousy. The gentleman walked up to them and greeted Malik first and then him. It turned out he was Bradley, Malik's friend, whom he had met on two occasions on the basketball court. Joshua had always considered him a man of few words. Bradley got his order to go and left them.

"Hey, are Melanie and Bradley a thing?" Joshua asked Malik a few minutes later

"Nah. Not in this life. Very good friends, though. Some people even consider them siblings."

"Oh." Joshua was glad he wasn't going to break any bro code should he decide to go after Melanie.

He made sure to leave her a huge tip and planned to return in the evening, but the rest of the day had not gone as planned. He had gone the next day and was told she had the day off. He did not want to seem obvious, so he ordered something to go. He had stopped by yet again the following day and was happy to see her seated at a corner in a booth having a chicken burger by herself.

"Hello, Melanie, I'm Joshua Doyle. I was here the other day with my friend, Malik." Joshua stretched out his hand for a handshake.

"Oh, hi. Please call me Mel. Did you lose something the other day? The lost and found items are in a box in that corner," she greeted warmly and pointed out the corner to him.

He laughed half-heartedly. "No. Please, may I sit?"

"Um, sure. I'm on a short break, though," she said as she waved over another waiter to take his order.

"Malik says you are friends."

"More like acquaintances. He's a friend of a dear friend. How do you know each other? Clearly you are more mannered than he is."

Joshua laughed.

"Our families spent summer vacations overseas together when we were growing up, even though we attended different high schools and colleges. He attended college here; I went up North."

"I see."

"My turn. How long have you worked here? You seem to enjoy it still," Joshua asked with keen interest.

She looked surprised at his question, like not many people noticed she enjoyed her work.

"This is my fifth year, and yes, very much so. Most people like to hear they are loved; I like to hear the ding of my microwave. And I look forward to owning my own diner or restaurant someday too." She spoke dreamingly with that fire he had seen two days earlier.

Joshua smiled at her as he began to eat his pasta and chicken wings.

"So what do you do?" she asked with a bite of her burger in her mouth.

Joshua held up his fork as he hurriedly swallowed his food.

"I'm an investment banker," he eventually managed.

Melanie laughed. "Have you ever spoken with food in your mouth? You should try it. It's a new level of freedom, I tell you. Anyway, so you are one of those who help people invest their money, yes?"

Joshua was mesmerized by her carefree spirit and genuine curiosity. He smiled at her remark of him not being free.

"Pretty much. We help companies and governments raise capital by issuing stock or borrowing money. We also act as advisers and the go-betweens on mergers and acquisitions, like the professional link between a company and investors."

"Mm-hmm. That explains the suit and constant tie," she said as she finished her lunch.

Joshua laughed.

"Part of my job requires making my client at ease enough to trust my pitch, and they wouldn't be if I didn't look the like the persona they have in their minds as trustworthy. You follow?"

"Uh-huh. Well, Joshua—"

"Please, Josh."

"Josh, it was nice chatting with you, but my lunch time is over."

"Oh, thanks for the company. Do you mind if I gave you a call sometime? I really hate to be a bother at your workplace." He had decided he was going to come back anyway if she declined, but he had also hoped she would make his life easier.

"Sure, if you do one of two things: Ask me with food in your mouth or lose your tie the rest of your lunch." She grinned, her eyes widening with eagerness to see which he settled for.

Who is this woman? Joshua thought as he weighed his options. Then he dropped his cutlery to loosen and take off his gray-black-and-white striped tie. He had worn a black suit with a white dress shirt that day. Melanie laughed and handed him her cell phone number. And so their journey had begun.

* * *

It had not been the smooth and easy one Joshua was used to. Convincing her that he was worth the chance, had taken daily and weekly deliberate efforts and commitment on his part. Many times, she had tried to brush him off, but for reasons he had not understood at the time, he simply refused to be pushed away. Eventually, after months of proving he was not budging on his decision to earn her trust, she begun to warm up to the possibility of them. Thankfully, his getting closer to Bradley had helped his cause, and admittedly, that could not have happened either without Malik.

She had later told him she'd expected he'd go with the tie option really. And she still enjoyed taking off his ties.

Joshua smiled at the memories and fired up his engine to go home. It was getting late, and he'd been in Malik's parking lot a while. He'd check around for Melanie again the following day, before he went to the office. If she was choosing to believe Malik after all they'd shared, and all he had done to be where they were, he didn't see why he had to defend his trustworthiness and commitment to their relationship. She ought to have trusted him over Malik or anyone else, whether he said it or not.

* * *

Abigail had left Melanie a voice mail almost every day since the episode at her diner four days previously. "Melanie, still Abi. We did not mean to... I'm sorry... I'd really like to speak with you. Please."

She had checked for her at the diner and at her house the following two days but hadn't found her. She was tempted to call Bradley, but it would have been awkward, given the way things were with them at the moment. She had gone online and done a lot more reading on autism and the variations of it in different people.

Autism spectrum disorder (ASD), she learned, was a group of complex neurodevelopmental disorders characterized by repetitive and characteristic patterns of behavior and difficulties with speech and with social communication and interaction. The symptoms were present from early childhood and affected daily functioning. The different symptoms a child could exhibit included repetitive behaviors like hand-flapping, jumping, twirling, and constant hyper behaviors. Symptoms also included fixation on certain activities or objects, as well as specific routines and getting upset when there was a change in the routine. People with ASD often showed exceptional brilliance in some certain academic areas but struggled with writing or maybe other motor skills, and they may have sensitivity to touch, light, or sound.

Basically, every child or adult on the spectrum was as distinct and individual as any other human, and no one solution or remedy fits all. Some people were completely nonverbal and had to depend on Picture Exchange Communication System (PECs) or devices for communication, while some did not have that challenge or outgrew the cards and all once they became verbal and then built on their vocabulary.

Abigail noted that several factors influenced the development of autism, and it was often accompanied by sensory sensitivities and medical issues such as gastrointestinal disorders, seizures, or sleep disorders, as well as mental health challenges such as anxiety, depression, and attention issues. She also read up on the challenges the child could face at the different phases and stages of life and the possible challenges a parent could go through in providing the needed support. More shocking was her discovery that some people may never fully recover throughout their lives. Some very bright and capable adults with autism could have problems dealing with unexpected challenges, such as a power outage or a clogged drain, and may have problems planning too far into the future, so it was best they stayed around an adequate support system.

While some people overcame the spectrum or some aspects of it, some still had challenges in certain areas and did their best to manage in those situations. An autistic adult might read and decode a huge range of data faster than most adults and still find it difficult to understand what others were thinking or feeling. For some, the challenge was in communicating, and they found it difficult to make friends and would rather be by themselves. Some exhibited the challenge they felt by being blunt or rude, while others could be very anxious in social situations. Some people with ASD might not even be officially diagnosed, especially if they are outgoing and, although not always intuiting every nuance or cause of another's reactions, are very self-aware. Abigail learned that the capacity for love, concern, affection, empathy, and compassion was the greatest similarity. It was just communicated in different ways.

Abigail felt both empathy for Bradley and angry at him, and she was scared for herself at the same time. What he must have been through growing up! And his parents and family as well. She could understand now why Melanie seemed so protective of him and why losing his mom was a huge loss for him especially. Where in all she had read did Bradley fit? To what degree or extent was he still autistic? Was she even ready to find out? And why had he not shared? Did he think she was that shallow? He had not even given her a chance to try and fail or not.

She was not sure herself if she could be supportive, but so far she had been denied the opportunity. One thing was certain, though, she should have handled it better than to totally ignore him for so long. Now it seemed harder as they days went by, and more importantly, she had yet to decide what she wanted going forward. Work had been tiring that day and she was beginning to feel as physically drained as she was mentally. She closed from work early, planning to just hit the sack, but then she decided to check on Melanie. She had resolved not to call again so as not to be a pest. But fortunately, Melanie was home.

"Hi, Mel, thanks for seeing me. Can I give you a hug?" Abigail greeted with remorse in her voice.

Melanie smiled and gave her friend a hug.

"Hey. I'm sorry I haven't returned your calls. I've been...doesn't matter really," Melanie began.

"And I'm so sorry you had to find out that way. I just couldn't find the right time and words..." Abigail sighed deeply.

"It's fine. Abi are you happy with Bradley, though?" Melanie asked in all seriousness. The concern in her voice could not be missed.

"I am—*was*—more than happy with Brad, Mel." Abigail closed her eyes and sighed deeply.

"Brad was the one I met at the airport in January," she added softly, as she headed for the large sofa. She didn't see a need to wait any longer before telling her friend.

Melanie stared at Abigail in disbelief for a few seconds. "What?" she asked when she finally found her voice.

"Bradley was—" Abigail tried again.

"I heard you, Abi. I just... What?!" Melanie cut in as she recollected all her friend had shared with her about the hot mystery man she was holding out for. *What were the chances?* she thought. Suddenly she felt faint and moved to the kitchen for a glass of water. She gulped it down in minutes and poured herself another while offering Abigail wine. Then she joined Abigail on the sofa and handed her the glass of wine.

"I was as stunned when I saw him at your diner, Mel. And considering all I had shared with you, and how protective you are of him, I did not see how you would have seen us as anything other than an accident waiting to happen. And Bradley had wanted to talk to you, but I promised him I would find the best time to tell you myself."

Melanie thought for a while and sighed deeply.

"You know, Malik was right about me being judgmental of people, and for that, I am sorry, Abi. Bradley has a large heart, and I'm just used to being there for him when others try to take advantage, you know. But that's water under the bridge now. I'm definitely happy you guys are good and happy together, unlike little-miss-perfect-Cleo who couldn't take a hint." She smiled and raised her glass of water towards Abigail.

"Yeah, about that, technically we are not at the moment." Abigail sighed and placed her glass down.

"You know, don't you?" Melanie asked quietly.

"Yes."

"And? Are you now sorry you were involved with him?"

"Not a chance, Mel. I'm just angry that he chose not to tell me," Abigail explained with a frown as she ran her hands through her hair and leaned back on the sofa in exhaustion.

Melanie was surprised at that because she knew Bradley usually was up-front when he was interviewing for a job. He really must have been taken by Abigail to have decided not to share. She sensed there was more on Abigail's mind so she kept quiet, hoping her friend would know she was there to listen and be the friend Abigail clearly needed at the moment.

"I showed up at his place unannounced last week, again. Not my first time, but in fairness, he did tell me he was not having the best of days. He was struggling to make us cereal, and he wouldn't let me help. I was already irritated by that because it did not make sense to me. But then his housekeeper showed up, and it turned out he was having difficulties because a particular measuring cup was missing. I lost it at that point." Abigail added with teary eyes and took some sips of her wine.

"Oh, Abi, I'm so sorry." Melanie spoke softly.

"So I kind of had a hunch all along, but associated it with him being an introvert and the fact that he was grieving... He's just always seemed like the perfect imperfect human like we all are, you know. Or maybe I unconsciously decided not to question my guts."

Melanie gave her some time before speaking.

"Just so you know, meeting anyone with ASD is meeting that person. No two people have the exact same disorder," she said softly. She had found that out in elementary school, as Bradley had some other classmates in his special education sessions.

"Right. And what's worse, even Ms. Lopez knew how to help, Mel, and I just stared, then up and left," Abigail added.

"She has been his housekeeper for over three years now Abi. She had to be informed before she even started the job so give yourself some credit." Melanie tried to lift her spirit.

Abigail sighed.

"Abi, I'm not trying to sugarcoat it, but autism just means "different" not "less." For example, instead of going to baseball games or practices, Bradley went for sensory programs or therapy sessions. Of course, he still developed the skills he had an interest in, but you get the drift, right? And like you may have stumbled upon, some days are beautiful, but some days are hard. Besides, you were just "officially" finding out, and you tried to be patient with him the best you could. It doesn't happen overnight, Abi. We kind of grew up together, and like you found out, he also needed loads of support from everyone and professionals back then. Sometimes even his mom did not know what to do. He's way better now, trust me. And yes, the passing of his mom most likely aggravated things," Melanie added.

"I just...I feel bad how I handled things, though. He did send me a message later, apologizing, but I've ignored it this whole time because, well, I was angry with him, but I also wanted to be sure what I wanted first. And now, he's left for California."

"Call him. I'm sure he's itching to hear from you, too. Believe me, Brad has the most childlike heart." She chuckled and gave Abigail a squeeze on her shoulders.

"And I'm not saying you have to be with him if you'd rather not anymore. Honestly, he should have been up-front with you. But please let him down easy. I know he values your friendship at the very least," Melanie added, careful to not seem as though she was taking sides. She could tell her friend was confused and also felt bad enough. Still, she needed Abigail to know she was under no obligation to continue the relationship if she was not up for it now that she knew Bradley had ASD.

Abigail thought for a while as she poured out more wine for herself in the kitchen.

"Who is Cleo?" she asked gently, making her way back to the sofa.

Melanie laughed out loud at her obviously jealous friend. She was clearly smitten by Bradley.

"You do love him, don't you?" Melanie asked with all the joy evident in her voice.

Abigail pressed her lips firmly together, as she tried her best to control the smile that crept onto her mouth. She knew she failed terribly because despite her tanned skin, she could feel the heat on her cheeks, which only made Melanie laugh out more.

"Oh, come on." Abigail finally gave in and laughed along with Melanie.

"Cleopatra is no one to be bothered about. She's a friend from our local assembly who liked or likes Brad, but he did not pick up on her advances and assumed she was just a friendly church acquaintance. I had to spell it out to him in the end so he could tone down his friendliness toward her if he did not mean to lead her on," Melanie assured her.

"Mm-hmm. Interesting." Abigail responded with a suspicious narrowing of her eyes.

Melanie chuckled.

"And how are you, really? And Josh? Please tell me it was a stupid joke. I left the diner angrily the other day and haven't spoken to Malik since then." Abigail sat up seriously and looked at Melanie.

"I don't know, Abi. Josh did not exactly confirm nor deny it, and I know Malik can be an a**, but this would be out of his league just to get at me, right?

And right now, I'm just mad at Josh and not wasting any emotions on Malik. Although it seems Josh tried to reach me that day or the next, but well, here you are almost a week later, and he has not tried again." Melanie added with a scoff and laid back on her sofa.

"Melanie, for what it's worth, I honestly don't think Josh would engage in a scheme like that. He really loves you, and he's proven that time and time again, right? Please don't doubt or give up on what you guys have nurtured for over a year now," Abigail told her softly and gave her hand a squeeze. They sat quietly for a while, each in her own thoughts.

"Thank you." Melanie sat up eventually and gave her a hug. "Will you be staying for dinner? Although everything seems to nauseate me these past few days."

"Oh no, thanks. I had a long day and closed early so I could turn in early. Maybe I can sleep better today now that we are fine again. I also need to see some apartment listings my agent sent me, starting tomorrow." Abigail smiled as she emptied her glass and grabbed her purse.

"Okay, then. Thanks a lot for stopping by. Take care of you." Melanie gave Abigail a hug as she got up to see her to the door.

"You, too. Have a good night." Abigail waved back and left her apartment.

Chapter 9

Bradley slowly opened his eyes and saw that the sun was setting through his bedroom window. It had been a short nap but a refreshing one. It had been four more days since he'd had the talk with his dad, but their conversations since then had been lighter. And that afternoon he had dreamed—or remembered in his subconscious state—a random episode that had happened when his dad was away on a business trip.

* * *

His sisters were still babies, and his mom had just put them down for a nap. She had lain down, really worn out, and had barely shut her eyes when he came into the room and tugged at her hand.

"Use your words, Brad," she said softly.

It took him about six seconds to process his thought, and then he asked gently

"Mommy, please come." He had wanted to take a walk, and dad was not available. Grandma had gone shopping.

"Mom is very, very tired now." She had squeezed his small hands, hoping he would understand.

He had watched her shut her eyes, and though he did not understand at the time why he did it, he felt compelled to climb on the bed next to her and hug her tightly with a smile. She had hugged him back, and with a sniffle, she had thanked him.

* * *

He sat up on his bed, grabbed his laptop, a hooded jacket, his wireless headphones, and a bottle of water. He informed his dad he was going out for a bit and would be back soon.

Bradley took a cab and then made his way to his mom's private graveside, listening to Michael W. Smith's "Be Lifted High" and "You Get the Glory" by Jonathan Traylor for the umpteenth time. The Michael W Smith song had been one of his mom's favorites, which she had put on replay on several occasions, while the Jonathan Traylor song seemed to capture where he was at the moment. The sun had finally gone down, and the wind blew gently every now and then. He stood a while just staring before placing the fresh flowers he had picked up on his way carefully on the ledge, then he took off his loafers and socks to feel the grass between his toes. He sat down cross-legged and rested his back against the headstone. He fired up his laptop and started to type.

Dear Mom,

5:58 p.m.

It's been nine weeks and two days since I was told of your departure from earth.

Hope heaven is more beautiful and "heavenly" than we are told or read.

I miss you, mom. Every day.

I literally had a heartache when I had to perform some rites at your funeral. I was still not ready to accept your departure. Your exit has left several of us in pain and with scars that only God can heal.

I'm also a few weeks late in writing this...but anyway, here I am.

I would have given anything to still have you here, but I realize now you were in pain and would not have wanted us to remember you that way.

I remember the hugs, our songs, our smiles, your disciplines, your subtle jabs at unaccommodating folks, your rants, the many tears, our prayer times, the scriptural confessions, your zeal, your passion, your cheers, and your constant belief in us. And moments before I came here, I remembered an episode when I am certain I did not act of my own accord.

I am certain you are definitely resting without pain now.

You were a loving mother, a caring wife, very hardworking and quick to defend your faith and family, no matter where or whatever the cost. You did not open just our homes to people but your heart too.

I am particularly happy you insisted on visiting in February even though we had just spent the Christmas holidays together. You had even mentioned a line of prayer for me when I told you about the woman I met at the airport. I did meet her, Mom, and you would have spoiled her silly with love. Her name is Abigail. I don't know where we stand now, and like you would have scolded, yes, it was totally my fault, but I'm still hopeful.

Just so you know, I am laughing now, imagining you taking her side if we ever had a fight.

You can be sure I miss your meals also, even though my recipes are largely based on yours.

We all really miss you, but God has been helping us dwell only on the best of times.

I'm listening to a Michael W. Smith song that I know you loved and placed it on repeat like you would have done. Any guesses?

I realized late that I was angry. I could not understand why God did not heal you. And why you to begin with? You had been through so much already; it just was not fair.

This was not the plan. You were supposed to meet Abi, help take care of Emma's baby, take pictures at Emily's graduation parties, hold dad's hands as you grew old together, and so much more. I suppose when we do see you in heaven, you will still be as young and vibrant while we would have aged.

I still have questions. But I am trying my best every day to release you, though. My assurance of you resting with the Lord, and that we will see you again, also helps the process.

Dr. Heather says I should move from the place of wishing as that's past and focus on what will be. I have decided to believe you just changed your physical home address for the time being.

I'm crying right now, but it's fine. It's one of my "release processes," okay? Things will trigger this from time to time, so when you look down and see me cry when I miss you, it's out of love, not so much pain, okay?

Oh, mom, I loved you. So much.

I loved making you proud, not like any of us could ever disappoint you. Emma's baby girl would have been fond of you as well.

You always made it a point of duty to know everyone important in our lives, and we were always so proud to show you off too. A lot of the time, I shared my hurts with you because your subtle support was always sufficient.

I'll explain to your grandchildren as they arrive that you have gone to heaven to wait for us, because I'm not going to hide any pictures, and if they are anything like us, I know they will ask.

I still hear your voice from time to time, and I know in time, I will hear it and smile. Perhaps strike up a conversation like we did with Mr. T.

I'm grateful you were my mom and no one else. I know every child in the world says their parents are the best in the world, but you really were the best of the best. My twenty-eight years on earth have had more meaning because you were in them, but with God, I promise you I'll keep trying my best to continue making you proud.

I miss you, mom. But I'm happy heaven gained a soul and the devil lost the battle and the war.

It's been almost three hours but I'm glad I finally did this.

A lot of times I still hope this is all but a bad dream I will wake up from, but till then, we are coping the best we can, even as we all miss you, with God healing us from the inside in the capacity we each need.

Above all, thank you for the honor of being your son. The takeaway from my life has always and will always be that God gets the glory. And now, even with your departure, I'm choosing to believe God is getting the glory.

PS, Now listening to the message in another song I know you would have loved.

I don't know how, but I'm again choosing to believe in all this heaviness, our crushed spirits, and my life's story as a whole, that God will get the glory.

I love you, mom. Always.

See you later.

8:50 p.m.

Brad.

* * *

Bradley fell asleep with "I Still Believe" by Jeremy Camp playing on repeat in his headphones. His dreamless sleep was more restful than any he'd had in the past weeks. The smell of his dad's patties of sausages brought a warm smile to his lips. All was going to be well. He got out of bed for a shower then went downstairs to join his dad. "Gone, Gone, Gone" by Phillip Phillips was playing in his head, and he felt a need to do a few dance steps as he descended. His dad laughed at him.

"Someone woke up bright and merry," he greeted Bradley cheerfully.

"Yeah, I did. Good morning, dad. That smells great." He leaned over to have a peek at the cooker. His dad had dipped the patties of sausages in crushed black peppercorn before placing them on the toaster, and Bradley could hardly wait to have his teeth in them. Several ears of yellow corns wrapped in foil were also steaming at the side of the grill. Bradley laid out their plates and offered to make them a mocktail. He grabbed some raspberries and blended them with some orange juice with pulp. He poured the blend into glasses and squeezed in some lemon. By the time he was adding the crushed ice, his dad had dished their patties and corn and was dressing the plates with some lettuce and sliced red tomatoes.

"This taste fantastic, dad! I think the only other item mom may have added would be buns with sesame seeds," Bradley said after a few bites.

His dad smiled.

"Yeah. She also may have thought some onion rings dipped in sauce were a necessity too. She put the 'H' in a huge breakfast. But thank you," he responded with a chuckle.

They enjoyed the rest of their breakfast, chatting easily, and after cleaning up, Bradley decided to have a video call with his sisters.

"Hey, you! You look well." Emma had picked up first and smiled at her brother.

"And you look like you could use a good massage," Bradley responded with a chuckle. His sister was heavier now with their first child, who the ultrasound technician had pronounced was going to be a girl.

"I could, actually. Hello, dad. Hi, Emily." She sat on a couch and stretched out her legs on a cushioned stool. His sisters had grown to be very beautiful, hardworking, passionate, and self-reliant women, although each was different from the other. Besides not being as identical anymore, Emma was more home conscious, a lot like their mom, while Emily was career driven and almost always on the go.

Emma was generally more reserved, while Emily was outspoken and made friends easily. But no matter how long they'd been apart without communicating, they always picked up right where they had left off. The twins had obviously kept in touch with each other more than he did with them, but their bond of love was never doubted.

"Hello, everyone. Good to see you," Emily called, waving.

"Do you and Ian have names yet?" their dad chipped in.

"Sort of. I like Gemma, Annabelle, and Hannah. Ian likes Britney and Cece."

"Riley has a sweet ring to it," Bradley added.

"Or mom's name," Emily said with a smile.

"Mm-hmm, and the list keeps growing. Oh well, we'll see. Hey, when do you return?"

"I plan to this Sunday," Bradley answered.

"Aw, nice. I'm sure dad will miss you," Emma said.

"Any progress with the nursey yet?" their dad asked.

"Yes, actually. And it's so pretty. I could show you if you want." the soon-mom-to-be offered with enthusiasm.

A chorus of "Definitely, Of course, Yes, please," answered her.

Emma chuckled and got on her feet with a lot more effort than she thought she would have required before she offered. She was about to reconsider her decision, but she hated to disappoint them, so she carried on.

"I'll be right back, guys. Take baby steps, sis." Emily said as she dashed out of her office. They all chuckled. It was a miracle to get Emily fully concentrated away from work unless she was about to sleep.

"So, here we are," Emma said as she opened the door to their nursery.

"Naturally, I wanted a soft-pink-themed nursery, but Ian wanted all the walls and furniture to be white just so it was a room she could grow into. Which made sense, but I also wanted some fun in it, so we settled for the soft-gray walls," she explained as she walked into the room.

"Wow! This looks really pretty," Emily exclaimed as she joined the call again.

"Totally," Bradley agreed as he beamed next to his smiling dad.

The muted pinks and soft gray two-toned theme looked really cute indeed. They dresser was gray just to ensure it was not gender specific, and the crib was also gray, but she had lined it with soft-pink button cushions, and the bed covering was a floral one. A golden floor lamp stood next to the dresser and two small woven baskets filled with small stuffed animals. There was a big stuffed giraffe next to the crib, though. Its head was high enough to look into the crib. A tall plant dominated the opposite corner, and Emma pointed out a space next to it where the expected mirror was going to be. A cream center rug had been laid over the dark-brown of the wooden floor. At a corner of the room were a smaller sofa and a table with a lamp.

"A big wooden soft-pink letter of the alphabet that will represent the first letter of her name, will also go above the dresser, highlighted in gold. The baby monitor and maybe television will be set up here, and well, we'll figure out the rest as we go along," Emma explained, pointing to some corners and wall space as she moved around the room.

"My granddaughter is going to love this," their dad said quietly but with a big smile across his face.

"I love it. May I sleep in there when next I visit?" Bradley asked, also smiling proudly.

Emma laughed.

"Well done, Emma. It's absolutely gorgeous," Emily added.

"Ah! Thank you all. I can't wait for us to be totally done, though. Moving around and making decisions gets harder by the day, I tell you," Emma responded as she shut the door of the nursery behind her.

"Guys, I need to jump off now. My break is over. Safe trip, Brad. I love you. Love you, dad. Love you, sis." Emily hung up after they all waved back.

"I have to get off soon too. I'm having my weekly prenatal tele-med session in a bit, and I still have a couple of chores to finish up before then," Emma shared with a weak smile. Bradley chuckled. She really looked like she would pop in a few weeks.

"Take care, darling. Love to my princess when next she kicks." His dad waved.

"Will do, Dad. Safe trip, Brad. We love you." She blew them a kiss.

"Love you, too, sis. Regards to Ian." Bradley responded and hung up.

* * *

III

PERFECTLY IMPERFECT.

Chapter 10

It had been almost three weeks since the awful phone call with Melanie, and Joshua was angry she could go on seeming so unaffected while he was a mess. He had started to call several times, but each time he changed his mind at the last minute. He buried himself in his work, and once when he had absolutely nothing to do, he went to a club with Malik and stayed until he was so tired he knew he would fall asleep as soon as he got home.

Her fragrance was in his car, his bed, his living room. On his desk at work was a photo taken during their first weekend together. He had been replying to an email on his phone and wasn't looking up, but she had her arm around him and was smiling into the camera from behind him. The image was real, and her smile had been genuine. The framed picture was the only personal item in his office. He was barely there anyway. Most of his meeting were at the clients' sites. He had avoided her diner and, instead, tried reaching Bradley, but he got his voice mail on both occasions. He had even doubled the laps he ran in the mornings or evenings just to redirect any excess energy or concentration. It was another Sunday, and he knew Melanie would have classes, so he decided to visit his mom. She had been inviting him for the past month or so anyway.

"Josh!"

"Hey, buddy!" Joshua hugged his excited eleven-year-old half-brother, and they carried out their rehearsed handshake that ended with a fist pump and an exploding sound they made with their mouths. Joshua then handed him a CD. It was a game for his Xbox 360.

"Whoa! Thank you! Mom, Josh got me a game…" Daniel ran off excitedly to get his mom. Joshua laughed. It was always warming to bring joy to his not-so-little-anymore half-brother.

"The prodigal son returns." Joshua's mom hugged him with kisses on both cheeks.

Joshua laughed.

"Hi, Mom. You look well."

"Oh well, Danny keeps me on my toes. It's been too long, Joshua! I've missed you."

"Yeah, I'm sorry. I've been swamped with work since I made project manager. Not that I'm complaining, though," he added with a smile.

She narrowed her eyes at him, and he chuckled.

"I'll repent."

"You don't look too well, though. Are you eating well?" She placed her hand on his cheek, inspecting his eyes and neck.

Joshua laughed. He suspected that even if he was a hundred years old, his mom would still baby him.

"I'm okay, Mom. Maybe my extra workout sessions have got me losing weight. Or my lack of adequate sleep, but nothing to worry about, I promise."

"Right. I'm making lasagna. Do you mind keeping me company?" she invited as she walked toward the kitchen.

"Hey, how is Melanie? I had hoped when you finally showed up, we would be meeting her, as well."

"Well, I hope she's fine. We haven't really been in touch for about two weeks now." There was no point mincing words with his mom. She was going to press till she got it out eventually. Since she found out he was in a relationship, her song had changed from "get a woman" to "bring your woman home." Joshua chuckled silently.

"Oh, whatever happened, Josh? I've never met her, but she sounds so sweet I'm convinced you were at fault and your pride, like your dad's, has gotten the better of you," his mom scolded.

"Really, mom?"

"Yeah…well? Go on. What happened?"

Joshua sighed and shook his head. Taking a seat, he summarized as best he could and waited for the verdict he knew was inevitable.

His mom placed the casserole dishes in the oven, set the timer, and then faced him.

"So, what are your plans?" she asked casually as she removed her oven mittens.

"What plans? I called her and went to her apartment, punched my friend, and had him rectify the truth with her, but she is holding on to the fact that I was disoriented at the time and did not give a direct answer. What more could I have done or do?"

"Josh, you called her after work and checked on her the first two days. Her best friend was out of town, and Malik did not get to see her until another two or three days later. Can you imagine what must have gone through her mind? And while we are at it, I'm going to have a word with Malik when next we meet. He may have gotten away with such childish pranks back then, but you all are grown men now. He should behave like one," she added in all seriousness.

Joshua was quiet. He'd been so angry with her for not trusting him in the first place and consumed with himself for being the victim. He massaged his eyes and stretched his neck, then sighed deeply. Melanie once told him Mrs. Madison had taught them to pray about everything, no matter how trivial. He prayed for wisdom to fix this. His mom gave him a tight hug, which made him smile. She could tell he was already down and out. There was no point beating him to pulp.

"Thanks, Mom," he whispered.

"I love you, Son. Hope you are hungry. I went all out on lunch today." She chatted happily as they headed for the dining area.

* * *

Bradley was grateful for the time out at home, but he had missed Chapel Hill, strangely enough. He felt like a fresh start awaited him, and he was hopeful. He had turned on his phone three days before when he decided he was returning and listened to his missed voice mails.

Melanie had left him three messages. "Hi, buddy, sorry I missed your call. Safe trip, and my warm regards to your dad. I'm here anytime, okay?"

"Hello again, wondering why I still haven't heard from you. I know you and Abi were an item, and she's asked for some space. Brad, you should know she liked you since you first met at the airport. I mean, she shared a lot of inappropriate things about the hot stranger she just met. And honestly, she has been happier and more energetic these days. I assumed it was coincidence, but I know now it was your influence. Please don't be too hard on yourself or on her. She was not prepared; that's all. And oh, Josh and I… We are on some sort of break. I hope. I miss you, buddy."

"Hey, Brad, I don't feel so good. Please call me when you can. I miss you."

Abigail had left one message.

"Hi Bradley, I had hoped to do this in person, but it's been almost ten days, and you're still unreachable. I want to apologize for reacting poorly. I'm sorry. I was surprised and upset you did not tell me yourself, and I was having to piece things together… Um, not important now. I hope you are okay. Please call me when you can. Looking forward to seeing you. Hey, also, the promotion came through. Yup. I'm an

160

assistant manager at the gallery now, and I finally got an apartment too. I move out next week on Monday evening. I'll text you the address. I hope you can stop by. By the way, this is Abigail. Okay, then, bye."

Joshua had two messages for him.

"Hey, man, you good? Wondering if you'd got ahold of Mel... Anyway, it's fine. Thanks."

"Hi Brad, learned you were leaving the bank. Jason's brother works in an engineering and architectural company, and they are interviewing for a structural engineer and 3D modeler. We are happy to introduce you if it's a role you are interested in. I'll expect your feedback. Cheers."

Dr. Heather had also left a message for him.

"Hi Bradley, simply checking in. How was or is your time at home going? Let me know when you can. Take care."

Bradley called Melanie first.

"Hi, Mel."

"Hi, yourself. But thanks for calling," she rushed at him. Bradley smiled. All was definitely going to be fine. He and Melanie were good.

"I'm sorry. I'm okay now, though. Dad says hi. You are not feeling good?" He sounded concerned.

"Yeah. For over five days now. Elka gave me the day off again, insisting I see a doctor this time, so I'm home now. It's probably just a bad flu or food poisoning or something. I'll be fine. Hey, when do you return?"

"Sorry about that. I return Sunday afternoon."

"Thank God. Safe trip. See you then," she said with a smile in her voice, happy to learn he was coming back.

Then Bradley called Abigail but got her voice mail.

"Hey Abi, Brad here. Thanks for the call. And I am sorry for the surprises. I return Sunday afternoon. Congratulations on the promotion. You earned it. And of course, I'll be happy to come by your new apartment on Monday. I'm super proud of you. Bye now."

He listened to his message just to be sure he sounded casual enough with no pressure. He did not want to assume he understood where they stood. If being a friend was all she wanted, he would take it. It would be better than not having her in his life at all.

Bradley was in the middle of a message to his dad to let him know he was home when his apartment buzzer went off and Melanie spoke up. He opened his front door to find his best friend looking shaken with teary eyes, and his heart ached. He hugged her tightly, not caring what could possibly have been responsible for her looking like she was falling apart. She sobbed quietly, and he just held her, not saying anything. A few minutes later she scoffed and tried to wipe her face.

"Hi, please, may I spend the night?" she muttered.

"Shh, of course you may. Ms. Lopez folds the clean sheets into the wardrobe in the guest room, so help yourself. I'll get dinner started if I still have anything in the house. Or we can order. Whichever you prefer."

He led her to the sofa to help her relax. He still did not know what was wrong, but he needed her to be comfortable to start with. He decided to get her a drink and headed for his kitchen.

"I'm pregnant, Brad." Melanie informed him softly as she sat on the soft sofa with her hand on her tummy. Bradley stopped in his tracks and turned around to stare at her.

"I swear we always used protection. I don't understand how this happened and now of all times. Oh, my days!" Melanie dropped her head into her hands as her elbows rested on her knees. She could almost hear Mrs. Madison's voice saying 'Be ready to accept the consequences of your actions or inactions'. Well, she had not been ready for this consequence, but she was definitely taking it head-on.

"Mel, sweetie, everything will work out fine, okay?" he whispered as soon as he got back to her side.

"Bradley, I said I am pregnant not that I added unhealthy weight!

God must be punishing me for not taking Him seriously all these years." she sobbed.

He chuckled.

"I heard you, Mel. With all the world peace issue on God's plate, I really doubt punishing anyone, especially you, is a consideration. Plus, I don't think God works that way. He is love, He's kind and merciful." he said.

"I also know nothing catches God by surprise. But what's done is done. Question is, Will you wallow in self-pity or revel in the miracle of carrying a child? I for one already have a list of girl names for you to pick from. And if he's a boy, we just add a consonant to all the girl names." He smiled warmly at her.

Melanie laughed. "Oh, Brad." She hugged him tightly.

"I'm so scared," she whispered softly after a while.

"I know."

"But I'm going to love him—or her—and never walk away, no matter what. Even if I have to give up on my own dreams," she added with her hands over her belly.

Bradley smiled proudly.

"You'll be fine, Mel. You need to eat, though. Mom stuffed my sister with food as soon as she found out she was pregnant." He gave her a quick hug from the side and headed for his kitchen again to serve her an array of avocados, plums, honeydew melon, and berries to choose from.

Chapter 11

The following morning, Bradley fixed Melanie two meals in case one made her nauseous, though she had ended up eating both options the night before, so he suspected she may devour both again that morning. She seemed to have had a better appetite when the food was made by someone else. Or Bradley's cooking was just that good. He left her a note to say he needed to take care of an errand and then go for his morning run. "Help yourself to some fruit, as well." he added to the note before he headed out. He had a session with Dr. Heather later that morning and planned to see Abigail later in the day.

Bradley had been to Joshua's place a few times, usually with either Melanie or Malik, so he called him to inform him he was on his way. He arrived about twenty-seven minutes later in his uber. Joshua's apartment was as detailed as he was. His furniture was straight-lined and geometric, with chrome and black metal as furniture legs, bases, and lighting fixtures. He had a single gray sofa with black-and-white throw pillows, a big black beanbag, and a wooden long chair next to a wall-fitted bookshelf under a circular mirror. The stools for his kitchen and minibar were dark-brown and complemented the twenty-by-twenty-four-inch abstract black-and-white picture that hung on a wall next to a ceiling to floor window. His flat-screen television stood on a white console, and a tall green plant stood next to a three-legged floor lamp of the same height. Melanie had added smaller potted plants to his study table and a small light-beige ottoman. She had requested that he frame and put up pictures, but he really did not have any.

"Hey, man, good to have you back." Joshua hugged Bradley cheerfully.

"Good to be back. And hey, thanks for the introduction," Bradley mentioned.

"Oh, don't sweat it. All the best with the interviews, man. And with Abi too," Joshua added with a smile.

"Yeah... Anyway, thanks."

"What brings you by so early, though? Are you fine?" he asked with a raised brow.

"I am. Mel's not, and I believe you are who and what she needs right now." He stated matter-of-factly as he slid his hands into the pockets of his hoodie.

"I did not mean to hurt her, Brad. I just don't know what I could possibly say at this time that won't sound cliché after almost three weeks..." Joshua sat on his sofa with his hands covering his face, feeling guilty and helpless as he remembered what his mom had said the day before.

"Look, whatever happened is past now, all right? You both need to quit trying to be right and plan your future. Oh, by the way, she's pregnant," he added with a straight face.

Joshua stared at Bradley for what seemed like eternity.

"She's what?" He sat up slowly to be sure he had heard right.

"Melanie is expecting, and she plans on keeping it. I'm guessing she just found out, too, so she can't be that far along. She came around crying and disheveled last night. I have no doubt in you both, and she will be a great mother, so could you..." Bradley continued to speak but Joshua had stopped listening at "crying and disheveled." He needed to hold her, and he was running out of time already. But best he showered and got dressed before he did.

"Brad, I have to go. Thanks a lot, man. I owe you."

Joshua dashed up the stairs, his heart pounding, and ran into a bedroom that oozed effortless style within. Against a modern 3D-textured dark-gray brick wall, the cushioned headboard of the king-size bed brought memories of Melanie. His lights were basic but hung low and delivered a soft light the white walls.

He turned off his fifty-five-inch flat screen and dumped his T-shirt on the wooden chair by his ceramic reading table next to his wide window and hurried off into his large bathroom for a shower. Most guys dressed in the bedroom or bathroom, but he had his dresser in the middle of his walk-in closet. His mirror was all the way to the floor, as he did not like surprises in any part of his dressing. His comfort, style, and personality in one space, just the way he liked it. He was rarely downstairs unless he had guests or had to eat a big meal, which was not often.

In the time he and Melanie were together, however, she sometimes cooked meals when she came over and made him enjoy his living room. Her presence was warm and made him not mind sitting on his sofa all night watching whatever boring show she was interested in. Even the guys seldom came over because he did not have much with which to entertain them, other than drinks. They either played games at Bradley's or watched a game at Malik's, or he went out with Jason and Malik. He'd rather just work till late, then come home to his quiet house and sleep. His exes had not been able to break his routine. They were in his bedroom or out.

He still did not have the words, but he knew when he held Melanie, all was right with his world. And they were having a baby. A mini him or her. He was going to be a dad with the woman of his dreams and reality.

Dear Lord, how did I get so lucky? Joshua thought as he sped out of his apartment.

* * *

By the time Joshua arrived at Bradley's apartment, he had a plan. A proposal, really. He made cases for a living, but he knew with Melanie, he had to choose his battles if he wanted to win the war.

As soon as Melanie heard his voice in the intercom, she knew he knew. And Bradley was responsible.

She concluded Joshua was there either to get back together with her for the sake of their baby, or he was merely stepping up to his responsibilities as the father of her child. He always thought way ahead. While she was not going to plant either of the ideas in his head, she was determined to fight tooth and nail to have custody if that was the card he chose to play. His family obviously had the wealth and influence to win hands down, but she would try her hardest and pull every possible string at her disposal to keep her child. She would have been more confident if Mrs. Madison was still alive—Melanie could always have counted on her to have their back.

She quickly wiped the tear that had rolled down her cheek and braced for his arrival. She was not going to give him the satisfaction of seeing her as less than fine. Melanie opened the door reluctantly. She had already buzzed him up, so there was no turning back.

"Hello, love." Joshua whispered as he shut the door behind him. He was dressed for work in a dark gray-suit, black shirt, and a slim black tie just to get Melanie to stare at him at the very least. It seemed to be working thus far.

"I'm going to have a strongly worded talk with Brad. What do you want, Josh? Cause the last time we spoke, you hung up and reduced me to tears."

She folded her arms across her chest in defense of what was to come. She had not been expecting any guest. If he didn't like her looking unkempt, he could leave.

167

"I am so sorry, Mel. I wish I had other words other than those, but I don't, and I really am sorry I hurt you, Melanie." Joshua said softly, hoping she heard the sincerity in his apology. He took a step closer to her, then paused for her reaction.

"Why? So you can be a part of the baby's life? I won't deny you your right, Joshua Doyle. You don't have to be sorry," she retorted without an ounce of emotion on her face.

Joshua hadn't anticipated that this would be easy, but he was beginning to lose confidence in his plan. He had expected her to be a bit bigger or rounded, but she was still his hot little tornado with maybe slightly bigger breasts. Even with the robe and tousled hair. He really had missed her.

"I'm sorry I let my job get the better of me that day and pride the days after. I'm sorry it took me eighteen days to realize you just needed my assurance and that Malik really was being a...well, Malik."

Melanie stared at him. This was not the fight she had been expecting. She had missed him terribly and just wanted him to hold her. But he had hurt her, and her stubborn self wanted to prove to him she could be fine. Except she wasn't. She hated that she was about to give him the license to hurt her again but trusted that he would not. She also did not want their child feeling rejected or unwanted by either of them, so it only made sense not to drag this out. A few weeks had not changed how she felt about him. And like her, he never promised to be perfect.

"He said you punched him?" she said softly, looking down at her chipped toe-nail polish.

"I did. And I'm usually not a fighter, but I'll gladly punch anyone again for you, babe." He smiled and finally closed up the little space between them. She took some minutes to process his apology. He waited, hoping he was back on plan.

"Thank you. Now what?" she swallowed.

He untangled her hands and put them behind his neck and used his hands to make her look at him.

"Now you tell me how much my tie is annoying you."

She chuckled and bit her lower lip. She grabbed his tie and loosened it a little, and he ran his thumb on her lips. She pulled him close till their heads touched and whispered to him, "I was scared, Josh, and you were not there."

His heart sank.

"I'm here now, and I'm never leaving, Melanie. Please don't ask me to because I could not. I prayed about us yesterday, and here I am today," he added softly.

Melanie smiled at him and stretched up on her toes to kiss him. He kissed her deeply, holding on to her head and waist as if she was the most fragile thing in the world. And she was carrying their baby. She was crying, though.

"Babe, did I do something wrong?" Joshua asked in a panic, worried he probably pressed against her belly too much.

"No, no. I've been tearing up a lot for a few days now. I guess its pregnancy hormones or something. This phase should pass soon enough, or so I've read, anyway." She smiled at him and wiped her eyes. She had been listening to one of Bradley's mixed CDs with Chris Tomlin, Skillet, Jeremy Camp, and the likes, playing low in the living room, and it was currently playing "Jireh" by Elevation Worship and Maverick City.

She loved the message of the song. It reminded her of Bradley's mom, who was like a mom to her. And now she was going to be a mom herself. Not exactly the way she had planned to, but she was going to be there for her child, no matter what.

"Have you eaten?" Joshua asked as they moved to the sofa.

"Argh! That's not all pregnant women do, you know. Or did Brad put you up to this?"

Joshua laughed. He had missed her drama.

"You know I like your curves well fed, and now you're feeding my baby, too, so I'm not sorry but I'm going to baby the heck outta you, Candytuft."

She rolled her eyes and tucked her feet underneath her thighs as she took her seat, only to find Joshua take a knee in front of her, revealing a small black Tiffany box. In it was a rose-gold band with an inner circumference that served as the base for the delicate four-pronged setting for the diamond, so that the height blended with the circumference of the outer band.

"Melanie Reed, I usually would have planned this better with precision and rehearsed lines, too, but I promise you I have never been surer of anything in my life than I am about being with you. Will you marry me?" he asked gently, looking into her eyes.

"Josh, you don't have to do this." she whispered, trying her best to quickly recover from the surprising turn of events.

"Babe, I've carried this in my pocket for over two months now, thinking up the best way and time to ask you. I asked Brad for his blessing as soon as we got back from our weekend out last November. Believe me, our baby is just icing on the cake." he explained without changing his position.

Melanie was crying again. "I'm sorry," she sniffled.

He smiled at her. "Take your time. Okay, not really. I need to know you'll be mine forever."

"Yes, I'll marry you, Joshua Doyle. I love you, and I'm in love with you. And God with us, I'm committed to loving you forever and always," she said with her hands on his cheek and chin. He tried to tuck her hair behind her ears, but it seemed to have a mind of its own, so he kissed her, hair and all. She pulled him up to her, and they lay on the sofa. She removed his jacket and was removing his tie when he sat up suddenly.

"You little minx. You almost had me sending my proposal plans out the window."

"What are you talking about?" she chuckled trying to pull him back down on her.

"I haven't even placed the ring on you!" he smirked as he took her hand. He pushed it in gently on her finger. It was perfect on her, just like he imagined. It was official. She was his fiancée. He watched her admire her fingers and made a mental note to have their wedding bands engraved with a message or their names. He had chosen rose-gold, rather than silver or gold, because he wanted something that reminded whoever saw the band that she was different, and he had been fortunate to have won the price of her precious heart.

"Mel, please listen with an open mind, okay. With the baby coming, I am happy to have whatever ceremony you ever imagined. My mom will be more than thrilled to have a daughter. Or we have it later after the baby is born, just so you are not stressed. However, I believe its best we move in together as soon as possible so I can help take care of you in the course of the trimesters. I promise I'm not trying to take over your life. You can have friends over, go to work and school for as long as you can before the baby is born. I told you I'm here now and not leaving your side. I meant it. I mean it."

Melanie thought for a minute, which seemed like two decades to Joshua.

"Can I wear sneakers for our ceremony?" she finally asked.

"Babe, we can all wear sneakers if you want."

She laughed. "Okay."

"I'm sorry?" Joshua was taken aback by her indulgent response

"It's fine. I'll move in with you. My bed now seems small, and I'm not even big yet. I suddenly don't like staying by myself, especially when I need to hurl or get aspirin in the dead of the night. And my lease is due for renewal in less than two months. Let me warn you, though, it's not all rosy, Josh, so be sure you really want this. And I'll need loads of pillows. Everywhere."

"I do. I do, babe. Pillows everywhere. You got it." He smiled triumphantly and kissed her. He also needed to get her another car, but he decided one battle at a time.

"I get to take you for prenatal appointments when I can, or at least, you will take my car just in case 'your girl' decides to give up in the middle of the road," he added.

"Don't push it, but I'll think about it. Your Jeep can be intimidating. Anyway, are you done proposing? I'm not sure if it's just me having missed you silly, but I'm choosing to blame it on pregnancy hormones." She purred into his neck, this time successfully removing his tie. Joshua chuckled.

"I'm happy to oblige, babe, but I feel weird slumming it on another man's couch. Especially when the said man is Brad." He made a face at the thought of it, and Melanie laughed.

"Let's go into the guest room. His housekeeper will change the sheets after I'm gone anyway."

"That works." He lifted her carefully and headed into the guest room, kissing her the whole way, then he locked the door behind them.

* * *

"Hey, did not think I'd meet you. Um, you guys did not make up on my sofa or anywhere in my living room, did you?" Bradley asked frantically when he got back from his run and saw Joshua grinning from ear to ear like a boy who just got his first bike on a Christmas morning.

"No, man. Fear not. You will change the guest room sheets, though, yeah?" Joshua chuckled.

"I may even change the mattress at this point, but that's fine." He sighed in relief.

Melanie came out looking flushed and proudly showed off her ring to Bradley.

"Ha! Finally. Nice. Congratulations, sis." He hugged Melanie.

"Thank you. I'm also moving in with him."

"Awesome! When do you leave?"

"Hey!" she punched him on the arm playfully.

"Mel, you have eaten one week's worth of food in one night and a morning. I'm happy to keep offering, but I fear Josh will feel left out, you know," he said sarcastically with a wide smile.

Joshua laughed and walked up behind her to plant a kiss on her head and hold her belly.

"We'll show him, babe."

Bradley rolled his eyes at them and gave her a peck on the cheek.

"Thanks for folding the sheets into the laundry bag for Ms. Lopez," he said with a wink. Knowing that was her cue to do so, Melanie sneered at him before responding. "Will do buddy."

"And I'm serious about the baby names. Have a good one, Josh. Got to run. Congratulations to you both once again." He hugged Joshua and ascended the stairs to his room to get prepared for the day.

"I have to get to work, babe. I'll order you some lunch ahead and pick you up by six. You are spending the night with me," Joshua said into Melanie's hair.

"And so it begins. Mr. Bossy Fiancé. I'll be at my apartment by then, though," she said with her hands round his neck.

"Okay." he said with a grin.

"Anything else?" She caressed his cheek.

"I love you. So much."

"I love you, too, Joshua Herberman Doyle."

Their lips brushed briefly, then he knelt to kiss her on the tummy. His steps were definitely going to have a spring in them the whole day.

"Later."

Bradley had a missed call from Malik and dialed him.

"Hey, man, I was on a run when you called." He spoke up as soon as the call got connected.

"Sure. I wanted to apologize again for spilling about you and Abi to Mel. It wasn't my place to, and I was way out of line."

"Thank you. Mel was bound to know at some point anyway, but no, it was not your place to."

"Right. About Mel, could you also... It escalated really fast, and I have apologized and tried to..." Malik sighed deeply, sounding really sorry.

"Hey, it'll be okay. I'll speak with Mel. She and Josh are fine again, too. Just dial down 'the Malik' in future, please?" Bradley chuckled. He did feel sorry for his friend and hoped he and Melanie would go beyond tolerating each other in the nearest future.

"You don't have to tell me twice. Thanks a lot, Brad."

"You're welcome."

* * *

Bradley was feeling exceptionally bright and gay as he rode the elevator to Dr. Heather's floor. He had carefully selected his recently laundered plaid brown-and wine-shirt so he did not appear too serious but sharp enough to get the day started out with. He was excited about Melanie and Joshua and their soon to be family, but he was also really looking forward to seeing Abigail. He had played out every possible scenario he could think of, and he had been unable to come up with one that ensured she would still want more with him. He was going to have to keep trying or find out for himself the hard way that evening.

"Good morning, Bradley, you look very well." Dr. Heather shook his hand with a smile.

"I am very well. Good morning."

"Please." She ushered him in and stretched her arm for him to take his preferred seat. Bradley chose his favorite sofa but sat up this time, his hands resting comfortably on his thighs, and looked at his therapist with a lazy smile. She pulled up a couch and sat across him.

"So, when do you resume at work?" She asked as she crossed her legs to raise her writing pad and flipped through her notes.

"At the bank, not again. I, uh, turned in my resignation before I left for home. I do have an interview coming up soon, though. Structural engineer at an architectural company. Full time."

"That's great. Congratulations. How do you feel about that?"

"At peace. I'm looking forward to it." He smiled at the thought. Dr. Heather nodded and jotted a few notes.

"And how was home, generally?" she asked.

"Well, in one word, refreshing. Pretty much." He rubbed his brows and eyes and stretched out his legs in front of him.

"Mm-hmm. Good. That's good." She observed him and waited patiently. He looked like he had something on his mind and was trying to decide if he wanted to share.

"What made you change your mind about taking some time off?" She nudged again.

"I sort of had an episode...woke up on the wrong side maybe." He shrugged.

"But Abi showed up, and it went downhill from there. She was angry she had to find out rather than me informing her and asked for some space. I'm... We are seeing each other later in the day, and I honestly don't know what to expect," Bradley added softly.

When Dr. Heather was sure he was done sharing, she went to her bookshelf for a printout mounted on a large piece of cardboard. There were two separate circles that looked like they had been hand drawn. One was colored in light maroon, the other in light blue. She grabbed a black marker and headed back toward him. She wrote "CAN

175

CONTROL" in the middle of the blue circle and "CAN'T CONTROL" in the middle of the maroon circle.

"I believe you may have had this exercise before?"

"Maybe. I'm not sure at the moment."

"Right. Well, the essence is to help remind you to focus your energy on things you can control and not on what you can't. So, could you share with me a few examples of what you can or can't control?" she asked.

He cracked his knuckles and thought for a bit. "I most likely can control myself and can't control others."

"Let's get more detailed," Dr. Heather encouraged.

"Er, I can control my thoughts?" he tried again.

"Yes. Keep going." She wrote that in the blue circle.

"I can control my choices, my attitude, how I express my feelings, my boundaries, my reactions, and how I treat others."

She tried to pen down as many as she remembered him say, as fast as she could, then looked up at him with a smile.

"Nicely done. I believe we can also control how we treat our bodies, asking for help when we need, and how we bounce back after a fall."

Bradley stared at his therapist, soaking in her additions, but did not offer any more than he had already shared.

"All right, then. And things we can't control?" Dr. Heather forged ahead. Bradley took a deep breath and scratched his head as he thought it through.

"The weather, what others think, their actions and reaction, the past, the future—although I know my actions and decisions today can influence my future—and other people's mistakes." He added to his list.

"Thank you," Dr. Heather said when she was done filling in the maroon circle. Bradley stood up to walk around and change his sitting place. He reminded himself he needed to stay positive and cheerful before he saw Abigail. He also realized, though, that he could only hope she decided to give them another shot. Dr. Heather grabbed another similar looking printout but on a smaller sheet and handed it to him. On this printout, the circles intersected at the middle.

"I'll have this emailed to you. Each of the circles of the Venn diagram represents what you can control, and what is important to you. Naturally, the intersection will have what matters that you can control," she explained.

"Seems straightforward," Bradley responded with a nod.

"Great. Again, the aim of this is to remind you what to expend your energy on. The intersection should be your focus. Needless to mention, you may expand the sizes of the circles to your desired circumference size."

"Got it," he confirmed as he handed the paper back.

"Also, I finally got to write the letter." He smiled proudly.

"Ha! I'm so pleased to hear that, Bradley. Do you mind sharing with me? Even if it's just the first paragraph," she asked politely.

He pulled out his phone from his pocket and surfed through his cloud documents. He opened it in a few minutes and stared at his screen. He wanted to read but the words wouldn't come out. Instead, tears had welled up in his eyes. and though he tried blinking them away, they rolled down his face and landed on his phone and hand. He wiped his face, turned off his phone, and slipped it back in his pocket.

"I'm sorry," he whispered.

"Don't be. Feelings are much like waves, Bradley. We can't stop them from coming, but we can choose which ones to surf. Allow yourself to grieve when you have to; it's a valid and important part of the healing." She gave him some time to compose himself and handed him a bottle of water.

"Just consciously dwell on the good memories more. And keep looking forward to how you'll keep making yourself and her proud.

Remember you have other loved ones around who care deeply about your pulling through, Brad." she added.

He nodded as he took more gulps of water.

"Is there any other thing you want to share?" Dr. Heather prompted.

A few seconds later Bradley's alarm went off, and he reached for his phone to turn it off.

"Uh, no. I believe I'm good," he said curtly and got up to head for the door.

"Okay, then. And Brad, be patient. With yourself. And with her. Enjoy the rest of your day." She smiled as she waved him off.

"Thank you. Bye, Doc." He smiled back and exited the room.

Chapter 12

Bradley parked his black 2018 Tesla Model X by the curb in front of Abigail's rented U-Haul truck with a smile. He turned off Micah Tyler's "Amen," which he had been singing along with as he drove down, and grabbed his hoodie off the passenger's seat. His session with Dr. Heather had been short and lively, but he felt really positive about seeing Abigail again. He had picked out his Michael Bublé and Rush of Fools CDs and put them in the gift bag, along with a purchased congratulatory card and a bottle of sparkling wine, to gift Abigail for her promotion and new apartment. He wore beige cargo pants, a navy long sleeve Henley shirt, and his navy Vans with white soles. He remembered Abigail had teased him about not going a day without a hoodie, so he dropped it back in his car. He had also sprayed a little more cologne than usual because he knew she liked it. He had prayed for her to be willing to give them another chance, but he was more than happy to be her good friend—for now.

"Hey, you," Abigail greeted cheerfully when she caught sight of him. She could smell his cologne already, and all the memories and "inappropriate thoughts" came rushing back to her. He looked more handsome than she remembered. His neat sideburns defined his cheek line. His beard had grown out but was also neatly trimmed. His thin moustache had been cut just above his upper lip, and a matching front proportion had grown out underneath his lower lip, and his hair was definitely recently cut and neatly shaped. Maybe her mind was playing tricks, but could he possibly have become more gorgeous in less than three weeks? He could easily have passed for a model. He flashed her his widest smile, and his dimples popped. *Crap!*

"Hi...Abi." Bradley had almost added "love" but caught himself just in time. He walked up to give her a warm hug. Her hair was packed up with her favorite black scrunchie, and she had on an orange T-shirt with black jean shorts with frayed ends. She did not have any makeup on, not even a gloss, but he could have sworn she had never looked more beautiful and relaxed and inviting all at once. Being just friends was going to be harder than he thought. He had to find the right words.

"These are for you," he said as he handed her the bag. Abigail smiled suspiciously as she inspected the content of the parcel.

"These are old, plus I don't own a CD player. Actually no one does anymore, Brad."

He shrugged. "Now you have a reason to come over—to use my player. And hey, your car does have a CD player?"

"Oh, right." She laughed.

"Hey, don't you really love this 2007 Rush of Fools album? I doubt you can get it replaced easily," she said.

"I do love it, and I don't intend to replace any of them, Abi. Maybe I'm hoping they'll find their way back to me somehow. Will you just thank me and get on with off-loading the truck already."

"Thank you. I love them. The card too." She smiled widely and gave him a light kiss on the cheek.

Finally, he thought and then said to her, "You're welcome."

"Okay! So I tried to label the boxes according to their destination. I don't have much, anyway. Living with one's mom and her new family has it perks. I have to do some shopping soon. Um, could you help with the pillows or the boxes marked 'clothes'? I'll start with the boxes labeled for the kitchen," she explained with all seriousness, but Bradley stared at her because he was sure he did not hear right.

"What?" he asked with raised brows.

Abigail stared at him, unsure how to explain her reasoning. She had dreaded their meeting because she still wasn't sure how to act around him now or what he would now expect of her.

"Abi, having autism doesn't mean I'm a feather," Bradley said as normally as he could, but he could not mask his hurt. He groaned nervously and ran his hand across his head and down his neck. He knew things got different once his condition was known, and he really did not want her of all people treating him like an egg. Unfortunately, she still did not look convinced. He remembered her apartment number meant climbing up a flight of stairs, but he had to do what he had to do. He closed the gap between them and lifted her carefully with the box labeled "utensils" she had with her. It took a nanosecond for Abigail to realize what he was about to do. His hand scooped up her knees and the other supported her lower back. She put an arm around his neck for balance in his arms and guided the medium-size box on her lap with the other hand. She kept her legs crossed and tucked in to remain as upright as possible, but his face was still so close, and his breathing did not change as they climbed up the stairs. She hoped no one was in the lobby or hallway. It was supposed to be an innocent gesture to prove a point, but his smell and obvious strength had her mind wandering.

"Here, yes?" he asked after some minutes. Bradley's voice and penetrating eyes brought her back to the apartment.

"Er, yes, please."

He set her down gently and held her by the waist to keep her steady till she had both hands on the box.

"So, are we good?" He smiled down at her.

She straightened her T-shirt, cleared her suddenly dry throat, and wet her lips with her tongue, but in the end, she just nodded.

"Okay. I'll join you in a bit. Let me grab more boxes," he added with a smile and left for the van.

Abigail unlocked the door and waltzed proudly into her new one-bedroom apartment. It wasn't much, but it was hers, and she could picture it in the near future, with tall chairs by the kitchen top, paintings hung all around, lamps, a cute wall bookshelf, plants, and a glass center table on a centered rug to bring the room together. There was a recessed corner just before her hallway that could readily be her small work station. Her well-lit bathroom had a bathtub and a small glass-door shower corner on opposite sides of the rectangular space, with a mirror above the basin wash area in the middle of the room. She had come the day before to have the Internet set up for her, and the cable man had been kind enough to help her assemble the new burgundy sofa that her mom had gifted her. Her television set and queen-size mattress had also been delivered earlier but were still in the truck. At least she could sleep, eat, and keep herself company as she settled in gradually. She plugged in her Echo Dot and turned on the music. *What is moving day without some music to move to while working?* she thought with a smile.

Bradley brought up the boxes in batches while she took them from the living room to the wherever their content would eventually be arranged. Her clothes, shoes and purses had the most boxes. The one labeled "hair and accessories" was just one big one. She joined him to maneuver the larger boxes along the stairs. After the truck was emptied, they stretched out her mattress in her bedroom, and he offered to set up her television set while she arranged the necessities in the kitchen and refrigerator. She told him about her house hunt with the agent and how she eventually looked up this listing online after a client mentioned he stayed in another building managed by the same company. She also shared how her interview process at work went and how excited she was when she was invited a week later for her letter.

"I'm so proud of you, Abi," Bradley cheered her in all sincerity. He had listened with keen interest to all her tales without chipping in much, enjoying her subtle movements to the music. He liked the sound of her voice and the positive energy in her voice.

"Thank you. Hey, how was home?" Abigail called back at him.

"Very good, actually. It was strange not having my mom there for the first time. That was why I hurried back after the funeral really. But my dad and I had a great time sharing with each other. I spoke with my sisters, too, and ran into an old friend I had not seen in over ten years. I'm glad I took the time out. Really." he added with a smile.

"That's awesome. I'm happy you are okay." She smiled back. He finished with the setup of her flat screen and was running through the default stations and services she mentioned she wanted to subscribe to, when he noticed she had stopped arranging and was dancing fully to a song he remembered she had told him was Party Favor's "Give It to Me Twice." She danced toward him, collected the TV remote to place it on the wooden floor next to the TV, and grabbed his hands to dance with her. He complied. He'd liked to dance when he was growing up, but had stopped as he got older. They moved their hands in the air and their bodies to the beat, bumping hips every now and then, which made them laugh. The music changed to "Work from Home" by Fifth Harmony, a slower but equally intriguing song. Abigail swung her head back and forth, which made her hair fly, and swayed her hips to the rhythm. Her smooth, graceful movements looked well-rehearsed, and while Bradley was clearly no match, he placed his hands on her waist from behind and moved his hips in rhythm with hers. He held her hands to spin her out and back into him a couple of times, and she flashed smiles at him each time their eyes connected. He always had a swell time with Abigail and hoped she enjoyed his company as much.

"What was that?" Bradley asked frowning at the Echo Dot.

"Did I just hear 'Shout Out to my Ex'?" He stopped moving and listened even harder. The track had changed to a song by Little Mix, and Bradley struggled to understand the reasoning behind the song. He laughed but decided he was done and took his seat on her sofa. Abigail laughed at his confused face and picked up a wooden spoon from one of the open boxes to sing along as she danced, using the wooden spoon as a microphone.

She sang along into the piece of wood in her hand with so much energy and concentration, swinging from side to side and choreographing. Bradley chuckled as he watched her enjoy herself. He stretched out his arm on the lower backrest and placed his left foot on his right knee as he slid down against the throw pillow to enjoy his private show. Some minutes later she found them glasses and grabbed the bottle of the sparkling wine from the refrigerator to pour out for them.

"Cheers," she smiled as she drained her glass in seconds, then poured out some more.

"Cheers." Bradley responded as their glasses clinked.

"Did I mention your hair stylist did a terrific job?" Abigail finally told him after several minutes. She had been contemplating whether or not it would be appropriate to comment about it, since they were kind of still undefined—thanks to her. But sitting so close to him and, well, not doing much at the moment, she had noticed it again, and her femininity got the better of her.

Bradley chuckled. "Thanks. Elaine did it."

"Uh, Elaine?" she questioned.

"My childhood friend I mentioned I ran into. Yeah, she owns her salon. A really nice outfit too," he explained.

"Awesome. Well, I'll be sure to do a recommendation should anyone in Nevada County ask."

She emptied her glass and leaned back into the sofa. Bradley frowned slightly, wondering if he had unknowingly done or said something wrong. She suddenly looked disinterested in anything he might have had to say, and it took him a few seconds to realize maybe he should have explained that Elaine owned the salon, but her staff carried out the service. But still, he wasn't sure why that mattered.

"Hey, you've been a little too quiet." Bradley nudged her after a pause, while they just listened to the music that played on and stared at the muted TV screen, watching nothing in particular.

"Uh-huh. Just enjoying my break from unpacking."

Bradley laughed at her attempt to conceal her sarcasm this time around.

"Did I miss something?" she asked as she looked at him with a frown.

"Abi, Elaine was and is my friend. I did not even notice if she had a wedding band on or not," he explained softly. He hoped that what he sensed was a hint of jealousy would mean she still cared as much as he did. It was probably best he left out the part of them having been somewhat of an item back then.

"And you are sharing this unsolicited information with me because?" she whispered, hoping he did not notice the sarcastic smile she was hiding.

He stood up and walked to the kitchen top to put his glass down, then pushed his hands into his side pockets and faced her.

"Because, Abigail, I am happy we are in a good place, and I really don't want to mess it up." He chose his words carefully and thought through how best to express himself.

"You know how when you miss something or someone, you build them up in your mind toward seeing them again, and then when you do, it's not as great? Except with you, it is always better than I imagine," he added.

"Bradley…" Abigail started to get up, but he held up his hand, so she decided to let him finish.

"I'm again sorry how we started off. Most people experience miracles a few times, but for me, every day of my life is a miracle. And I could say keeping that fact from you was poor judgment on my part, but you know, I'm not sure I would have gone about it differently if I had a do-over. I'm usually not the hero in the scripts, but for the first time, I really wanted to be in yours. I learned early enough that my path was different, and I don't even bother comparing my life journey, but I couldn't help but wonder if you would—you know, if or when I had to tell you."

He paused for a bit and did a quick read of her facial expression to determine if he should give up right there and then or try a little more because she was maybe giving his words any thought.

"Anyway, I've been wrong about assumptions and cues and sarcasms...but if being friends with me is what you want, I am happy to have you in my life in any way, rather than not at all. Just let me know if I cross the line or whatever. But please, please don't go cold on me."

He let out a deep sigh and wiped down his mouth with his hands. Then he chuckled and rubbed behind his neck as he faced Abi again.

"Okay, I'm done," he informed her, and pressed his lips firmly together, hopeful about what was to come.

Abigail ran her hands through her hair and packed it up, thinking of the many things she wanted to tell him and the best way to convey them to him. That she was just caught off guard and freaked out, but she was ready to be on the ride with him the best she could. She was still scared, with questions, too, but ready. She wanted to tell him that she missed him in every possible way, and she was definitely not fine with them being just friends. He made her a better version of herself, and she'd never felt so secure and alive in a relationship. She was usually the overly trusting one who got hurt in the end because they were the wrong people to have trusted in the first place. That she had in fact compared other men to him since they first met, and none had matched.

She also wanted him to know the only way she was ever walking away was if he said so. Even then, at this point, she would possibly put up a fight. In the end she decided to show him instead and prayed he heard everything she wasn't saying out loud. She took a deep breath, her heart pounding fast enough for her to hear it, and walked slowly toward him without breaking eye contact. She smiled, took his hands out of his pockets to wrap them around herself, and stretched up on her toes into him.

"Is it okay I really want you to kiss me right now?" she whispered softly as her hands went round his shoulders and neck to pull him down on her.

They had shared a couple of kisses before, but Bradley was not prepared for what he felt at the moment. She had taken a few minutes in gathering her thoughts, and he had begun to dread what her response was going to be. He had missed her. So much. The smell of her hair always reminded him of lavender, and her perfume was soft and inviting. Her hands tightened around him for support, and he bent to lift her from the waist. The trip to the sofa was his longest walk he ever had with boxes all around. He ended up knocking a box over, but neither of them noticed as he kicked off his shoes and stretched out the best he could.

She kissed his neck, and a groan escaped his lips. He removed her scrunchie so that her hair fell around her face as he ran his hands through it. He kissed her neck and went up her cheeks to her hairline, then cradled her head as he took her lips again.

Abigail had unbuttoned his shirt to have her way with his larynx and the lateral depth of his collarbone. He had tasted as good as he smelled, and his squeeze on her waist had encouraged her.

"Abi..." Bradley breathed heavily against her lips.

"Mmmm."

"Abi, we should stop."

"Cause of the boxes? I don't mind, I promise," she responded in short breaths, as she buried her face in his neck again.

He chuckled then, but with all the willpower he could muster, he straightened her T-shirt and willed his hands to stop roaming. His heart was pounding so fast against his rib cage, he could swear she was probably hearing it too. Abigail eventually sat up, and he followed, placing an arm on the backrest of the sofa, leaving the other on her waist.

"I'm sorry." Abigail whispered without looking up at him.

"Me too." He tucked her hair behind her ears and raised her chin to look at him.

Abigail smiled and placed her hand over his. He was so principled. His mom would have been proud. Maybe she would have hated her for tempting her son, but she would definitely have been proud of how he had handled it.

"No pressure." She frowned and forced a smile through her pressed lips.

"I should...um...get the boxes out of the way." She tried to sound casual as she stood up from his reach. Sitting so close to him still had her riled up. Bradley turned her back into him and gently pulled her to rest her head against his chest, with his left arm around her. He rested his back against the arm of the sofa and stretched out to give her legs room to stretch as well, but she kept them folded next to his.

"I cook and bake with measuring cups and spoons because I can't estimate. Same reason I measure my detergent to do my laundry and weigh the basket before loading. The dishwasher is easy cause it uses a brick of soap," Bradley told her.

"I also don't like my space being invaded," he continued.

Abigail listened to his heart beat against her ears as he talked on.

"I have to repeat a process and create a system about six to ten times before I can get the hang of it. I like to stick to some routines, as well.

"You won't find an analogue clock or watch in my house because I can't tell the time accurately unless it's digital."

Interesting, Abigail thought. She wondered why she had not noticed that before in his apartment.

"I do not like sudden noises and do not do well in a large crowd, so I probably cannot attend a concert with you. I also avoid movie theaters, but I can survive those if I absolutely have to.

"Numbers and creative thinking for problem solving come naturally to me. I have a great ear for musical sounds and express myself a lot through music. I actually enjoy singing, and I sing well enough but usually to an audience of one.

"Speaking of which, music and art can be therapeutic for me. Sometimes I have to use anxiety pills when it gets frequent or elongated.

"I take a few more seconds than most to process things. I usually read faces, micro expressions, and hand gestures to understand, sometimes. So I can more often than most people, tell if it's a genuine positive energy or not.

"I do not know how to hold a grudge. Mel says people take advantage of that, but I just happen to see the best side of people.

"I can be unaware of the time passing so have to set alarms for almost everything, including making my dinner.

"Sometimes I enjoy white noise. I have an app that plays birds chirping, or waterfalls, or raindrops.

"Again, I don't easily pick up on cues."

Abigail chuckled against his chest, which made him smile.

"I didn't use to understand sarcasms, but you don't grow up with my mom and sisters and not pick up on them a few times.

"I could be withdrawn for no apparent reason, or very excited at something flimsy. I could be...uh...intense."

The last he said slowly as he had struggled to find the right adjective. He took a pause to think through any other major peculiarity of his that he thought she deserved to know immediately, because he probably could not exhaust the list at the moment, but he was going to try to reduce any further future surprises for her.

"I could be fixated on a task until I get it sorted before I can move on to another. I ponder such things as why one says 'heads-up' when they in fact need you to duck down?"

"I have to change my clothes for the tiniest of stain, or if I believe I've sweated on one in the course of the day.

"I love gadgets and figure them out more easily than most people. I don't do so well in emergencies and was medically approved to have my car's accelerating pedal taken out, so I drive on auto mode. I can use the brakes if I have to. Or just ride an uber.

"I don't take alcohol. That's mostly a personal decision though.

"I have a photographic memory. I may not remember what you said but I'm sure to remember what you wore and the expressions on your face at the time.

"Sometimes, very few times these days, I may find it difficult to express myself, but if you are patient with me, I'll eventually get to it.

"And I like my space as often as possible. But I also want you, Abigail Sogal, in it as much as possible."

Abigail listened without interruption, and when she thought he was done, she looked up at him with compassion.

"Thank you for sharing with me," she whispered.

"Mm-hmm." He smiled back. "Are you going to be okay with me though? Knowing I don't have a manual you could study..."

Abigail smiled at his last comment but took some minutes to think about all he'd said and what she had researched on her own.

"Um, not that I have doubts so far, but have you ever...been with a woman?" she asked coyly.

Bradley chuckled. "No, Abi. Not yet."

"Oh."

"But if you're asking what I think you are, my doctors confirmed I'm a hundred percent just like the next man. And I've proven time and time again that I'm good and really fast at learning." He leaned in to whisper the last part into her hair for emphasis, which sent the intended chills down her spine.

"Plus, my parents always thought it important to assure me my instincts will kick in with the right partner." He added on a lighter note with a shrug and pulled her in closer.

She smiled and hid her face in his chest and muttered, "Okay."

After a while, he turned her to look at him so she would know he meant every word and said softly, "I am really sorry I wasn't up-front with you, Abi. And I truly, truly appreciate you wanting to ride this wave with me."

"Apology accepted, Bradley. And I hope I'm as fast a learner as you, you know, without a manual to study…" she added with a lazy smile.

He grinned at her sarcasm and responded in relief. "Thank you."

"Now, about that photographic memory of yours —" Abigail started to ask after a few minutes, but he jumped right in, interrupting her.

"The first day I saw you, you were in a red dress with black polka dots. I learnt your 'upset' and 'excited' faces that day. Our next meeting at the diner, you had a white top on, and you were mostly on the edge that day—for reasons we now know." He added with a chuckle, and she playfully nudged at his side.

"I learnt your 'concerned' expressions from my first visit to your workplace. I suppose you were concerned because you were unsure how Mel was going to handle our situation. I also remember you had a green and white outfit on. And one of my big ones, was learning your 'after a mischief' laughter! That happened in my apartment, and I particularly remember your sandals were red. Should I go on?" he asked proudly, with a grin on his face.

"Wow! I'm not sure if I should be impressed or concerned you would remember every detail, even when I upset you." Abigail said with all sincerity, but Bradley laughed.

"I remember memorable moments, both good and not so good ones, but not the whole event. And I usually let only the good ones linger. Believe me when I say every moment with you has been good Abi. Even when we were not." he replied.

"Well, my disclaimer; I am human, Brad. And I'm a woman. It won't be all good moments, so brace yourself."

He chuckled lowly. "So I'm told. Besides, like you now know, I'm not exactly a smooth ride at a park."

"Right. I guess we'll work hard at it the best we can." She said with a smile.

"Yes we will".

When his alarm went off at 7:30 p.m., he wasn't ready to leave her.

"Do you need me to stay longer to unpack some more boxes?" Bradley asked reluctantly, hoping she'd also want him around.

"Oh no. I couldn't finish unpacking today anyway. Besides I promised my friends to call them for a virtual tour after I unpacked a bit—Mel being one of the said friends. Thank you so much for the help and company, Brad." She smiled up at him. Her eyes glistened, bright and inviting. Bradley pulled her gently into him for a kiss that went longer and deeper than he had planned. Her lips always tasted softer and better each time. When he raised his head, he smiled down at her.

"My friends and I typically hang out away from the crowd at CBR on July Fourth, to enjoy the band and fireworks at night. If you don't have plans yet, do you mind coming with?"

"If the fireworks I'm experiencing right now are any indication of how the evening will end, count me in."

He paused for a bit and then asked her slowly, "Are you sure you want me to leave?"

Abigail laughed at his hesitation. It was good to know he really did not want to leave her just yet.

"I know you have to, so yes," she responded.

"Okay. So will I get to see you tomorrow to start with?"

She nodded with a smile, her hands still behind his neck.

"And the next?" He held her tighter, his head leaning in closer.

"Mmm...now, that depends." She turned her head sideways, looking serious in deep thoughts.

"Oh?"

"Yeah...just the dimples tonight," she teased. "Next time I may ask for a kidney, but till then, the dimples will do fine."

Bradley laughed, and his dimples naturally appeared for her viewing pleasure.

"I'll call you. Later love."

"Okay."

He gave her one last quick kiss and a squeeze, then headed out.

Chapter 13

Could I really attend church looking like this? Abigail was concerned nothing in her wardrobe was small-church worthy, and even though Bradley had given her lots of time, she wasn't sure what she would buy even if she'd gone shopping. At best, Melanie would have made her wear a skirt suit, and she would have been miserable. Bradley had assured her he was proud to be by her side no matter what she had on.

"You look breathtaking as always." He winked and smiled his widest, revealing his dimples so she would smile back at him. She had settled for a very loose kimono-style V-neck dress with slim stripes of coffee and dark-brown, with a fitted plain black long-sleeve halter neck underneath so the sleeve showed underneath the kimono in case she had to raise her hands. She tied the ends of the halter neck to the front to form a bow on her neck. Her stilettoes were mostly see through, with a patch of plain black velvet that covered the toes areas. Her purse was black, her studs were white pearl, and she had bought a cute dark-brown mat hat that had a short crown but a very wide Victorian brim. That could hide her face in the event it upset anyone.

Bradley smiled at, and was waved at, by almost every human they passed by as they ascended the stairs into the medium-size church building. Abigail was grateful for her hat, even though Bradley held on to her right hand as they proceeded. The elderly usher probably decided she was not front-row worthy and led them to the third pew even though the first and second were not fully occupied yet. A petite elderly woman joined them and whispered to her, "My dear, worry not about Yolanda. She doesn't approve of anyone at first. Not even the pastor." They all laughed softly.

"Hello, Bradley, and a happy Sunday to you, son."

"Thank you, Mrs. Peterson. Meet my girlfriend, Abigail." he added proudly with a smile.

"Oh my. You are most welcome, dear. I hope you enjoy the service."

"Thank you, ma'am." Abigail was still shy but glad someone other than Bradley seemed to be happy with her presence.

"I'll be sure to get fashion tips from you, though. You look great." Mrs. Peterson added. Abigail thanked her, and they all prepared to start the service.

"Hey, Brad. Nice to see you again." A slim, pretty redhead in a fitted red dress with a boat neck and a long slit greeted Bradley a little too cheerfully for Abigail's liking and blew him a kiss, as she took her seat at the front row. Bradley smiled and nodded curtly at her. *Interesting,* Abigail thought, *That must be the Cleo Melanie mentioned'.*

Bradley gave her hand a reassuring squeeze and a smile before they had to stand up for prayers and the opening hymn.

The church service ran for about two hours, and it was better than Abigail had anticipated. The pastor's sermon on God's grace being sufficient was short and concise with relatable examples to illustrate the Bible passages shared. One that stuck with her was Mathew 11:28–30: *"Come to me, all you who are weary and burdened, and I will give you rest. Take my yoke upon you and learn from me, for I am gentle and humble in heart, and you will find rest for your souls. For my yoke is easy and my burden is light."*

"First, Jesus frees us from the pressure to be perfect. There is no way we could by ourselves measure up to God's perfect standard, no matter how hard we try. Come as you are. Secondly, Jesus fills us with the power to be faithful. Like the oxen in His parable, He is the bigger one bearing the weight of the yoke, showing the new and smaller oxen how to plough," the pastor had shared.

"And we could mistakenly equate God's love with a trouble-free life. Or assume if we worship, serve, and love God, our lives will be void of problems. But for as long as we are human, in this imperfect world, Jesus admonishes us to seek shelter in God's grace when we experience seasons of difficulty. And His grace speaks of His great love for us," he added.

Abigail knew she wasn't hearing this for the first time, but it had been so long since she fellowshipped in a similar gathering that the reminders got her reflecting. The pastor ended the message with an altar call, and then the praise team led the Phillips, Craig, and Dean song "Your Grace Still Amazes Me." It was familiar to her from when she attended Sunday school with her mom as a teenager.

Abigail had spotted Cleo hanging out by the door, and when she moved toward Bradley, Abigail slid in front of him and stretched out her hand with a wry smile.

"Hi there, I'm Abigail, Brad's girlfriend. You missed me earlier."

"Cleo. Cleopatra Wright." Cleo retorted reluctantly as they shook hands.

"Well, nice to meet you, Cleo. It's my first time here, but I enjoyed the service so much, you'll definitely be seeing a lot of me. Hope to see you again soon. Bye now."

"Yeah, sure. Same here." Cleo replied, her lack of interest evident in her tone. Abigail nodded curtly, put on her sunshades, and folded her arms around Bradley's left arm as they walked off.

"Later, Cleo," Bradley called back before they walked out the door.

As soon as Abigail got to the passenger's side of his car, he pressed her against the door and leaned in to kiss her. She had thought he wanted to get the door for her like he usually did. She placed her hands between them and pushed back lightly, just enough for him to raise his head.

Bradley chuckled against her lips and asked, "What is it?"

"Well, we are in church parking lot. I don't want God or anyone thinking I'm making you backslide or anything."

"You do know God is everywhere every time, right? Germs, too, by the way." He laughed. She rolled her eyes at him and moved her hands back up behind his neck.

"So, are you upset? I'm sorry, but I had to straighten things with her," Abigail apologized.

He smiled and gently held her head in place. "I love you when you are cool. I love you when you are feisty. I love you. Don't forget, okay."

He removed her sunglasses to look into her eyes and dropped a light kiss on her lips. She squinted a bit at the sun in her eyes, but she was fine otherwise. She smiled at him and said with a whisper, "Okay."

* * *

Joshua and Bradley waited patiently at one of their usual tables at the far-right end of The Griddle diner, each of them busy on their mobile devices. Joshua suddenly chuckled and glanced up at Bradley.

"Malik says he's stuck in traffic and coming with a 'Simone,'" he said.

"Ah, guess it didn't work out with Trish after all." Bradley shook his head as he smiled. Malik never had a problem with wooing and wining a woman. He just found it challenging to stay committed when things got a little rocky. Rather than be a jerk, he ended things as cleanly as possible. He never two-timed, and he was up-front with whatever arrangement worked for both parties. He just wasn't patient enough to go the long haul. Or, in his words, he had not "found the one that could make me go the extra mile."

"Abi apologizes for running late too." Bradley added.

"Oh, no worries. Elka is probably just making official introductions to the staff members. All the papers were penned over the weekend with both lawyers and Elka's sister in attendance. So was I."

"Nice. You didn't bother going home to change after work?" Bradley observed

"No, but it was intentional. Mel and I are meeting my dad for dinner," Joshua explained as he took off his tie.

"Whew! I was worried I did not get the memo about the dress code." Bradley laughed

"Nah, you're good man."

"Hi, guys, meet Simone." Malik joined them with a smile as he introduced his date for the evening.

"Hello, Simone. Nice of you to join us. I'm Joshua Doyle." Joshua shook her hand with a smile.

"Thank you." Simone responded politely.

"Hi, Simone. Brad." Bradley also smiled warmly as they shook hands.

"Hello, Brad. Nice to meet you." She smiled again.

Simone and Malik ordered their drinks and were weighing in on their meal options when Melanie walked up to join them.

"Hey, entrepreneur. How does it feel?" Bradley greeted her with a very wide smile. Melanie laughed.

"Still feels like I'm in a beautiful dream. It's just 25 percent partnership for now, but we added the 'right of first refusal' clause in the event they are ready to retire before I make the offer," she explained. "But I am excited! It's a dream come true. Thank you all for being here. Really." she added with tears welling up her eyes. Then she caught sight of Simone.

"Oh, hello. I'm Mel."

"Hi, Mel. I'm Simone and congratulations." Simone added with a smile as they shook hands.

"Thank you."

Melanie would typically have passed a snarky comment at Malik, but she was learning to be more open minded, and with their baby on the way, she really could not be bothered by trivial things at the moment.

"Hi, babe, sorry I couldn't pick you as planned," Joshua whispered when she finally sat down next to him.

"It's fine. I took a while deciding on my dress anyway."

She had struggled to find the best outfit for meeting Joshua's very principled and almost-perfectionist father for the first time. Her outfit couldn't be too much, either, so she did not come across as trying too hard. Meeting his mom had been warm and loving and natural. She was the daughter his mom never had, and well, she was her new mom now. The woman checked on her almost every other day and kept counting down to their next visit. Melanie was about eleven weeks gone now and had added a bit of weight. Plus Joshua had made it his project to ensure she ate well and used her supplements, so her options were further narrowed. He had stocked the house with enough food to last many months, even though he rarely made it home early enough for dinner and she usually ate lunch at work as. He'd also ensured there were peppermints and dry crackers at every corner for her to reach, and fresh lemons were in the kitchen at all times for days she couldn't hold down her meal. Most days, though, he stayed with her in the mornings till she was fine enough to go to work or school. But once, he had asked his mom to come over when he couldn't get out of a meeting. Melanie had protested to no avail, but she was grateful for his efforts and care of her and their currently strawberry-size baby.

So she had settled for a simple sleeveless midi baby-doll dress that had bold pink and orange horizontal lines and an invisible zipper at the back. Her low heels and clutch were black, though.

"You look perfect. Always." He kissed her softly with a smile and placed his free hand on her belly.

Malik cleared his throat a little too loudly and longer than necessary, just to remind them they still had an audience.

"What!" Joshua growled at him, but Bradley and Melanie had a laugh while Simone simply smiled.

"Please go ahead with your orders. Everything is on the house tonight." Melanie chimed in.

"Hi, everyone. Hey, girl, congratulations. So sorry I'm just getting here." Abigail joined them with a warm smile and hurried to give Melanie a tight hug.

"It's fine. We were just about to order."

"Great. I had a long day at work and had to dash home to freshen up. You look like a dashing CEO by the way. Really happy for you, Mel," she added with a wide grin.

Melanie laughed. "Thanks. Again, 25 percent partnership for now. But thank you. Really."

"Hi, Josh. Hey, congratulations as well. You must be really proud." Abigail hugged Joshua too.

"I am. Thanks, Abi."

Bradley grabbed a seat for Abigail while she hugged Malik and shook hands with Simone, before coming around them to join him.

"Hi, love."

"Hi. You look good." He smiled down at her.

"Hold on, you've got an eyelash on your cheek," he noted and carefully picked it off with his fingers.

"Thanks."

"Wait, there's something on your upper lip too." He said with a frown and leaned in to kiss her.

"Mmm. Did you get it?" she asked, smiling, her hands still holding on to him.

"Not yet—" Bradley started.

"Guys! Please. Are we ordering, or what?" Malik interrupted with a hint of frustration in his voice.

Melanie and Joshua smiled while Abigail and Simone chuckled, but Bradley gave Malik a daunting look that made him roll his eyes and wave a waiter over. Abigail observed that only she and Bradley were casually dressed—well, she was. Bradley was semiformal in his white Henley hoodie, black chinos, and white sneakers. She had gone with her brown Lulu shift dress with a wide multicolored strap that ended as a bow at the back, and white flat slides. She had thought it was their regular night out or something, and she wondered if Melanie minded. The waiter came over for their orders, but Melanie was having only a drink just in case another person's meal got her nauseated. Also, she did not want to be filled up before their dinner with Joshua's dad. She asked the waiter to please take their pictures with their phones. She did not want to forget this night and her friends who had been kind enough to take time out to celebrate with her. They let the waiter go and took turns taking random pictures with each other. Simone volunteered to take most of them since she wasn't exactly supposed to be a part in the first place. Although Melanie had insisted that she join in a few shots that she had with Malik. Perhaps she would stick around long enough. Or not. But she was there that night and happy for her; that's all that mattered.

"I'm so sorry I'm underdressed for your big night" Abigail whispered into Melanie's ear as she stood next to her for a picture.

"Don't be silly. Josh and I are having dinner with his dad afterward. That's the only reason we are this dressed up. And I guess Malik and Simone were coming from his or her office, maybe," Melanie explained as they smiled for the photo.

"Oh, that's a relief then. Thanks." Abigail hugged her, and they took another shot.

* * *

Abigail stood in front of the mirror in her bathroom in her mint-green silk robe and finished up her makeup with a subtle pink lipstick. The pink rollers were still in her hair, and she had considered wearing her yellow off shoulder ball dress since Bradley was going to be in a tux, but she had told him she was wearing a blue outfit when he'd asked her the night before, so she decided to stick to her plan. They were going on a date to celebrate his new offer as a 3D structural engineer in an architectural company.

His case study practice had been challenging for her, but he insisted she was doing a great job, just so he did not have to ask Melanie. She googled practically every technical term and had to study some other papers to give him suggestions when he prepped with her. In the end, she had been happy he had given her the opportunity. He had come back after the interview to say the forum ended up being a chat about his past projects, what he was looking to bring on board, and what he hoped to achieve with them, as they were also big on ensuring their staff were fulfilled in their career with them. He'd learned and was always encouraged by his therapist that it was best he be up-front about his medical condition to avoid unpleasant surprises in the course of carrying out his projects, and this job was no exception. He had Justin, Jason's brother, inform the hiring team. So even though they had not interviewed him like they may have done with other regular new intakes, they had been professional and put him at ease. They were up-front about the expectations and possible challenges he could encounter but thrilled at his enthusiasm and the ease with which he described how he would handle some of the specific deliverables when a case study was shared with him. He had also negotiated to be allowed to visit the physical sites of their projects and not just behind the systems, which they had been more than willing to oblige with safety measures in place.

He was optimistic, but the wait had been heavy on his mind. It reminded him of the project opportunity he'd lost a few years back at a powerhouse. He was supposed to be part of the team and had sailed through the first sets of interviews. He had been up-front as always, but this time, that was the one reason they had not proceeded with his application. The team had called him about three weeks later for a chat. and somehow he sensed it was not positive. They told him their decision had not been easy but that they could not take any chances with unexpected outbursts or reactions should an emergency occur. This was one of many that he had lost out on because he had been up-front.

From a business angle, it made sense for the companies to want to mitigate their risks, but from his end, it had been heartbreaking every single time. It made him question all over again why he was the way he was. And so this time, he had been hopeful like always but was also prepared in the event it went south. He had been so excited when he got the call about four weeks later to confirm his earliest availability to begin, that he left Abigail a voice mail about their dinner that weekend. It would be just them, he had emphasized. He had also informed his dad, but he decided he wasn't ready to tell Melanie and the others just yet. He could not trust his sisters to not blab to Melanie, so he did not inform them either. He figured they would all go overboard with wanting to celebrate, and he really just wanted to spend the time with her. They always celebrated his small and big wins in big ways. Every milestone he ever achieved was always a big deal because it had taken them all a whole lot to help him get to where he was. Also, he knew Melanie had been close to signing off with Elka and had not wanted to take the attention from her big break when she finally did. It turned out that closed out earlier than anticipated, but he still wanted to have their private dinner date before telling them.

Abigail heard her buzzer and went to let Bradley up. She unlocked her door and ran back inside. He knocked lightly when he got to her apartment, so she had to yell from her bedroom.

"It's open."

"Abi?" Bradley stepped in cautiously and locked the door behind him, wondering why she had sounded far away.

"Hi, love. Help yourself to a drink or anything. I'm still getting dressed and did not want you to see me in my rollers," she yelled out again.

Bradley chuckled and made his way to her flat screen to turn on Alexa.

"O-kay," he mouthed to himself.

He downed a glass of water and tossed some of the red grapes he found on her kitchen top into his mouth. He saw an empty branded thermal cup that had a small teaspoon inside, near the bowl of fruits, and he pushed it off the top to the floor. The loud clangs made Abigail rush out to him, looking worried. He had a grin on his face as he admired her—pink rollers and all. Abigail's worried expression was quickly replaced with an upset smirk when she realized his trick, and she rested her hands on her hips, giving him a questioning look.

"I had to see them." Bradley shrugged with a wide smile as he made his way to her.

"You look good," he whispered as he kissed her lightly on the lips with a smile, after he closed the space between them.

"Thank you. So do you."

He did look really clean and sharp. Perhaps his choice of navy-blue suit and a black shirt was to match her cobalt-blue? Abigail thought. His leather belt was black with a silver rectangular buckle, and his monk strap leather shoes were also black with double silver buckles. She remembered he once told her he wasn't a fan of laces but could work them if he had to. It just took him a longer time, and he had a pattern, so the lace had to be of specific length. She had worn her collared mini cloak-sleeve dress that was double breasted with bold black buttons. The lapels overlapped snugly to form a V on her chest revealing just enough to make other men jealous of the man who had her in his arms.

She was in the middle of deciding on her shoes when she heard the crash of the cup and spoon. She probably still had a lot to learn as their days went by, but in the weeks that had followed their getting back together, she had learned he was brutally honest about anything and everything, he could not thread a needle, he loved nature and enjoyed going on walks with her even if they did not say a word throughout. He even enjoyed watching animal documentaries as much as the basketball highlights, but he also always looked forward to their indoor movie nights.

She had yet to watch him paint, although he often played the piano for her. He had quite a few pieces of his art in his bedroom and walk-in closet, but he refused to take them downstairs for display when she suggested it. And while he had not had a serious episode like she had first witnessed, she mentally took note of songs he sang along with whenever something triggered memories of his late mom, like "Scars" by I Am They or Jonathan Traylor's "You Get the Glory." She had learned also to say exactly what she felt or meant rather than leave him to figure out or read between the lines. She was still learning to return his stuff exactly where she found it, especially in his home office or kitchen, but he also was getting better at cutting her some slack and fixing anything she did not set right. He'd also learned to check with her, or in some cases his housekeeper, if he ever was looking for something before freaking out.

He seemed to usually let her win their small arguments, even though she wished he would hold his ground more, just in case the argument was with someone other than her, or if he was right. But she also learned from him that, just because someone perceived something differently, it wasn't necessarily wrong. It was just different. If she ever was pacing around him unconsciously or worried about work, he grabbed her gently to sit on him or next to him and held her without a word till she calmed or moved away to pace elsewhere. And he always marveled at how she estimated her flour or eggs or spices or anything when she made them pancakes or any other meal she was proud of. She usually just left the major dishes to him, anyway, and assisted only when called upon.

"Dance with me." Bradley took her hand in his and drew her in by the waist. Owl City's "If My Heart Was a House" was playing, so it was mostly slow movements, but they did not seem to mind or notice. Bradley twirled her out a few times and back into him, but the third time he turned her round in a full circle, a roller fell out.

"Okay, I need to take these out and get my shoes so we can go," Abigail chuckled.

"You could be bare foot for all I care," Bradley smiled.

"Okay, that's not true. It's going to drive me nuts, so please put on your shoes," he added almost immediately.

Abigail laughed at his confession.

"Hey, these are for you." Bradley slipped out a slim black rectangular box from the inner pocket of his jacket and opened it for her to see.

There was a pair of square silver studs with big, square cobalt stones in the middle of each and small, white diamond-looking stones around the edges of the studs. The matching necklace was a choker and had the same small square-cut diamonds around the circumference, but ended at the center with a matching big square cobalt stone.

"Bradley, these are so gorgeous. You really shouldn't have," she whispered as her hand gently ran over them.

"May I?" he asked, very pleased with her reaction.

She turned around for him to place the necklace on her, which he did as gently as possible, while she clipped on the earrings.

"Perfect. Just like I pictured," he exclaimed.

"Mm-hmm, were rollers in this picture of yours too?" She laughed as she stretched on her toes to kiss him deeply. His fragrance made it longer than she planned, and she did not care that she'd have to reapply her lipstick.

"Thank you. I love them."

"You are welcome, love." He smiled, staring down into her eyes.

"But you've got to let me pay for dinner, please."

"Ha-ha. Very funny," he retorted as he placed her down gently.

"I'm serious, Brad. This night is celebrating you, and I did not get you any jewelry, so it's only fair."

Bradley laughed.

"Abi, please get your shoes and purse, and let's go."

She was going to have find a way to make their waiter take her credit card before he could tell, Abigail thought, as she slipped on her high black patent-leather boots. The zip ran all the way to just below her knees. She reapplied her lipstick and took out her rollers. Her hair was curled nicely and had a bounce. It fell nicely on her shoulders, and her necklace made her looked exquisite. She smiled at herself in the mirror, sprayed on her perfume, put on her wristwatch, and grabbed her black box-shaped clutch.

"Wow..." Bradley cleared his throat when she emerged from her bedroom. "You look..." he tried again as he used a finger to loosen his shirt collar, not that it was tight to begin with.

"I mean..."

Abigail laughed and made her way to the door.

"Keep trying. And I really hope the ends of these sentences are positive," she called back with a wink.

Epilogue

Abigail went into the bathroom to apply her eye liner and mascara. Though her dressing table had a huge mirror with adequate lightening, she still believed the bathroom concentrated and bounced the light better for finishing touches. It was as large as their walk-in closet because Bradley liked his space, and it had two square ottomans for days either of them needed to sit while the other used the room for whatever. He usually showered with the overhead, so they had a bathtub installed for her when they got married and bought their house. The shower could comfortably fit five of him, but he preferred that a wall be moved for her tub rather than reduce his bathroom space. He joined her in the tub on very few occasions, so she usually just showered with him instead. Each of their two basins was wide enough for them both, and they had separate cabinets just so she did not disorganize his. Other rooms had their bathrooms separate from the guest restroom just so there was no chance of having to share theirs with any guest.

Bradley had been playing his cover of "I Will Go" by Kutless and then "Old Church Basement" by Elevation Worship and Maverick City downstairs on his digital piano and singing along, too, while waiting for her, but she didn't hear him anymore. *Perhaps he's having a snack,* she thought. She had bought him a mini complete studio kit with microphone and audio interface for his birthday two years ago, with the hope of him warming up to also play and sing to an audience, either in church or at the gallery.

"Does your husband have good taste or what?" Bradley spoke softly behind her.

She turned around to see him leaning against the doorframe, legs crossed, both hands in his front pockets as he admired her. He had been fully dressed for the past hour in his white jeans, white long-sleeve shirt, light-brown Timberland laced boots and black smart Fossil wristwatch. She smiled at him. He had shopped for her dress by himself and surprised her with it two days earlier, as she had been too busy and apparently overworked in preparation for the opening. Her white sheer voile dress had a soft Lycra underlay that sat snugly on her. The top was a fitted backless halter neck that thinned out by the neck, but spread out as it descended and ended with gathers at the fitted waist. The lower half was designed to appear as three layers that could twirl if she turned round but swayed nicely as she walked. It had a bold silver flowery applique attached to the center of the fitted waist, and she had worn her black shimmery strap heels and decided on the black clutch purse to pair. Her hair was pinned up nicely with a loose strand or two by the sides of her face, and her drop earrings where silver with black stones. The only other jewelry she had on was her gold wedding band and silver wristwatch. She felt like a princess and was excited about their gallery opening that night.

Bradley moved in to give her a hug from behind and a kiss on the nape of her neck with his legs between hers.

"Mmmm. That feels good. I'm sorry we will leave later than planned on my account. I know you're never late," Abigail said with a smile as she put her hands over his, on her middle.

"And we are going to be even later." He whispered back as he let her hair down.

* * *

Abigail parked her white Porsche Cayenne and did a last makeup check in the rearview mirror. She'd had to reapply her lipstick for the third time that night, thanks to Bradley. She had changed her car when she needed more room for paintings and deliveries. Her dream car had always been something small and cute, but Joshua had advised her that her arrival at a meeting was just as important as the meeting itself and she needed to woo the big-bucks clients, so she had settled for a vehicle with more room and a color that commanded respect and attention. She had always liked a Porsche. Though she was only familiar with the small and cute models and not the SUVs, but they were not as roomy for large paintings that she chose to deliver herself rather than ship, plus she was hoping their family of two was going to increase soon and she was going to be one those Volvo moms she always dreamed about. So for now, she settled for the 2020 Cayenne model. Even though the exterior was not important, she had preferred the Cayenne Turbo over the Macan or any other Cayenne at that. Something about the semi box-shaped back and a less lengthy hood caught her attention. Her husband had not understood why that was a factor in her final decision for what model to go for, but oh well, it was her car, and it served the purposes of both an art curator and a mom.

Bradley unbuckled his seat belt and went around to the driver's side to open the door for Abigail. They were about thirty-five minutes later than planned, and he wasn't sorry. Seeing his wife looking so angelic needed some acknowledgment that couldn't wait. He chuckled at his thoughts as they walked into their art gallery.

It was a beautiful sight to behold even from the outside. A professional window dresser had arranged the front display with a black metal sculpture of a male figure on one end and placed a yellow hat on it. On the partitioning wall was a vertical rectangular canvas with a short write-up about the gallery—their mission to bring art, events, classes, and performances to the community, the expected vintage and modern mix of the art curated, and the existing and upcoming artists' exhibitions to look forward to. There was a square black-and-white painting of three birds on a branch on the wall as well and two single polygon-painted columns closer to the middle of the glass each displayed a smaller painting. At the opposite corner of the display window, a gray armless cushioned chair was positioned by a wooden table against the wall. A small table lamp with a white shade was next to a sheet of blank white paper and a sharpened pencil, as if the room was waiting for the artist.

Bradley and his team from work had seen to the design and maximized the 3,580 square feet the best they could. The floor space was all wooden, and each opposite wall painted white and light gray. Overhead lighting on each painting was separate from the fitted lights in the white ceiling. Flat disconnected partitions had been placed around to create false rooms and more hanging space for the paintings. They were sturdy enough but could be rearranged anytime in the event they wanted a new look for the gallery. Small benches in the middle of each viewing area provided temporary seating.

The gallery currently had seventy-six paintings displayed and about thirty more in their storage to replace paintings on display as the evening went on, not to mention the forty they were expecting in the course of the week. Abigail had arranged the paintings according to size, and in one of the partitioned rooms, only the monotone paintings. The biggest paintings were on the middle walls so that they were the focus once anyone entered the gallery. The center frame, however, held one of Abigail's favorite quotes: "A work of art is above all an adventure of the mind."—Eugene Ionesco. In the middle of the open floor were glass-cased sculptures and a glass-top table with art books opened to specific pages.

Abigail's office space was hidden behind electrochromic glass that they switched between translucent and opaque. It also doubled as a screen for their projector just to save space. They had been able to work in stairs that led to the current storage rooms for incoming paintings and extras and for sorting out deliveries. An empty room would have the workstations for staff members as they expanded. For now, the team was Melanie, a receptionist, and her assistant, although she had three other contract staff who could come in as the need arose—the opening event, for example. The music console had been stationed at the receptionist's work area so she could easily control the choice of music and volume. Abigail had also hired a chef to manage the kitchenette, which would sell coffee, tea, cocktails, and finger foods on weekends. However, all was complimentary for the opening, as it would be when the gallery offered collaborative or solo exhibitions, since the expense would have been worked into the ticket fee.

"Hi, Mom. Thank you so much for coming." Abigail hugged her mom tightly as she had really missed her.

"Oh, darling, I'm so proud of you. Everything looks great. I have no doubt you'll have clients trooping in and out pretty soon. I have taken a handful of brochures myself to spread the word," her mom encouraged with a smile. Abigail returned the smile, then hurried along to join Bradley and his dad.

"Hello, Mr. Madison. So kind of you to fly out on our account. I was disappointed to learn neither of you was staying with us for the weekend though." Abigail hugged Bradley's dad and then his younger sister Emily.

"Nah, the consultant and I have some catching up to do anyway, rather than disturb you lovebirds. Awesome work with the gallery. I always knew you two were the best of teammates," Bradley's dad said with a broad and very proud smile.

"Yeah! And I know this is about our third or fourth time meeting in person, but we are family now, so any help I could render, please shoot right at me," Emily chipped in with a smile.

"Hey, how come I don't get such blank-check offers from you?" Bradley complained with a smirk.

Emily rolled her eyes and ignored her brother but winked at Abigail.

"Please help yourself to some refreshments at the entrance. I'll be right back." Abigail gave Bradley a kiss on the cheek and hurried away. They had sent out the invitations in batches with about forty minutes intervals just so everyone did not arrive at the same time, but it looked like the earlier guests were still taking their time. There had also been a projected version of the paintings from the website in case anyone preferred not to walk around, and a little crowd had gathered there as well. She hoped they were also subscribed to the mailing list. They had sold a number of paintings and had to take them down to display new ones. A friend of one of her past clients had bought the set of two lines & shapes women painting by Bradley. She was really excited about this as she had included it in the "New Artist" section so as not to be misleading.

One of the part-time assistants beckoned to Abigail, and she headed to the front to speak with the guest. "Good evening. Thank you for coming." Abigail greeted each person professionally but with warmth in her voice. The music was low enough for people to hear each other, and most of the guests were working class and spoke softly to each other. Few had come with kids, but the general atmosphere was lively without being wild.

"Hi! You have an outstanding gallery. I'll be sure to attend your future exhibitions as well." The woman her assistant had been attending to, responded politely with a smile.

"That's so heartwarming to hear. Thank you for your kind words." Abigail beamed with pride.

"My pleasure. I'm an interior designer, and I'm told a gentleman has bought these paintings. I know my client would absolutely adore them in his space. Is there any chance you can reach out to the artist on my behalf? I see they are in the New Artist section," the woman explained.

"Thank you so much. I'll be sure to do just that. Kindly leave us your details, and we will get back to you as soon as possible," Abigail responded, and the assistant came closer swiftly, ready with her tablet and stylus. She also had Abigail's complementary card handy and handed it to the client.

"Thank you." The woman seemed hopeful.

"May I ask, in the event the artist doesn't have duplicates of his work, would you be open to works by other artists with similar style?" Abigail thought to add. Bradley was the artist in question, and she suspected her husband would not want to paint with the intention of selling the painting, but maybe he wouldn't mind selling off the ones he did therapeutically. They were fast filling their walls at home, and they were, in her opinion, too beautiful to stay hidden from the rest of the world. But she made a mental note to ask him without being pushy. Her business side also really wanted to satisfy her client, and she was looking for alternatives to meet her request.

"Sure, if it comes to that. But I'm hoping this comes through, though." she answered, crossing her fingers.

"Okay, then. We'll try our very best." Abigail assured her with a smile.

"Uncle Bradley…" Gabrielle ran as fast as her little legs could allow her to jump on her favorite uncle.

"Hey, kiddo." Bradley caught her and swung her in circles until they were both dizzy. This always made her laugh

"I'm going to be three in three weeks," she said holding up three fingers.

"No way! You are a big girl now," Bradley said with as much enthusiasm.

"Yes, way! And I want a pony or a unicorn for my birthday. Will you get me one, please?" she asked with all the innocence in the world.

Bradley laughed. Smart a**, like her mom. She probably got away with a lot by making the "innocent" face.

"I'll see what I can do. But I'll be sure to come see your pretty princess dress."

"Ah yes, it's going to have lots of colors. Dad says I'm going to have a castle for me and my friends." She chatted excitedly.

"Gabby, sweetie, that's enough now. We also want to speak with Uncle Brad, you know." Melanie said when she finally got to them, looking like she could use some sleep.

"Hey, buddy. Congratulations!" Melanie gave Bradley a kiss on the cheek as he set Gabrielle down gently.

"So sorry we are late. Still yet to hire a manager for the diner, which is fast operating like a restaurant by the way, since the exquisite remodeling you all did, so my presence is still needed a lot of the time. We are thinking to perfect our services online and maybe create a drive through as well to decongest the hall. Thank God I can always trust Josh to get Gabby dressed up." She explained.

Bradley laughed. "Thank you. But you should slow down, Mel. Please. Abi is at the back with Emily. I'm sure they'll be happy to see you."

He watched his friend walk away with her daughter. He was always so happy she and Joshua found each other. She was more business oriented now and put some effort in her appearance, especially since they had bought out Elka's family and had taken full ownership of the diner, making her the CEO. Joshua's offer had been too irresistible for them to turn down. It had been his gift to Melanie when Gabrielle was born.

"Hey, man, wow! This is huge. Congratulations." Joshua greeted him with a hug.

"Thank you very much. It's Abi you should congratulate, though. This is her dream in the flesh." Bradley smiled proudly.

"Nah. It's you both, but I will be sure to speak with her too. How have you been? Work and all?"

"Good, good. New challenges now and then but taking it one day at a time," Bradley responded with a nod.

"That's great to hear. Jason sends his regards by the way. I invited him, but he had a business meeting and couldn't commit to stopping by. I'll save him a brochure, though, or just send him the link to the website."

Joshua had moved on to another investment bank to be one of the vice-presidents, three steps below a director, but he and Jason were still good friends.

"By the way has Malik arrived yet?" Joshua asked looking up from his phone

"Thanks. Malik had called to say he was running—"

"Hi, guys. Sorry I'm late." Malik walked up to them and hugged his friends one after the other.

"Hey, good to see you! It's been what, five months?" Bradley chatted heartily.

"I know. But it's been good really. Expansions never come easy," Malik said with half a smile.

Joshua laughed.

"Welcome to the club, mate. But what's going on with you? No woman in your arms tonight?" he asked with a raised brow.

"Nah. Tonight is about my friends' gallery opening. Besides, I do admire what you guys have, you know. Having your own woman is a blessing."

Joshua and Bradley stared at Malik, finding it difficult to believe their ears.

"Oh come on! Why is that so shocking?" Malik laughed as he grabbed a glass.

"Uh, because it is. Who are you and what have you done with my friend?" Bradley asked with caution when Malik turned back to him. Malik waved them off and turned around to admire the floor. Since he also had made vice-president, his social life had dropped drastically. These days, he mostly rode his Santiago silver Hyundai Equus as his days were filled with one meeting or the other, and his condo was beginning to feel more like a hotel with no one to return to after his long trips. But it was always refreshing to see his friends who were more like family now. He made sure not to miss any major occasion any of them celebrated, and they checked up on him regularly, as well.

Shortly after, Melanie and Abigail joined them. Emily had carted Gabrielle away to give Melanie some girlfriend time.

"Hi, Josh. Hello, Malik. Really good to see you and thanks for coming." Abigail hugged Joshua and then Malik.

"Congratulations, Abi. You outdid yourself this time I tell you!" Malik greeted cheerfully.

"Yeah, you did. This is mind blowing. The design, the architecture, the arrangements of the paintings and sculptures, the window display—you thought of every detail! Nice plan with the weekend café, too. Kudos, woman." Joshua cheered.

Abigail beamed proudly as she stood next to Bradley with his arms around her.

"We really appreciate your continued support guys," she answered, beaming.

"And may I say, with Brad's permission, you look absolutely stunning," Malik added with a wink.

"Thank you," Abigail said with a wry smile. Bradley chuckled and gave her a light squeeze.

"Hey, Malik. Good to see you. Are you in town for long?" Melanie hugged Malik and moved back to Joshua's side.

"For now, I believe so. It depends on how my meetings this week go, though. What's up?"

"It's Gabby's third birthday in three weeks. If you're still around, it would be nice to have you there."

"Oh wow! Three already? I am getting old. But yes, I will be there if I'm around," he promised with a smile

"She wants a pony or unicorn. Just so you know," Bradley added with a smile, which made them all laugh.

* * *

The rest of the evening went by slowly and eventfully. It had been a successful opening, indeed. After the last of the staff gave Abigail his report and headed out, she and Bradley locked the door and went back inside to catch some rest before heading home.

"I just realized I haven't had anything to eat. I did have a glass of orange juice, though." Abigail said, exhausted, as she took off her shoes. Five hours on her feet in heels, talking, shaking hands, and transacting was no piece of cake, but she had enjoyed every moment, and come Monday, she was going to be ready for it again. They already had a number of deliveries from the evening to start off with. The anticipation made her smile.

"Yeah? I'm sorry, love. May I whip you up some noodle soup? Or gravy?" Bradley offered in all seriousness.

"Uh, I don't think the chef has all the measuring cups for the condiments for you to use."

"I'll see what is available, and you can guide me when I need help. Sound good?"

"Okay." She smiled as she watched her man take charge of the small cooking station. She feared they may have to increase the size pretty soon with the influx they saw that evening. Even though the café was to operate only Fridays and Saturdays, some passersby had come in simply for the coffee and finger foods. When they noticed it was an art gallery, they had stayed to interact.

"Brad, I got a mail from my OB-GYN earlier but chose not to check it then, just so I didn't dampen my mood." Abigail said quietly.

"Oh, okay. Have you checked it now? What did she say?" Bradley turned off the heat and went to stand by her. They had run the tests, his especially, and were aware of the low chances of their baby receiving structural genetic variant from him. But they were hopeful and choosing to trust the higher chances of that not happening. Especially since he was the only abnormality in either of their family lines.

"I'm about four weeks gone," she said with tears in her eyes.

Bradley stared at her, registering the words she had just said, and then he hugged her. Tightly.

"Congratulations, baby girl," he whispered into her ear.

"Mm-hmm." Abigail was too shaken to speak but had her arms around him too. They had been married for almost two years and had decided about seven months earlier that they were ready to have kids. While there was no pressure from anyone, she had been worried. Bradley, on the other hand, had been assured God was going to gift them their children. He did not know when or how, but he was at peace with the knowledge, saying he was a testimony himself that God definitely answered prayers. She had tried to be at his level of faith, but it had been so difficult. Some days her work distracted her, but on another day, they might pass a store with a baby stroller, and she would put her hands over her belly and pray silently. She'd had a false positive before with the home pregnancy kit, so this time she decided not to get her hopes raised when she missed her period.

"So, technically, I'm cooking for two now, huh?" Bradley broke the silence, making her smile. He was so grateful to God for bringing Abigail into his life and he always prayed that he made her smile all the days of their lives together.

"Finally, I'll get to share trimester talks with Mel," she added with glee.

"Ha-ha! I suspected so but decided not to say since they didn't share yet. How far along is she?"

Abigail laughed.

"About five or six weeks, if I remember well," she told him.

"Well, congrats to them. Gabby will get two or three younger ones at once. Yikes!" Bradley laughed and went back to complete the soup for her.

"Moment of truth. Well?" he asked as she tasted off the wooden spoon he held to her mouth.

"Mmm. Yum. It's perfect." She smiled. "Thanks, love," she added as she began to eat her mushroom gravy soup. He had done a good job following her directions without the tools he was used to. And he'd cleaned up nicely after himself too. She was famished by the time he was done, but she was proud of his determination to not have her take over.

"If you are too exhausted to drive, we could pick up your car tomorrow and just get a ride home instead."

"Yeah, sounds good, thanks," she said as she finished her glass of water.

"Okay. But before then, it's time for the best part of today's opening. Dessert," he said as he walked around the chef table and led her to her office. It wasn't as big as their home office but was large enough that Bradley could feel comfortable if he had to be there. Her L-shaped desk was backed into a corner facing the door with her workstation set up and a framed picture of them when they had arrived at the airport after their honeymoon on it. She had a minibar next to her standing bookshelf, and an opal-gray Kannon chaise lounge with a light gray cylindrical throw pillow. A painting hung on the wall, and a framed write-up next to it read, "Be stubborn about your goals, but flexible about your methods." A giant plant sat at the other corner of the office.

Bradley turned on Little Mix, simply because he knew his wife loved their songs. He would have played the sounds of crickets chirping if she so desired at this point, but thankfully she was not as insane as his sisters! He turned the volume down a notch and made his way to her on the sofa.

"Um, I think I know what, but I've been wrong before. So just for clarity, what's for dessert?" Abigail asked eagerly, grinning from ear to ear, the mushroom soup and upbeat music seeming to have given her a new level of energy. Bradley leaned in, making her recline against the headrest and throw pillow as she propped up a knee, and he kissed her lightly at first then whispered against her lips,

"You."

Author's Note

Thank you for taking the time to read *Uneven*. I hope you enjoyed reading it as much I did writing it. If you connected to the story of hope, be kind enough to spread the word and gift someone a copy. There is a very high possibility that the story is not yet ended, so sign up to for the bi-monthly newsletter to receive my updates: **bit.ly/TATieriBoo ksNewsletter**

My inspiration for the main character springs from the personal journal I had kept for about two years. However, the decision to publish came after the testimonies from my journals were of help to someone, and I thought *"why not many more people?"*. Of course, I did not have all the details, and had to research, and speak to a few others with a better bird's eye view on some subject matters, but *Uneven* was eighty-seven percent personal, and was penned down in faith, believing that any child of God with ASD will have a future better than the fictional literature I have penned down. And to the supportive community of any said individual, I pray you draw grace anew to press on with the promises from the word of God.

If you happen to be remotely associated with individuals like any of the characters, I hope you also find the strength to never give up.

I would really appreciate if you could review this novel on as many digital platforms as you are comfortable with, starting with my website www.tiwaadetoye.com. Or send me a message or tweet **@ta_tieri.** I'll really love to read from you.

Till next time, remember to have faith, hope, and love because God loves you.

T.A. Tieri

Acknowledgment

A successful project usually comes with a team, and *Uneven* is no exception.

First and foremost, I thank God Almighty for the desire to write, the inspirations, and the many helping hands He sent my way to accomplish it.

Crown Jewel, my first and loudest cheerleader, thank you for always believing in my many adventures in the creative space. It's been easy making my leaps because I know you're there calculating the risks and making the plans to mitigate them.

Thank you, TJ, for your love and understanding the days I had to be away or was present but buried in piecing this together. Even more, for the blessing of you, I will always be grateful to God.

I would not have gotten this work done without the continued support and constant encouragement from my biological parents—Lanre Adenekan, PhD, and Kehinde Adenekan, and every parental figure in my life who steered me onto the right path. Thank you to my sisters—Adun Adenekan, M.D, and Feyisope Adenekan, Esq. I am forever grateful for the hours you devoted over the many months.

To Marshawn Evans Daniels, Christy Young, Bimbo Davids, Andrew Kim, Lara Cole, Afua Osei, Molly McGinnis, Benedicta Dzandu and all my advance copy reviewers who gave me a chance and took on the book as theirs, thank you all for making this novel eminently more readable than it otherwise might have been. I genuinely appreciate the time you devoted and your candid reviews and feedback because they helped the final structural development.

In addition to many others, Nathan Reed, Funmilola Adetoye, Toyin Poju-Oyemade and Anne Kingsbury, perhaps sensing this project was beyond me, took the time out of their very busy schedule to personally encourage me either through discussions, prayers, emails, voicemails, and/or virtual meetings. A million times, thank you all. I am so excited to share this book with you sooner than later.

And finally, my dynamic support team: Detan Oyedele, Paula McGinnis, and all the voluntary members of my launch team, I owe each of you thirty-two more hugs for the networking platforms; Alison Imbriaco, who copy-edited this book with enormous skill, warmth, and precision; and Liam Relph, who designed the book cover only after painstakingly reading my complete manuscript. Your professionalism and patience with me cannot be overemphasized. Thank you all.

About the Author

T.A. Tieri is an entrepreneur in the fashion industry by day and a novelist in the publishing industry by night, affirming one of her favorite quotes by Maya Angelou: *"There is no greater agony than bearing an untold story inside you."*

'Tieri's unique wry voice shines in her write-ups and blogs and now in her debut novel, *Uneven.* She strives to write contemporary stories that promote faith, hope, and love, centered on imperfect characters finding their own perfect endings. And when she is not working, 'Tieri spends her time reading, cooking, or watching animations and comedy with her family.

You can connect with me on:
- https://tiwaadetoye.com/books
- https://twitter.com/ta_tieri

Subscribe to my newsletter:
- https://bit.ly/TATieriBooksNewsletter